How To Live Happily Ever After in the Highlands

ALSO BY ELIZABETH COLE

Honor & Roses

Choose the Sky

Raven's Rise

Peregrine's Call

A Heartless Design

A Reckless Soul

A Shameless Angel

The Lady Dauntless

Beneath Sleepless Stars

A Mad and Mindless Night

A Most Relentless Gentleman

Breathless in the Dark

ELIZABETH COLE

How To Live Happily Ever After in the Highlands

SKYSPARK BOOKS

MILWAUKEE, WISCONSIN

SkySpark Books
Milwaukee, Wisconsin
skysparkbooks.com
inquiry@skysparkbooks.com

Publisher's Note: This is a work of fiction. Names, characters, places, and incidents are a product of the author's imagination. Locales and public names are sometimes used for atmospheric purposes. Any resemblance to actual people, living or dead, or to businesses, companies, events, institutions, or locales is completely coincidental.

Ordering Information:
Quantity sales. Special discounts are available on quantity purchases by corporations, associations, and others. For details, contact the "Special Sales Department" at the address above.

HOW TO LIVE HAPPILY EVER AFTER IN THE HIGHLANDS / Cole, Elizabeth. – 1st ed.
ISBN-13: 978-1-942316-63-3

Chapter 1

Edinburgh, 1816

"Damn and blast!"

Catriona cursed softly under her breath, then immediately glanced up and down the hallway to make sure no one had overheard. She was a lady (according to all her family history and the dictates of society), and ladies didn't swear like soldiers, even when tested to the limits of their endurance.

Cat's current test was surviving an evening of social drivel and the assessing gazes of unmarried—as well as married—gentlemen who were in attendance, despite the fact that she was not actually even supposed to *be* at this event (according to her personal preference and the dictates of society). Lord, one glance at her outfit should make that clear as day!

Tonight's party was one of the biggest of the Season in Edinburgh, though a far cry from the pomp and extravagance of the London Season. Cat liked to believe that was because the Scottish people were less silly and wasteful. In reality, she suspected it was because there wasn't as much money to be spent, and not nearly as many participants in the marriage mart. Several school friends of hers had gone down to London for their debut Season. A few even persisted in repeating the ordeal the following year—particularly the young ladies who hadn't garnered a suitable proposal, their families desperate to make all their efforts and expense pay out. Cat had not gone to London for any Season, to no one's surprise.

But Cat wasn't thinking of parties or proposals just now. She was thinking of birds. It was a stroke of luck that Lady Balfour, the hostess this evening, had managed to lose her favorite pet songbird less than an hour ago. Cat leapt at the chance to recover it. She would have anyway, since she held a great love for nearly all animals. But tonight, the missing bird gave Cat an excuse to escape the ballroom and all the curious stares at her *very* inappropriate attire, and instead search for the fugitive.

She greeted a woman she knew well as they passed each other in the hall.

"I'm looking for Lady Balfour's bird," Cat explained, skipping any pleasantries. "Have you seen one flying by?"

"No, indeed!" Miss McGregor responded. "Is bird-rescuing your new cause, then?"

"Only until this one is found," Cat assured her. "You'll see me at the meeting next week as usual."

Her acquaintance wished her luck and continued on.

She hadn't been the only volunteer to recover the bird, but it still felt like a solitary mission as she made her way through the halls, checking rooms one by one, and closing doors once she determined that the area was bird-free. (Or in the case of a particular room on the floor above, determining that no bird could be inside, to judge by the passionate and frankly alarming sounds emanating from within.)

Thanks to her habit of reading widely, especially those books and other materials deemed unfit for ladies, Cat was aware of what was going on behind that door. But although she was nearly twenty-five, she had no personal experience of it, nor did she expect to gain any for a long time, possibly ever. Marriage was an outdated and oppressive institution, unsuitable for a modern young woman such as herself. She would rather *die* than be married off to some man who just wanted her to raise his children so the next generation could perpetuate the cycle.

Cat would do something different with her life. She intended to forge her way alone.

Lost in her musings about future goals, she was startled when her present goal suddenly appeared in the form of a bright yellow songbird flitting across the hallway.

Cat took care not to make any moves that might be mistaken for a predatory pounce. She hated the idea that the bird might be too frightened of her to allow her to help.

Instead, she called softly to it, keeping her voice mellow. "Pretty bird, pretty bird," she cooed. "There you are, Treacle darling. Let me bring you back to your home."

She extended her arms slowly from below, cupping her palms as if preparing to receive manna from heaven. "Come here, sweet little thing. I won't hurt you."

The bird tipped its head, regarding her with curiosity.

"Yes, come along. I fully sympathize with your desire to fly away. I don't want to be here either. But you'll be much safer back in your cage, you know. Especially with all these people about. Fly to me, little bird!" With every word, she kept her tone sweet and soft, hoping the bird recognized her as a kindred spirit.

Thankfully, the tiny creature was used to human contact, and fluttered into Cat's gently cupped hands. She inhaled, surprised by how light the bird was—she might as well be holding mist.

"Ah, wise decision. Now let's get you to safety, shall we?" Cat spread her fingers to form an airy enclosure, and turned around to go back downstairs. As she walked, she kept up a stream of gentle nonsense to soothe the nervous creature. If she had the gift of music, she would have sung.

But Cat lacked such a gift, and she didn't plan on subjecting any prisoner to *that* torture.

"Yes, you're doing well, little bird. Not long now. You'll get a treat, I'm sure. And it's still rather cold out, you know. Spring isn't here yet…"

With her eyes locked on the fragile creature in her hands, she rounded the corner…and promptly collided with another person rushing up from the adjoining corridor.

The bird went flying—literally. Cat cursed—loudly. And the man staggered, grabbing on to her as he did so.

She got a fleeting impression of what it must be like to run into a stone wall. Except that the man's body was warm rather than cold, and stone walls generally didn't embrace a person and curl big hands over her upper arms, bare between her cap sleeves and the tops of her gloves.In any case, this *far* too intimate touch was what finally made Cat realize that she'd been tumbled practically on top of the man, his body breaking her fall.

He looked completely dazed for a second, then said, "Where'd you come from, lass? Are you all right?"

His voice was deep and full of concern, and for the briefest moment Cat wanted to tell him everything in her life that was *not* all right. But she shook off the strange sensation (surely the result of being knocked to the floor without warning).

That was when she locked her gaze with rich green eyes only inches away from her own. They were, she noted with the calm that comes only from unexpected shock, very beautiful eyes. The irises had a little golden rim, like a ring of sunlight. If her assessment of the stranger's appearance had ended with his eyes, the next few moments would have gone very differently. But her assessment did not end there, to her eternal regret.

Because she saw what he was wearing: a military uniform. A disturbingly familiar-looking one. A uniform just like…

Cat's breathing hitched, and her vision seemed to narrow to a pinhole. She opened her mouth to say…something…but nothing came out. By instinct, she reached up to touch the little charm that hung on the chain around her neck, seeking the comfort it provided.

That uniform. Here. Now. Why?

He said something else, but she couldn't hear much past the sudden pounding of her blood in her ears.

"I'm alive," she whispered. "I'm still alive."

"You daft, lass? What are you saying?"

He stretched out one long arm and touched her, and the touch of that hand, extending from the sleeve of that uniform, was so utterly, shockingly wrong that it snapped her back to the present.

"Have you oats for brains?" she lashed out, now seeing only the uniform and the living body beneath it. She pushed off him and jumped to a standing position, yanking her skirts back into place. Thank God there was no one else there. "Next time, try a walking pace when indoors, sir. Though perhaps you've forgotten how to behave inside walls. You clearly haven't been in town very long." Why would anyone stroll about in his uniform unless he was on active duty? Why would anyone want to be *reminded* of the war, of what it took away from people?

He frowned at her words, getting up as well—with far more agility than she had, annoyingly. "True, I've been away for a while. I didn't know it was the fashion to dress like a raven. But it's still the fashion to apologize for nearly knocking a man to the floor, isn't it?" As he spoke, he stood up, brushing himself off. There was plenty to brush, since he stood well over six feet, with broad shoulders and, of course, the rock-hard torso that she'd smacked into a moment ago. "I didn't think Edinburgh was so dangerous."

"How dare you joke about danger now," she said, eyes narrowing. Without warning, a snakelike hiss of fury lashed out of her soul and she said, "After all, *you* came back."

He went still, a stillness that sent some signal to her body, a signal to flee in the face of a predator. Why had she said that? It was true, but it wasn't fair.

The bright red of the uniform's jacket was like a warning flag, waving too late.

"What," he said. It was not a question. He'd heard her perfectly. The low voice was not full of concern now. It was deadly.

The signal must have been palpable, because the second she felt it, she heard the shrilling of the songbird, drawing her attention from the predator in front of her to the tiny creature she'd hoped to help.

Despite the chaos, it was still nearby, flapping from spot to spot in confusion and distress. Determined to save one life, Cat hastily scooped up the bird, still half-stunned.

"Come along," she whispered. "Let's get to safety."

Her burden once again confined in her cupped hands, Cat turned to leave, refusing to look at the rough figure who'd knocked her down. Her heart was hammering in her chest, overworked from too many emotions in too short a time.

"Retreating so soon? Who the hell do you think you are?" the man growled to her back.

Without answering him, Cat fled. The brief, disturbing encounter with the unrecognized soldier in the recognizable uniform proved to Cat that she was by no means prepared to be among people, not yet. Her world was too fragile, her wounds too fresh.

She would leave the party the moment she returned the rescued bird to her hostess. And that way, she'd never see that man again.

Chapter 2

THANE MACPHEARSON WATCHED THE WOMAN stalk off, her dark skirts billowing and strands of equally dark hair flying loose to fall about her long, bare neck. For just a moment, he had the impression of a furious black swan.

Too bad she wasn't a swan, because in that case he could wring the bird's neck. Instead, he simply had to tolerate the harridan's cutting words and her misanthropic manner. And why the hell was there an actual bird in the house? Was she some sort of witch, capturing a creature for a spell, and that was why she was dressed in head-to-toe black?

I should never have come here, Thane thought, not for the first time.

He indulged in a moment's weakness and pictured what he wanted to do to that rude, cruel woman. He'd teach her a lesson about what happened when people ignored the rules. They were there for a reason, and without them, everything devolved into chaos.

It was a good thing she'd left when she did. If he had the opportunity, he'd scare some sense into her, hold her close so she couldn't escape the lesson, kiss her senseless until he heard the gasp from those plush-looking lips and she begged him to keep going, to taste every inch of her skin and make her his in the most primal way possible…

What. The. Hell. Thane's imagination had completely run astray, onto a wilder track than he wanted to be on, especially since his body was already reacting to the brief, unexpected fantasy, stirring at the mere notion of getting closer to that temptingly soft skin and the snapping eyes that showed such disdain for him.

He shook his head, willing the erotic images to dissipate. The woman had made him angry, not aroused. So what if she was gorgeous, with the sort of figure that could persuade him to want to stay in bed all day, playing the kind of games that would have her gasping his name…

There he went again. He needed to get his damn fool body under control, or he wouldn't be able to walk at all, let alone walk down a hallway in public. Why was he even feeling this way? It hadn't been that long since he'd bedded a woman, a week at most.

Maybe two weeks. Or four. Six?

Never mind. The point was that Thane was never going to think of this particular woman again, in any context. After all, she was a stranger; he'd never see her again, and soon he was leaving the city of Edinburgh for good. So it wasn't as if he was going to get to know the lass. He didn't want to.

You *came back.*

The venom in her words was overwhelming. There was something else in them too— something harsh and even frightening if he lingered over the intonation of her speech, trying to understand why she'd said that phrase, that way. He almost recognized the sense in the sounds, but then his mind slammed shut. He shook his head.

"This is why I don't go to parties," he muttered, avoiding the curious regard of a passing older couple, who were probably wondering if he was drunk. Thane wished he were drunk. The sweet, dulling numbness was a balm, taking away so much of the pain that attended him since his return from the war.

In a flash, he remembered that he could absolutely get

drunk, and quickly too, because he was meant to meet his friends up on the floor above at this very moment. They'd have drinks to hand, because they were good, sensible men who knew what was important in life—namely, avoiding any attempts to ensnare them in marriage by hiding out far from the matchmaking mamas in the ballroom below.

Already feeling more like himself, Thane adjusted his clothing, yanked on the hem of his jacket to restore his appearance to mostly respectable, and walked to the end of the hall where he knew the staircase to be. Even better, his path took him in the opposite direction from the black-haired harridan.

Who I am never thinking about again, he told himself, taking the stairs two at a time. *Wait. I'm thinking about her now because I'm thinking about not thinking about her.*

Damn, I need whisky.

A few moments later, Thane strode into a red-wallpapered room, his mind still occupied by the irritating woman he'd just run into. Not her words; he couldn't think of those. He focused on her black hair and black clothes. That was safe to consider.

"Why the stormy face, MacPhearson?" a voice asked. "I thought I was supposed to be the dour one." It was Struan who spoke, one of Thane's comrades and a veritable hulk of a man. He'd been born and raised in a part of Scotland even further north than the others, and was the main evidence for Thane's private theory that people grew more laconic as their home latitude increased.

"You *are* the dour one, McInnes," another man interjected. Calan Shaw was by far the handsomest of them all (a fact he was well aware of and used shamelessly in the presence of ladies). "No matter how often I try to get you out among people who like having a good time, you choose to hide."

"Let him if he likes." That comment came from Duncan

MacKenzie, one of the most dependable and steady men Thane had ever met. The red-haired Duncan sat near the fire with Kai Buchanan, who looked like a gangly youth next to Duncan's more mature figure. Not that that stopped Kai from sipping what looked like an exquisite whisky, to judge by the rich amber hue.

Kai noticed his gaze and raised the glass. "Looking for one of your own, Thane? Over by the window."

"No time to change your kit?" Duncan asked. All the other men were in typical evening wear. They'd wisely left their uniforms at home when they came back.

Thane shook his head as he made his way to where an open bottle sat near several cut-crystal glasses. He poured himself a healthy measure and walked to the last free chair. "Ceremony went late. Of course."

"Should we have come to it?" Kai asked. "Not sure if we ever established a tradition for that sort of thing."

"Our tradition is to avoid everything we're not directly ordered to do," Calan growled.

Their company was a young one, having been cobbled together from the dregs of a few others following a bad stretch of luck for the British and their allies on the Continent several years ago. That was why it contained men from all over the country, and perhaps why Thane's particular little group had bonded so quickly. And definitely why they had hardly any traditions or quirks like so many other companies had.

"You've not explained," Struan said as Thane settled into his seat.

"Explained what?"

"Why you looked like you wanted to take someone's head off when you walked in."

"Oh, that. I'd just been insulted, is all." Had he, though? *You came back* wasn't an insult, it was more of a…curse?

No, condemnation. She hated him for existing.

Calan's expression went from idle to deadly in a second. "By who? I'll set the man straight."

"You'll do no such thing," Thane told him firmly. "For one thing, it was a woman."

Kai bit his lip to avoid laughing. Duncan didn't bother trying to hold in his mirth. "Oh, Lord, what was it about? You've barely been in Edinburgh for a day, and yet you've already made enemies?"

"She can't be an enemy, for I've no idea who she is."

"What did she say?" Kai sounded curious now. "Most folks don't make a practice of insulting total strangers."

Thane paused, considering his next words. Like him, all his friends were veterans of the war on the Continent. They'd served with him, risked their lives with him. Repeating the woman's words about how *he came back* would be unnecessarily cruel. They knew too many soldiers who didn't.

"It was nothing," he said, deflecting.

"It had to be something," Calan pressed. "Or you wouldn't be so angry."

"She said I had oats for brains."

The other men laughed, not believing him. Though she did say that, before the other thing.

"Tell us, MacPhearson." This time it was Duncan who pressed.

"Let's simply say that she didn't respect my service to the Crown."

Struan's jaw clenched. "She's lucky she's a woman" was all he said.

Thane was glad he'd opted not to share the lass's harsh dismissal of his comrades who died. Struan would never hurt a woman—but Thane wasn't going to give him or any of the others more details about her appearance. His friends were exactly the sort of men who could identify an enemy with minimal information. It was how they'd survived.

The best battle is the one that's avoided, he recalled a hardened sergeant telling him once. Very true.

"It makes you wonder why we went over," Calan murmured. "Seems half the population of the isles wouldn't have cared if Bonaparte actually managed to cross the Channel and take over."

"They'd have cared if it happened," Thane said. "And we helped ensure that it didn't. So let's drink a toast to that."

"Aye," Duncan agreed.

They did, and the whisky made a smooth trail of fire down Thane's throat.

"By the way, you know who's here tonight, against all odds?" Kai said brightly after he'd put his glass down. "One who will assuredly appreciate our service—none other than Miss Ross."

"Ach, Brodie Ross's wee sister," said Duncan, his eyes crinkling at the corners. "The stories he'd told about her!"

"She's not that wee, for they were twins," Kai pointed out. "A quarter hour apart, according to Brodie."

"So? She was born second," Calan said. "That makes her the wee lass, doesn't it?"

"Not now," Thane muttered. The mention of Brodie Ross had thrown him—all the way back to the war. Brodie's death had ripped Thane into pieces. He would never get over the guilt he felt, living and breathing and walking while his friend did not.

After all, you *came back.*

The taunt echoed in his head once more. Was that why the unknown woman's words seared him so? That fact that, all unwittingly, she'd hit upon his sorest spot, his guilt at surviving what his dearest friend had not.

"Thane, you with us?" Struan asked. For such a bruiser of

a man, he was surprisingly astute at noticing people's reactions.

"Of course." Thane lifted his glass again. "To Brodie."

"To Brodie!" they all echoed.

"You'll come downstairs to meet her while she's here, won't you?" Kai asked. "I know she'd love to meet you, Thane. And see Calan and Duncan again. And someday, I think it might help her to hear us talk about Brodie."

Thane nodded. "Hard to believe I haven't met her yet, considering how much Brodie went on about her."

According to Brodie, his sister was an angel on earth—though a rather mischievous one, based on the many stories of childhood pranks and jokes Brodie shared. It would be good to meet her, if only to remind himself that there were women in the world who viewed soldiers like him, like Brodie, with respect rather than disdain.

The conversation turned to more general topics, and Thane allowed himself to relax. At long last, he was among friends, in his home country. All would be well. Eventually.

So, having been fortified with good Highland whisky, Thane was willing to brave the crowded party below. Bowing to the inevitable, he went down with the others. They'd had their reunion, now it was time to appear as guests. Just another form of duty, Thane told himself, knowing how many of the ladies present were looking to make a marriage. Well, they'd have to look beyond him. Thane had no intention of marrying anytime soon. Possibly never.

That reminded him of something. "Struan, I wanted to ask you about that croft near Ben Nevis you'd mentioned… Struan?" Thane looked over to where his friend had been not five seconds ago. "What the hell?"

"We've lost him. Again," Kai said sheepishly. "I didn't notice till you said his name. How does he *do* it?"

Thane had no answer. The man was approximately the

size of a mountain, and yet he could slip away like a shadow when he wanted to. Thane never knew how he learned the trick. But he was well aware that crowds made Struan uncomfortable. That had been true ever since the war, and in particular since that horrible day when Struan… Thane's mind shied away from the memory, unwilling to plunge into the depths of battlefield trauma while about to enter a bright and sparkling ballroom.

It wasn't fair. Struan should be able to walk anywhere he damn well pleased. But he'd suffered an injury that couldn't be ignored, and he hated the way people looked at him now. No wonder he'd turned into smoke between the upper and ground floors.

In the ballroom, Calan and Kai divided the task of finding Brodie's sister as quickly as possible, before the men got ensnared by the gauntlet of traps laid by all the single women and their mothers.

"Ah, there she is," Kai said. "Obvious when you think about it. West corner, by the windows."

What was obvious? Thane couldn't tell yet, thanks to the crush. Trusting that Kai knew one young lady from all the others, he followed his friends though the sea of unfamiliar faces.

"Here they are!" Calan said cheerfully, putting his full charm on display now that ladies were present. "Mrs Tacita Murray, and Miss Ross, both looking lovely enough to put the sun to shame."

"Is that the whisky speaking, Calan Shaw?" a woman's voice responded, her tone rich with amusement.

Thane went still, because the voice was familiar. As he stepped past his friends, who'd blocked the view until this moment, he confronted the last person he expected to see.

The black-haired, black-clad harridan from before was none other than Catriona Ross.

Chapter 3

Cat regarded the sudden reappearance of the awful man from upstairs with alarm. Was she cursed? And how was he connected to the men of Brodie's company? Then her gaze locked on to the upsettingly recognizable emblem on his uniform, and it finally registered in her addled mind. *Of course*, she realized, far too late. He'd been *in* the company.

Meanwhile, Calan smiled at her, unaware of her turmoil. "Miss Ross, here's a man who you will be delighted to know, and honestly it's an oversight that you two are not already acquainted. May I present Major Thane MacPhearson."

Cat's stomach dropped into her dancing slippers. Not just a random member of the company, but someone Brodie had spoken of practically as a brother! She couldn't count the number of times Brodie mentioned Thane MacPhearson in his letters home over the years, always with genuine affection and respect. And Brodie had plenty of time to form such bonds, having joined the army the very first moment he was legally permitted to do so. (It had made for a rather sad sixteenth birthday party for them both.) Cat had formed a picture of a splendid gentleman who Brodie had admired and clearly would have taken a bullet for, and who she might even have developed a touch of affection for herself.

But considering how he was glaring at her now—and rightly so—she doubted there'd ever be anything like friendship between them.

"Mr MacPhearson," she said reflexively, using the etiquette drilled into her by hours of instruction. "How do you do."

"Where's your bird?" Thane asked, disregarding any pretense at politeness.

"*What?*" Calan muttered at this highly unorthodox greeting. Behind him, Kai and Duncan exchanged glances, probably wondering if their comrade had taken leave of his senses.

Even her aunt Tacita and the evening's hostess, Lady Balfour, looked thrown, and these women had both reached an age where surprises were rare.

Cat said into the horribly awkward silence, "It wasn't my bird, Mr MacPhearson."

"Oh, I understand! It was mine," Lady Balfour said. "Miss Ross kindly offered to find my sweet Treacle after she flew out of her cage when I'd turned my back. And she succeeded. Treacle is back safe and sound. You are truly a lifesaver, my dear."

Lady Balfour beamed at her, as if she were a saint on the level of Francis of Assisi.

"It was no trouble," Cat said, embarrassed at the praise.

"Brodie always said you loved animals," Kai offered, clearly hoping to smooth over the tension between Cat and Thane. "He'd read out your letters when you talked about your pets. What's the name of the dog you've got now? Big name for a small dog. Exchequer Houndstooth, yes?"

"Check for short," Cat said. "We actually just…we lost him earlier this week, I'm sorry to say." The dog's sudden death had been yet another blow to an already distressed household.

"Check belonged to the twins' mother, my sister," Aunt

Tacita added, in her always dignified tone. "Mrs Ross passed away only a few months after the news of Brodie's…" Tacita's voice broke for a moment. "So we were especially sad to say goodbye to Check, of course. And all unexpected too. He was only four."

Kai, Duncan, and Calan all expressed condolences. Thane didn't say anything, but Cat assumed he was mentally mocking her and her family for doting on a dog.

"We must speak of happier things," their hostess insisted. "I throw a party to brighten moods, not darken them. You young folks should be dancing!" She regarded the four men as if they'd neglected to follow a direct order. "Miss Ross has no partner for the next dance."

"No! I can't dance!" Cat protested, looking at their hostess in panic. "We were just leaving. I'm not even supposed to *be* here!"

"But you *are* here, dear," Lady Balfour said, "and it would be such a shame for you to be so close to a dance floor and yet not participate."

"I agree," said her aunt. "It would be so lovely to see you enjoying yourself for the space of a dance, dearest."

Cat could only stare at her, plucking the black fabric of her gown as if to provide tangible evidence of her inability to take part in the festivities. "But there are rules! Expectations."

"And when has that ever stopped you, Miss Ross?" Lady Balfour returned, echoed by Aunt Tacita's murmured, "*Indeed.*"

The hostess confronted the men. "Will not one of you provide Miss Ross with a small bit of respite from her dreary duty? As a new acquaintance, Mr MacPhearson, perhaps you'd like the honor."

"Dear Catriona does love dancing," her aunt added. The fact that it was true did not make Cat any happier to hear it.

Thane looked as if he'd rather run across a battlefield without a gun. But then he seemed to think of something else and bowed to Lady Balfour. "I know better than to refuse an order from my superior," Thane said, earning a winsome smile from their hostess. "And since Mrs Murray has informed me Miss Ross loves dancing, of course I'll dance with her."

Cat glared at him. She'd been expecting him to refuse. But Thane must be invested in torturing her, for he merely held out his hand in invitation. She had to accept, unless she wanted to cause a scene in front of her aunt and the hostess, not to mention her late brother's closest friends. And Cat would never force any of these people to share in her embarrassment.

"Very well," she said softly, and allowed him to escort her to the floor. The music started, and Thane swept her into his arms.

Oh, no. It was a waltz.

If Cat had realized that the next dance was to be a waltz, she would have come up with some way, any way to avoid accepting the invitation. She'd have set Treacle loose again! The waltz brought the dancing couple *so* close together. She couldn't even breathe without inhaling his scent.

At least he bathes, she thought, trying to maintain her usual tartness. For the primary note of his aroma *was* soap, a clean woody scent that she honestly couldn't hate if she tried. And it was good that she didn't hate it, because the dance forced her into his arms as he whirled her over the ballroom floor with a level of skill that she hadn't anticipated.

The thing about waltzing was that it felt rather like flying, and Cat had always loved the dance because it was one of the few times she could feel *light*.

Free.

Even in the arms of a man who clearly despised her. Well, why shouldn't he? He was Brodie's closest comrade, probably the last person on earth to speak to him before he died. And Cat had been appallingly rude to him upstairs. She ought to apologize, if only to reassure herself that she was civilized.

But it was hard to apologize to a man made of ice. She could practically feel the cold anger rolling off him. Because of what *she* so thoughtlessly said.

"If you didn't want to dance, Mr MacPhearson, why did you agree?" Clearly he wasn't going to offer any conversation, so she had to open with something.

"Mrs Murray is Brodie's aunt," he said, his tone as frosty as his expression. "I would not want to hurt her feelings when she obviously wanted you to dance."

Not her aunt. *Brodie's* aunt. As if Cat wasn't even a person. Cat stifled the stab of pain at his words, and said lightly, "We both had the same purpose in mind. I had no wish to dance either, but she wants to see me enjoy myself."

"Then you should smile," Thane advised, "so your aunt doesn't misunderstand."

"I should kick you," Cat said sweetly, beaming at him as though he'd offered her the greatest compliment.

"You should try," he suggested, returning her smile with one of his own, outwardly warm but freezing her soul, even as he spread his hand on her back a bit, and pressed her to him as if to say *You couldn't even move if I didn't allow it.*

Strangely, Cat felt a jolt of heat through her body when he did so. There was something perverse in her that *liked* the proximity of this despicable male, that urged her not just to accept his dominance but to test it. Without warning, prickles of sweat beaded at the small of her back and between her breasts. She inhaled, hoping a breath of air would help.

All it got her was the scent of Thane, and she felt a little dizzy when the dance steps swept her in a half circle, orbiting him. Momentarily disoriented, she looked up and caught his gaze, only to find that he was suddenly regarding her like she was a venomous snake.

Without breaking the rhythm of the dance, he managed to put a few more inches between them, and then he looked over her head to some other point in the ballroom, seemingly bored with her.

"Do you always offer to kick your dance partners?" he asked casually. "Is that why no one rushed to fill your dance card?"

"I don't have a dance card. I'm in *mourning*," she snapped, annoyed that he'd so easily goaded her into such a defensive response. "We only came tonight to perform a small service for Lady Balfour and this was the night it could be done. Then the bird got loose and I helped find it. I never intended to actually be present at the party, let alone dance like I haven't got a care in the world. Which should be obvious by my outfit!" Deep, unrelieved black. Cat was grieving for not one, but two family members, plus the dog now…and she didn't do anything by half measures.

"You don't look as if you're lost in despair," he commented, his gaze traveling over her quickly, and just as quickly condemning her for what he saw.

Was it possible to hate someone so thoroughly upon first acquaintance? She said, "You're trying to needle me, sir, but you must understand how little your behavior even registers. To be quite honest, as hideous as you are, you're not even the worst thing that's happened to me this evening, let alone this week. Why, my carriage nearly crashed on the way here!" She finished with a light, disdainful laugh, the one she'd perfected for the times when she wanted to crush a man's hopes and dreams.

Thane's grip on her hand tightened for a half an instant,

and when the dance called for her to turn, he swung her about with just a tad more force than necessary, making her almost lose her footing.

But then he pulled her closer to him. Anyone watching would think he meant to steady her, the sort of thoughtful partner a dancer would want. Only Cat knew it was just a way to make her uncomfortable, drawing her near so she couldn't avoid him.

His smile was polite enough, but his eyes told a different story. "What was the obstacle in the carriage's way? Your inflated sense of self-importance?"

"You jest, sir." Cat gave another laugh, but it didn't feel as triumphant this time. Thane was quicker than most of the gentlemen she'd sparred with over the last several months.

"So?" he asked. "What happened?"

Cat frowned, recalling the details of the event, which had been more alarming than she let on. "Well, I couldn't see everything, being in the seat behind the driver. But he'd just taken the turn by Bells' Mills…"

He nodded. "Where you can walk down to the Water of Leith."

"Yes, exactly. A group of Travellers had stopped their caravans just there, probably because it was so close to the river. Anyway, the front right wheel just detached without warning. Practically sent the whole contraption flying over the edge and down to the water. But luckily our driver was able to steer just enough to get out of the main road and not lose control. In retrospect, one might consider it a warning from on high that I should not have left the house tonight." She shot him a narrow-eyed glance, sure he felt *exactly* the same way.

"Yes, well. Even a carriage that looks well on the outside can be damaged or flawed." He offered the double entendre with a completely straight face.

Odious man! Cat refused to rise to the bait that time, or acknowledge the metaphor. "No, you're mistaken in your assumption. Aunt Tacita just bought the carriage a few months ago. And yet the wheel still went flying off. I watched it roll down the street," she added, an admittedly odd detail for her to focus on, considering that at the time she'd been in danger of falling into the river, a painful distance below.

"I see," Thane said. "Too bad I couldn't have arranged to be standing in the carriage's path instead. Then I could have been struck dead, as you so clearly wished I'd been during the war."

Cat closed her eyes and swallowed hard, feeling the awful tang of shame well up in her throat. "I should not have said that. Not to you, or to anyone."

"Then why *did* you say it?" he asked, his voice low and now hot, the anger no longer concealed.

"Your uniform."

He frowned. "What about it?"

Cat wasn't even sure how to put it into words. The bright red of the jacket, the company emblem on the arm, but not the arm she recognized. Not the arm that reached for her so many times and pulled her into a fierce embrace while her twin's voice told her she wasn't rid of him yet…

"I wasn't expecting…it's *so* similar to Brodie's, but it's not his. And…I think the truth is that I resent every soldier who was able to come back home, because the one person I needed to come home again never ever will." Cat's throat tightened up, and she struggled not to wipe her suddenly damp eyes. Why was it hard to breathe? She'd cried so much, but it still felt like a new wound every time.

Thane's expression changed for a second, losing the iciness. His voice sounded raw when he said, "He was a good man. Not just a good soldier, I mean. He was a good man."

The last two words were spoken as though Thane could bring him back to life through force of will alone.

But no one could.

Cat had to look away, unable to meet his gaze. "Then why did he have to die?"

Thane didn't say anything, and his body seemed to freeze once more. But what could anyone say to that question? Cat sensed the tension in his muscles, the thud of his heartbeat as he held her black-clad form in the scandalous embrace of the waltz.

Lord, this had to be the worst dance ever, for both of them.

Chapter 4

FINALLY, BLESSEDLY, THE WALTZ MUSIC ended.

Thane wished to hell that he'd escaped the party along with Struan earlier. Then he'd be drinking with his friend somewhere instead of worrying about this damnable female who set his teeth on edge every time she opened her mouth. And then her question: why did Brodie have to die?

As if Thane didn't ask that over and over and over in the silence of his own head. He couldn't give her the truth, the only answer he knew. It would be too harsh, for both of them.

Fortunately, he could hide his mind from Brodie's shadow because dealing with her presence was distracting enough. She didn't even have to talk. During the waltz, there'd been a moment when she stopped talking and just *looked* at him with a distracted and dreamy gaze, and suddenly all Thane could think of was seeing that same expression on her face, but in a bedroom.

The thought took his breath away.

He'd immediately stepped away from her, cursing his body's reaction to simply having a woman in his arms. Not just any woman. This woman. It was astonishing that Brodie's ghost didn't rise up out of the ground to wreak vengeance on his so-called friend.

God damn whoever invented the waltz.

It had been decried as a scandalous dance when it first arrived from the Continent years before, and rightly so. It was far too much fun to be able to embrace a beautiful woman in public and then spin her about till she circled back and was close enough to kiss.

And Catriona was an exquisite dancer, graceful and responsive to his lead. Even in her somber gown, which was totally unsuited in color or form for a party like this one, she outshone every other woman on the floor. A black swan among sparrows.

Thane reminded himself that he didn't even like her. His body dearly seemed to need that reminder.

It was a good thing that after tonight, he would never see her again.

"Let's get you back to your aunt, so that you no longer have to endure my company," he muttered, escorting her from the center of the dance floor as the dance ended.

"Now that's a wonderful idea," Catriona said, though she still looked as if she were about to sob in despair.

Christ. He couldn't return her to Brodie's aunt with tears in her eyes. Those eyes as blue and clear as her brother's had been. Far more suited to laughing than crying.

"Here," he said, offering her a pocket square of fine white cambric. "I don't want to be accused of making a woman cry."

The lady didn't so much as glance at the cloth, and instead produced one of her own from somewhere amid the folds of her skirts. How the hell had she done that? She didn't even have a reticule, and the current fashions made ladies' ballgowns so ethereal that one could practically see through them.

And yet Catriona Ross kept her own supply of handkerchiefs in hers. Black, of course.

"You're prepared," he said, stuffing his rejected offering back into his jacket, trying not to feel offended.

"It is common sense for any woman to see to her own needs," Catriona said, even as she wiped the trace of tears off her pale cheeks. "I don't wish to be dependent on a man for anything, whether it be as insignificant as a handkerchief or as important as a home to live in. To cede such decisions to men is to cede one's own freedom."

She talked fast, the words raining down like precise little bullets into the corpse of tradition. Thane remembered Brodie once saying that his sister was a rather free-thinking person. Apparently, Brodie undersold the fact that she was an outright political radical.

"You're a follower of Wollstonecraft and Robinson and all those other ladies, I gather."

"I am," she said, nodding firmly. "I hope to one day contribute a work as earth-shattering as they have done."

"Are you active in women's…issues, then?"

"I've written several articles for broad-minded newspapers in Scotland," she said, glaring at him as if he was about to denigrate her for the act. "And I've written letters to the editors of narrower-minded ones, though *they* are too scared to print them."

Color had risen in her cheeks as she warmed to this new subject. At least she wasn't crying anymore. That was an improvement.

Now safe from being called out, Thane walked Catriona back to her aunt and his friends. "Thank you for the dance, Miss Ross," Thane said, this time observing the exact dictates of etiquette and not going a step beyond them. It was very common for a gentleman to hint that he would call upon a lady at home on the day following such a party as this. It was an acknowledgment that he enjoyed the dance and the woman's company. Thane wouldn't be calling at Catriona's home, because he'd rather eat broken glass than chat with her again.

Kai leaned over to him the moment they rejoined the group.

"What did you two discuss out there?" Kai asked, his eyes wide. "I swear I witnessed a whole opera's worth of expressions in the span of one waltz."

What could Thane say? He didn't want to get into the discussion of women's rights, which he was hardly qualified to speak on, not to mention that he didn't pay attention to any sort of politics that didn't directly impact the battlefields he fought on. Thane was a very practical man.

"We talked about her carriage accident earlier today," Thane replied dryly, choosing the least controversial of her several conversational topics over the past few minutes. Though something about her recounting of it actually did bother him. Maybe just the sense that it had scared her more than she pretended. Even before the war, Thane had been very good at picking up on people's fear. His time as a soldier honed the sense to a preternatural sharpness.

And he could tell that Catriona Ross was scared of something.

Damn it. He didn't even like the woman, but he couldn't ignore that feeling. For Brodie's sake, he had to at least figure out the source of it. It was probably something inane. But until he knew, Brodie's spirit wouldn't let him rest.

During their short absence for the dance, the group had expanded slightly—there were now two more ladies, one wearing blue and the other green. Catriona already turned her attention from Thane to greet these other women. "Ah, Mrs Roberts. And Miss Fairchild. How good to see you both."

The lady in blue (now identified as Mrs Roberts) gave Catriona an affectionate peck on the cheek. "You as well,

Miss Ross, though I must say I did not expect to see you here!" She gestured vaguely to Catriona's all-black ensemble.

"I certainly did not expect to be here. It's a long story, involving a delivery and a broken carriage and an escaped bird, and some acquaintances of my late brother. I shall explain in full at some later time."

"Oh, perhaps after the rally on Thursday next," the lady in green (evidently Miss Fairchild) said, having eagerly followed the conversation. "You do still plan to attend the event, don't you, Miss Ross?"

"I wouldn't miss it," Catriona assured them both. "I have been working on my speech."

"Excellent! You always make such wonderful points that I think you could convince even the most hidebound man of your argument."

Thane sighed inwardly, watching this exchange. Miss Fairchild seemed to view Catriona with an almost worshipful regard, and Catriona looked a little embarrassed at the praise. "If I can convince anyone of the rightness of our cause, I shall count it a victory," she said, glancing at Thane as she spoke.

Perhaps she considered him the proverbial hidebound man. Thane didn't care.

Though part of him wondered just how convincing she could be. "Where is this revelatory speech to take place?" he asked, out of perverse curiosity. He added, "Just so I can avoid it."

Mrs Roberts replied, "The League for the Advancement of Scottish Women gathers on the second Thursday of every month at the park near Greyfriars to speak out on topics relevant to our cause. And to gather with like-minded people who are brave enough to join us, sir."

Catriona's lip quirked. "Mrs Roberts is one of our very

best advocates, as I'm sure you can tell." She turned to her friends. "I'm afraid Mr MacPhearson and his compatriots are not likely to see the worth of our aims. We would have better luck rallying a stone to our side. Of course, if we waited for men to come to their senses, we would be waiting until doomsday."

Thane didn't bother to respond, knowing a jibe when he saw one. Duncan raised an eyebrow, and Kai looked distinctly uncomfortable. Only Calan spoke, and when he did it was a very Calan response: "Well, if the audience is primarily ladies, it sounds like very good odds for me. When does it start?"

"One in the afternoon," Mrs Roberts chirped, clearly of the opinion that anything to raise the headcount of the event was acceptable.

"Speaking of the time, we had better be going," Aunt Tacita said, tapping Catriona's shoulder. "I told the household we'd be home well before eight! They will surely think we've wandered off into the Highlands by this point."

"Yes, I've kept you both too long," their hostess agreed. "Thank you again for rescuing my little Treacle, Miss Ross. Mrs Murray, I did tell the staff to be ready to call for carriages at any time. You will excuse me from seeing you out to the front hall?"

Naturally, she would be expected to remain at the helm of her party. Mrs Roberts and Miss Fairchild obviously just arrived, and Miss Fairchild was asking the location of the retiring room so that she could repair a rip in her hem that she'd noticed. Thane couldn't see a thing wrong with the gown himself, and part of him wanted to ask why such enlightened women cared about frivolous details like a skirt hem. But he didn't, because he didn't want to risk catching Catriona's claws in his face again.

"Allow us to escort the ladies out," Thane said, seeing

how busy their hostess was. Then he added in a lower tone to Catriona, "After all, the sooner you get to your carriage, the sooner you'll be gone."

Catriona shot him a poisonous sideways glance, which he rather enjoyed. She wasn't nearly as aloof as she pretended. She slid her hand over the crook of his offered arm with the absolute minimum of contact, which had the unanticipated effect of making the light touch of her gloved fingertips more noticeable than otherwise.

Duncan led Mrs Murray out, and the two other men formed a sort of honor guard ahead of them.

Passing him, Calan murmured, "Strategic move, using the ladies to cover our own escape. Well done." Thane didn't crack a smile—so he wasn't the only one who'd been unnerved by this storm of social danger. Even Calan the inveterate flirt knew it was best to flee from all these matrimonially minded women. Well, excepting Catriona, who seemed to disdain the notion of marriage.

The front hall was cooler and quieter than the ballroom... which was like saying it was cooler and quieter than Hell. Kai approached a footman and instructed him to summon a carriage for the two ladies.

The footman warned that it would take quite a while. "There are three parties happening in the street now, thanks to the neighbors not coordinating dates."

Kai gave him a commiserating grin. "Ach, isn't that always the way? Nip out to the side lane and flag down a hired carriage leaving one of the other parties. The ladies can walk to the corner and get in there."

As the footman darted outside to fulfill the request, Thane smiled to himself. Kai always seemed to have a workaround to any obstacle, whether back in the army or here in the city. As quartermaster, he'd shown extraordinary aptitude in procuring virtually anything their company needed, even when others couldn't get the same supplies.

Meanwhile, Catriona and Tacita retrieved their cloaks from a maid and put them on, since the early spring nights were still chilly in Edinburgh. Thane looked around the foyer, noticing the flow of people to and fro. He caught a glimpse of Miss Fairchild, evidently on her way up the stairs to the retiring room, her green gown bright against the shadowed walls. There were also two gentlemen standing in a corner, both wearing dark jackets, gesturing at Catriona, probably discussing her choice of attire. *Odd*, Thane thought, *that men wear black all the time and it means almost nothing. But a woman in black generates all kinds of comments.*

Kai had been keeping an eye out the open front doors, and he suddenly nodded. "Carriage is ready. Ladies, if you don't mind a short walk to the corner?"

"Of course not," Catriona said, bestowing a smile on Kai that was warmer than any expression Thane had seen on her all evening. "So thoughtful of you, Mr Buchanan, to find a way to keep our waiting to a minimum."

"No problem at all, Miss Ross." Kai actually blushed at her compliment.

She can be charming when she wants to be, Thane thought, once again offering his arm. Catriona took it, this time with a slight smile. He was struck by just how much she resembled her brother for a moment. Not that they'd been identical twins, obviously. But the tilt of her head, and that wry twist of the lips…he'd seen that same expression on Brodie's face dozens of times, usually right after he'd won some argument or dropped the punchline of a joke.

"Your ordeal is nearly done, Mr MacPhearson," she said softly, pulling him out of the past. "To the street corner, and then we'll never have to see each other again."

"I'd offer to race you, but I expect your shoes are not meant for running," he returned.

Her laugh was as rich as it was surprising. He could not get used to Catriona's reactions to anything.

They did not run. (For one thing, Tacita Murray was walking ahead of them next to Duncan, and she moved at a measured pace.)

So Catriona and Thane paused for a moment at the top of the steps, waiting politely for her aunt to proceed. Kai remained standing in the doorway, his eyes locked on the carriage at the corner.

Was it the unexpected hesitation that gave Thane the slightest warning of what was to happen? Or did some minute telltale sound alert him?

But before he even knew what he was doing, Thane was already moving, pushing Catriona to the side and away from the doorway, back toward the brick wall of the house, putting one hand behind her head to protect it from impacting against the hard surface. Instinctively, he covered her, using his own body to block hers from view.

A sharp crack shattered the night air. Several feet away, Duncan uttered a curse, and Calan echoed it.

But Thane noticed only Catriona's hushed gasp, and the way her body was fully eclipsed by his own.

She opened her mouth to speak, to scold or yell, but then came another crack.

"Don't say anything, and don't move," Thane ordered, pressing himself against her, lest even the smallest part of her be exposed. Another crack. Behind their heads, window glass shattered, and Cat gave a little shriek of alarm.

He felt her heart pounding in her rib cage, and heard her breath grow fast.

"Stay still," he hissed, ready to haul her back inside if necessary, to use the house as a fortress.

Because someone had just taken two shots at Catriona Ross.

Chapter 5

CAT WAS TOO SURPRISED TO do anything when Thane MacPhearson suddenly lost his mind and shoved her roughly against the wall, then had the audacity to warn her not to move. And what were those loud bangs? Behind her, she heard glass falling to the ground in a strangely delicate-sounding wave, like faerie bells tolling.

"What are you *doing*?" she finally asked, ignoring the bloom of pain in the back of her head from where it had hit the smooth stone.

"Are you hurt?" Thane asked in a low, urgent voice. It was utterly unlike his previous tone.

"Yes! What did you expect would happen when you pushed me into the side of the house?" She rubbed her neck, and cautiously reached up to the back of her head, surprised to find that there was no wound from slamming against the brick. It was as if her head had been cushioned somehow.

Still, she'd likely have a headache later.

"No, I mean did he hit you?" Thane looked her over, his expression anxious. Again, his attitude was so different from before that it left her confounded. "You look all right. No blood. He must have missed."

"Who missed? No one hit me." Was the man drunk and she'd somehow failed to notice until now? Or was he possibly unhinged?

Kai had darted back inside the moment after it happened, and now he returned, his usually pleasant expression serious.

"No one was hurt inside either," he reported. "Looks like a clean miss, except for the window glass. Found one where it buried itself in the doorjamb of the coat closet past the window."

Cat shook her head, hoping to clear it. "Found what?"

"A bullet," Thane snapped.

"What do you mean, a bullet? Why would Mr Buchanan find a bullet?" She realized that her heart was racing, her head was already pounding, and that she didn't feel at all well.

Thane stared at her as if she were dense. "He found a bullet because someone shot at you."

Things happened very quickly after that. Thane herded Cat and Aunt Tacita into the carriage at the street corner, accompanied by the innocent-looking Kai and the considerably less-innocent-looking Calan. Duncan had stayed behind to carry out some task Thane had given him in a whispered tone. Even in her shock, Cat noticed how the other men all obeyed Thane instantly, and how they worked smoothly together despite the oddness of the situation.

None of the men would answer any of Cat's questions, other than to say that they were taking her home, and that everything could be discussed later. Thane and Kai joined them in the carriage (after practically pushing them inside). Without a word, Calan had hopped up to sit next to the driver.

"I was supposed to be home long before now," Cat said softly, staring out the window. Well, she stared out the window until Thane abruptly pulled the shades down. "Excuse me!" Cat objected.

He just glared at her, so she glared back.

Then Aunt Tacita said, "Perhaps it would help us all to

remain as calm as possible." The statement was clearly aimed at Cat, though her aunt was polite enough to not look directly at her while saying it.

Kai nodded. "You are very wise, Mrs Murray. I hope your neighbors won't look askance at the arrival of unexpected guests at this hour," he added, as if the evening's most dramatic occurrence was a bungled invitation list.

"Our neighbors keep their noses out of our business, an example I wish more people would follow," Cat snapped, keeping her gaze on Thane.

"Tell Buchanan about your carriage accident earlier," Thane suggested. "He was curious."

Perplexed by the sudden change in subject, Cat sighed and recounted the incident. Kai did indeed look quite interested, and asked a barrage of detailed questions, only some of which she could answer.

"You'd have to speak to our hostler and driver for the rest," she concluded.

"Thank you, I will," Kai announced, evidently thinking she'd invited him to do just that. "And I think an examination of the carriage will be instructive."

"Ah…as you wish." These were the men Brodie spent his life with while in the army? Lord, they were all daft.

Back at the house, the servants seemed to all have purchased their colors in the time between Cat's departure and return, because from the footmen to the maids to the housekeeper, everyone obeyed Thane's word as they would Wellington himself. Kai followed one of the servants toward the back entrance, a path she'd never seen a guest take before. She'd lost track of Calan entirely. And her head was definitely beginning to ache.

One of the maids helped Cat off with her cloak, and everyone was startled by the sound of glass shards falling to the floor, souvenirs of the window breaking behind her when the bullet flew through it.

"Whatever *happened* to you tonight, miss?" the maid asked.

"That is a tale," Cat said.

"One that requires discussion, but not now," said Thane.

Cat turned to him, surprised. "Wait, what? Why not now?" Although Thane annoyed her every minute he was nearby, the thought of him just up and leaving with no explanation was somehow even more vexing.

"Our objective tonight was to ensure that you both got home safely. Now, you and your aunt ought to go to bed. Which bedroom is yours, by the way?"

Cat gaped at him. Gentlemen did *not* ask unmarried ladies where their bedrooms were located.

"Er, upper floor on the right, looking out toward the back," the housekeeper said when Thane leveled a look at her after Cat's continuing silence.

Thane nodded his thanks to the housekeeper. "Good. Make sure all the windows in that room are locked and that the curtains are drawn completely. Miss Ross, bolt your door from the inside as well."

"It doesn't have a bolt," Cat said, before thinking that this was also a potentially scandalous tidbit of information.

Thane looked heavenward. "Then prop a chair under the knob before you go to bed. I trust you are capable of that?"

"I'm capable of a great number of things, Mr MacPhearson. But I usually like to know why I'm ordered to do them."

"Tomorrow is soon enough for that. Good night, Mrs Murray." He bowed to Aunt Tacita, and then left without another word.

"What just happened?" Cat muttered, not to anyone in particular. "He left Kai behind, and did Calan even come inside? He explained nothing. And he's very rude!" She added that last observation just in time to notice Tacita regarding her with an odd expression on her face. "What?"

Tacita smiled slightly, but then shook her head. "My dear, I cannot put two thoughts together at the moment. But Mac-Phearson was correct about one thing. We ought to end this evening now. Go and get ready for bed, child. With luck, we'll understand more about what happened when the gentlemen return tomorrow and explain what they've found."

"Gentlemen," Cat said with a snort. "More like ruffians, the way they practically kidnapped us."

"Darling, one could only wish for a kidnapper to escort one home at such speed. Now go to sleep. And don't forget to say your prayers."

"Of course, Aunt." Cat gave her a fond kiss on the cheek and then climbed the stairs to the upper floor, a trek that seemed more arduous than usual.

Her maid helped her out of the black evening gown and into her night shift (which was her old white one, for Cat had drawn the line at mourning while unconscious). After declining the offer of a tisane, Cat climbed into bed and blew out the candle.

Staring up at the canopy above, she could hardly believe what had transpired in the last few hours. All that was certain was that from the instant Thane MacPhearson ran into her in the hallway, her life had spun out of control. The cause was obvious: Thane himself.

Where was the daft man now? Probably off carousing with his comrades, laughing about how easy it had been to pull a prank on Catriona Ross…

She shook her head, immediately revising the image. Thane MacPhearson wouldn't carouse or laugh or pull a prank. For one, the man was as dour as the grave, and for another, he obviously despised Cat as much as she despised him.

"Well, if he'd watched where he was going, none of it

would have happened!" she whispered, entreating the darkness for sympathy.

But if he hadn't been there, would the evening have possibly gone much worse for her? Cat's mind shied away from the full meaning of the incident on the front steps. Perhaps that was why it was easier to focus on the details, like the fact that he'd been pressed against her so tightly that she heard—or felt—his heartbeat, which seemed like far too intimate a thing to be privy to, considering they'd been aware of each other's existence for a grand total of one hour.

Though she'd been too shocked to register it at the time, now she recalled how his breath had hit her cheek, and the rumble in his chest when he spoke so close to her. She'd be living with that memory for a long time.

As Cat dealt with the secondhand embarrassment at reliving that moment, she frowned. His heartbeat. Something about it was a bit strange, wasn't it? (Aside from the fact that she'd been close enough to sense it at all.)

Then she realized. Her own heartbeat had trebled the moment he pushed her out of the path of the bullet. And he was far more aware of the danger surrounding them than she had been. Yet his had remained slow and steady.

He'd stepped into the possible path of a bullet with no more concern than most men would if they'd stepped out for a newspaper.

A thin sigh escaped Cat's lips. If Thane did that for someone he didn't even like, what would he do for those he cared about?

He'd move the earth, Brodie told her in her mind.

Cat half turned her head, as if her twin might be there in the room with her. The feeling in her chest surged from the mild fluttering of her silly heart to something too big for one person to hold.

"Brodie," she murmured in the darkness.

He wasn't there. He was never there, and that was the problem. She must be remembering a line from a letter home, or a story Brodie told her while on leave. One of his shaggy-dog tales of life in the army, told in a way that made the dangers feel remote, and the daily life amusing. He could have a whole room in rapture once he got going with a story—he'd had such a gift for voices and mimicry and that perfect command of his audience. Cat always wished she could talk like her brother, knowing just when to pause to draw out a dramatic moment, or drop a detail that colored a whole character. She was well aware that her own style had only directness to recommend it.

"I've got a speech coming up," she said aloud. "If you were here, you could tell me what I'm doing wrong."

You're never wrong, kitty cat. You're always right, and that's your problem.

"Oh, hush." How many times had he told her exactly that?

Then she whispered, "If you really want to help, tell me what to do about this MacPhearson character. I can't believe you could tolerate him, let alone call him a friend."

A brother in arms. I'd trust him with my life.

"Well, I shan't do the same. Though he did save my life tonight. Maybe." She told Brodie the whole story, mumbling the details as sleep settled over her while she communed with the other half of her own being.

* * * *

Cat slept surprisingly well, considering the disruption to her quiet life the previous evening caused. In the morning, she sat up in bed and noticed that the fire had already been lit —the maid slipped in and out without even rousing Cat. Perhaps she should have placed a chair under the doorknob, but the mere idea of acceding to the high-handed Thane MacPhearson's order set her teeth on edge.

"And I lived through the night despite it all," she told herself smugly. She couldn't wait to inform Thane that his silly instructions were unnecessary.

Once dressed in a morning gown in a dark grey (she couldn't abide black first thing), Cat went downstairs in search of breakfast. Not that breakfast was elusive—the staff always put the same items in the same room every day. Cat just liked the idea of doing something intrepid, rather than passively waiting as life slipped by.

But before she could manage to stalk some wild coffee—or whatever one did to obtain coffee in its native habitat—she heard voices coming from the servants' hallway. The tones of the conversation hinted at some consternation, so she hurried forward, only to see Thane MacPhearson standing just inside the tradesmen's entrance, looking like he expected to be allowed all the way in.

"Mr MacPhearson. It is rather early for a social call, is it not?" she asked, hoping to relieve the footman of the unpleasant duty of telling MacPhearson he could go away. "About five hours too early, by my guess."

"Good thing I'm not making a social call," he said, somehow managing to slip past the footman (who was not a small man). "Truly, Miss Ross, my only goal is to sort out what happened to you and why. And that only for Brodie's sake. We've arranged to discuss the matter this morning."

"What, here?"

"Where else? This concerns you, and you live here." He gave the footman a polite nod along with his greatcoat. *So much for telling him he had to leave*, Cat thought.

"And are your comrades equally early risers, or do we wait for all of them to appear on their own schedules?"

Thane shook his head. "They'll be here soon." He turned

and raised a hand to hide a massive yawn.

"I am sorry that my plight is so boring for you," Cat said as she turned back toward the room where breakfast would be.

"I didn't sleep," he said, following, still looking away from her. He seemed preoccupied.

"Why not?"

Now he glanced at her, frowning. "Because I was watching the house."

"This house? *My* house?" Not once had he intimated that he'd be doing that!

"Wouldn't make much sense to watch any other house."

"Where were you? There's nowhere to loiter all night, and it was *cold…*" She had a sudden image of Thane and the other men shivering through a watch, and the grimy touch of shame crept over her. Cat had slept in a very comfortable bed, after all.

"Never mind, Miss Ross," he said abruptly. "That is not relevant. Now, there are a few matters to address—"

"You can't just—"

"Ah, good morning, Mr MacPhearson!" Aunt Tacita had come down the stairs while they'd been talking, looking refreshed and radiant in a deep green dress dark enough to be acceptable for mourning. "Won't you join us for breakfast? I instructed the staff to make more than usual. Young men always have such an appetite."

Ugh. Cat almost lost her own appetite upon realizing that she'd have to endure a meal with MacPhearson. But she put on an icy-bright smile. "Mr MacPhearson will certainly want coffee." If only to stop the yawning in the company of ladies.

In fact, Thane seemed to prefer tea. And a lot of it, to judge by how frequently he reached for the pot.

Cat nibbled her toast in sullen silence, allowing Tacita to

grill Thane on his childhood and family, it being unspoken but understood that the real topic wouldn't be broached until the others had arrived.

Luckily, they *were* prompt, and soon Cat's breakfast table was quite filled with gentlemen all delighted to eat whatever food was offered to them. Tacita must have told Cook that an entire company would be dining with them.

"Struan sends his regrets," Calan said when he arrived (the last of them to do so). "But he'll help later if needed."

The other men all nodded as if this were an expected thing.

"Who's Struan?" Cat inquired. The name was familiar. Brodie had definitely mentioned him. "Another member of your company?"

"Aye. Captain Struan McInnes."

"Oh, yes! Brodie wrote about him. He's very tall and says nothing?"

"You've got him pictured, Miss Ross. He's sorry not to come, but he's been a bit...um..."

"Reclusive," Kai supplied.

"Yes. He's been a bit reclusive lately." Calan grinned at her. "But not to worry. With our combined intelligence, we'll get to the bottom of your little problem."

"Yes, about that. I'm still not sure there is a problem. Surely the response to last night's...incident has been overblown."

Thane put down his cup. "If everyone is finished, let's discuss that."

At Thane's insistence, the men ushered Tacita and Cat into the drawing room. Cat sat down in her mother's favorite armchair, which was upholstered in tan leather and kitted out with an embroidered cushion that did not match the chair. It matched nothing in the known world. It was a singular and shockingly tacky item beset with crude cross-stitch floral designs, tatted lace, mismatched shell buttons, and excessive ruffles.

Cat and Brodie had made it themselves when they were twelve years old as a birthday present for their mother, and they poured their hearts and souls into its creation, unbothered by fashion or indeed taste.

Their mother told them it was the most wonderful gift she'd ever received, and it would have a place in her home forever.

Cat sat in such a way as to shield the pillow from the scrutiny of the men, who wouldn't understand it if they tried. Not that they'd bother to try.

It was a fine day, and the drapes had been opened to let in the bright sunshine. Looking as if the sunbeams personally offended him, Thane ordered the drapes to be drawn shut, and Arnold, the youngest footman, leapt to carry out the command.

"Why do the curtains matter?" Cat asked, remembering that he'd done the same in the carriage last night, and also ordered the maid to close her bedroom drapes.

"A gunman needs a sight line. If he can't see you, he can't shoot you."

"You make it sound like someone's hunting elephants, and I'm the elephant. Why would anyone wish to shoot at me?"

"Well, I only met you yesterday, but I've already wanted to murder you a few times."

"Thane," Calan muttered in a reproving way. "Be serious."

"Oh, I am. But the fact remains that someone else actually did attempt to kill Brodie Ross's wee sister," he snapped to his comrade.

"You can't possibly believe that I'm being pursued by an...an assassin!" Cat burst out. It was ludicrous.

"Let's go over the few incidents that you happened to mention last evening. Your carriage suffered an odd mechanical failure. Despite the fact that it was less than three months old and driven only about twice a week, the pin dropped out and sent the crucial front wheel loose as it turned a corner more sharply than expected. Because your driver had to swerve to avoid the string of caravans that had parked along the side—which isn't usually there and authorities will surely clear out soon, if not today."

Cat blinked. Thane had done some serious investigation while he was shivering in the cold last night.

Kai added, "If you'd been any closer to the edge when the wheel broke off, the momentum would have sent the carriage over and into the ravine. If the impact didn't kill you, being stuck inside the carriage while it filled with water would have been a second threat."

"But in fact, I suffered no more than a bruise or two. It was just an accident."

"Miss Ross," Kai said seriously. "I often was in charge of requisitioning vehicles during the war. The sort of malfunction you describe does not happen to a new, well-maintained vehicle. And I know your hostler treated the new carriage with extreme care and attention, because I asked him and I saw the vehicle in question. He knows his work; your servants are of the best quality."

(In the corner, Arnold the footman's posture straightened even further.)

"Yes, but…let us say that incident was not random chance. It was still just one incident."

Thane shook his head. "Not the only one. You said the dog died."

Cat looked away. "I don't want to talk about that. Check was a wonderful dog."

"I expect he was. Guarded the house, yes?"

"Oh, aye. Check knew the milkman and the lad who brings the paper and everyone else who stops by. But as for strangers, he'd bark as if it were the Devil come knocking."

"Exactly. Not the sort of animal one wants around if they hope to gain entry to the house."

Cat swallowed hard. "What are you saying?"

Thane turned to the housekeeper, who'd materialized at just that moment. "Who found the dog?"

"Young Jenny, sir. She's always first up to collect the milk in from the stoop. She found Check on the kitchen floor moaning in pain."

"No wounds? Had he been struck?"

"Nothing like that," she said. "Just taken very ill, very quickly. He didn't make it to lunchtime, poor creature."

"Sounds like poison," Calan said quietly.

"Oh, my Lord," Cat gasped, suddenly chilled in a way she'd hadn't been before. "They killed Check just so there wouldn't be an alarm?"

Thane nodded.

Cat stared at him, her vision blurring, until she realized she was crying. And not just a few tears. Trying to remain sensible and rational, she intended to explain that Check was a good dog, and also *her mother's dog* and this would not stand, and she'd rip Edinburgh apart stone by stone to find the culprit because that's what justice demanded, but she couldn't even get the first two words out past her gulping breaths.

Chapter 6

THANE HAD LITTLE EXPERIENCE WHEN it came to women breaking down in tears in front of him, and he had absolutely no idea how to deal with it. Luckily, Tacita swiftly swooped down and shielded Catriona from the eyes of the men. As Thane looked at his comrades, he realized that they were no better off, and all of them had in fact already found somewhere, *anywhere* else to look, distinctly uncomfortable with the sight of feminine distress.

If it had been one of his sisters, he'd have bluntly asked what the hell was wrong and who did he have to speak to in order to set things right. If it had been a lover…well, Thane couldn't recall any lover crying in his presence. That was less because of some magical ability to always make a woman happy, and more due to the fact that Thane rarely kept a lover for very long. He liked women very much, but he didn't have a place in his life for one.

And in any case, Catriona Ross fit into neither of those categories, so his previous experience mattered not at all. It was a relief when Tacita helped Catriona from the room.

The moment they left, Kai exhaled in a whoosh, overwhelmed by the sight of a beautiful woman having her heart broken after breakfast.

"Pity the war's over," Duncan said. "Rather face a battalion of Prussians than that."

"It was a lot for her to accept," said Calan. "But I think she does at last realize the truth. The first time I truly registered that an enemy had shot at me, I nearly pissed myself. Think of how a civilian would feel. She never took the king's coin."

Thane nodded. It was one thing for a soldier to experience the violence of an attack. It was expected, and at least there were certain rules in place during war. It was quite another for it to happen far away from the field of battle, to an innocent person.

And not just any person. Brodie's *sister*. Once again, the acute sense of loss tightened Thane's throat up and made his vision blur. Without warning, he saw a vision of Brodie on the first day the two had met—still in civilian kit, he'd been wearing a green jacket and made a joke about emulating Robin Hood so that he could perch in a tree to pick off the enemy. Brodie seemed shockingly young, at a mere sixteen years old. But then again, Kai was about the same age, and so was a good portion of the company. They'd had to grow up fast, or not at all.

"We won't let her get hurt," he said, past the ache. "We owe him that." Thane owed Brodie far more than that, but that was all he could put into words. He couldn't explain to the others that the debt he owed Brodie could never ever be repaid, not even if he'd had a hundred lifetimes to do it. He was the reason Brodie was dead. He sure as hell wasn't going to have his twin's death on his account as well.

Duncan walked over to him and put a hand on his shoulder. "We'll do whatever needs to be done."

"Aye," Calan agreed, his usual charm and banter gone, showing the relentless man underneath.

Kai also stood, somehow looking years beyond his chronological age. "For Brodie." He frowned, adding, "And also, because we shouldn't just let some madman with a gun run loose on the streets of Edinburgh."

Thane always admired Kai's basic decency. A lot of soldiers lost it. Kai never did. None of his friends did.

I do not deserve these men, he thought.

A moment later, Catriona reentered.

Thane blinked, surprised. Now she looked like a queen, dry-eyed and in full command.

"Forgive my outburst, gentlemen," she said in a cool tone. "I promise it won't happen again."

Everyone made the usual noises of *Nothing to forgive* and *Don't think a thing about it.* Catriona sat down on the same chair as before—once again concealing the garish pillow it sported—and looked expectantly at them. "Well, I suppose we should resume the discussion if we are to find a solution."

Thane might need to revise his opinion of her, if she was that quick to recover from a shock.

Just then, Tacita returned to the room as well, bearing a squat pasteboard box. "It might be helpful to look at these items, gentlemen."

"What are they?" Thane asked, accepting the box from her.

"Letters, if one can dignify these communications with that name. Both Mrs Ross and now young Catriona have received many nasty notes in response to their views."

"Aunt!" Cat gasped. "You shouldn't show anyone those. I didn't even know you kept them."

"Dear lass, you know I never throw anything away. And since it was clear the authorities weren't going to take any action about them, I thought it best to hold on to them so I had proof of people's aggression."

While she was talking, Thane had already opened the box on the table and was sorting through the letters, handing them out to the others. "Half of these are signed," he said, surprised.

"Yes. Some writers were as proud of their own views as they were disdainful of Catriona's."

"Um, this is a sight worse than disdain," Kai said after reading through one letter, his face contorted in alarm and disgust. "This is…" He trailed off.

Thane took a few papers and leafed through them. The first letter was merely rude, suggesting that Catriona was poorly raised and educated, and needed to be set straight by her family who had indulged her foolish whims. *Possibly somewhat true*, he had to admit.

The second letter, by contrast, was vile. The writer explained in coarse language how they thought a woman could be put to the best use, and that if Catriona continued to speak and write about the dangerous notion of rights for women, he'd come and show her personally what rights he'd take with her. Living in army barracks for years, Thane was familiar with the language used. But he'd rarely heard it employed alongside such intense hate, and never in conjunction with a well-born daughter of society. In his world, ladies of quality were practically different creatures. It was one thing to speak of a camp follower or a common prostitute in such terms. To use that language to describe a lady…

Calan put down the letter he'd read. "Some of your correspondents are quite graphic in their description of what punishments you should endure for having an opinion." His tone was light, but there was a deadly glitter in his eye.

"Yes, I know," Catriona replied in a low voice. "Stabbing, beating, hanging… I first tried to make a chart with all the possibilities, but I decided not to continue."

Kai must have read through a particularly nasty one, because he looked sick when he finished. "Miss Ross…I am so sorry. You should not have to be exposed to that."

"It is not *your* fault," she told him. "And in fact, such vitriol only strengthens my resolve to enact reforms. Women, all women, should have the right to live freely and safely, on their own terms and not at the mercy of a man who might believe the same hateful nonsense as these letter writers do."

Thane could see the hints of her brother's personality in her words. Brodie had always been ready to jump into action when it came to defending the helpless.

"Have you mentioned these letters to the other women you work with?" Thane asked. "Are such letters common?"

Catriona nodded. "Mrs Roberts, our chairwoman, has received many, and I know other women have been insulted and threatened as well. It's simply something we must accept if we choose to participate in the process of change, just as someone who goes out walking must accept the risk of rain."

Except that rain generally isn't so vindictive, Thane thought. But he said, "Did you ever mention them to Brodie?"

"No, I wouldn't dream of it," Catriona said. "He had too much on his mind already. I wanted to ease his burden, not add to it. And anyway, these letters are just venomous. The people who sent them want to feel superior, and they know that I can do nothing to counter their nastiness. They're harmless bullies."

"The one last night wasn't harmless. You were lucky you didn't get hurt. Or worse."

Cat swallowed, looking chagrined. "I admit that last night's…incident was disturbing."

Funny how all of them kept referring to it as an *incident*, as if they were all trying to avoid the more accurate term of *attempted murder.*

Meanwhile, Catriona was saying, "But I'm sure that whoever it was is content to have frightened me like that. He's probably laughing with his cronies about it, and that's good enough for him."

"What if it isn't good enough? What if he tries again?"

To judge by her helpless expression, Catriona had no good answer.

"You've thought about this quite a bit since last night, gentlemen," Tacita said softly. "What do you suggest we do to protect Catriona?"

Thane said, "Considering that she's done nothing to protect herself so far, anything would be an improvement."

After shooting him a dark glance, Calan added, "We'll seek out the writers of these letters who've so helpfully named themselves, and perhaps we'll get an answer that way, and discourage the person from doing it again. But at least for the next several days, Miss Ross should behave with far more circumspection than she usually does. Stay at home, avoid being seen, that sort of thing. And one of us should remain here as well, in the event that the gunman returns."

Catriona looked puzzled by what Calan was saying. "What? You mean to have one of you stay here, in the house?"

"Yes."

"Who?"

Thane glanced at the other men. In fact, the issue had already been discussed and decided among them, and there would be no room for negotiation. Thane looked back to her.

"Oh, no." She shook her head as if to prevent time from flowing forward. "No, absolutely not. Anyone but you."

"I'm the only one who can be spared," Thane said, using a flat tone that permitted no argument. "I will stay in this house, and there's nothing you can do to stop it."

Cat spun toward her aunt, appealing to her, "Tell him he *cannot* be permitted to stay here. It's against all the bounds of society. We're in mourning. I'm unmarried. He's a stranger."

Tacita just shook her head once. "I'm afraid I can't agree with you."

"What?"

"There is nothing to prevent a household in mourning to offer a room to a guest, provided that the visit doesn't turn into an excuse for frivolity and social entertainment. Mr MacPhearson is going to stay here with a very serious objective in mind, and so naturally we will not be distracting him by hosting dinners or the like to entertain him," Tacita said. "And though he is a new acquaintance to us, he was a trusted friend to Brodie. I can think of no greater recommendation to extend that friendship."

"But *Aunt*!"

"And," Tacita continued, forestalling Catriona's objections, "I believe it's what Brodie would have wanted."

Catriona looked as if she'd been struck. The mention of her twin's wishes seemed to be the one thing that could silence her. Thane filed that fact away for the future.

"I promise to be a very discreet houseguest," he told Tacita. "You won't even know I'm here."

"I doubt that," Catriona said, and then spun on her heel and left.

"Excuse me, gentlemen," Tacita said. "I'd best go after her. She's had rather a trying morning."

Thane had no issue with Catriona retreating to her room after losing the battle. If she was in her room, she was safe. And in the meantime, he and the men could get to work solving the problem of who had shot at her.

He turned to them, saying, "So, assuming that the gunman objects to Miss Ross's social views, we ought to ask around and find out if other people in Edinburgh have had any experiences of a similar nature."

"I'll look at the newspapers from the last month or so," Kai volunteered. "Such an event is probably lurid enough to warrant being written about, if it was public."

"And I'll pay a visit to everyone who actually signed their names to a letter sent to Miss Ross." Calan slapped one letter down on the table in disgust.

Kai shook his head. "Can you even conceive of what Brodie would have done if he'd known about these letters? Thane, you have sisters. Imagine if one of them got a letter like that!"

"I'd hunt the man down," Thane said, his hands clenching as he envisioned what he'd do after getting the bastard alone.

Duncan stood, stretching as he did so (he claimed that every year of his service in the army gave him another creaking joint). "I know one of the magistrates in town. I'll go and speak to him. It may be that the local authorities are aware of such things happening but the news doesn't make it all the way to the newspapers or the gossip circuit."

"Good. You've all got your assignments. I'm going to stop by my rooms and pack a few things before I return here."

"Pack your pistols," Calan advised.

"You're sure you'll be all right, staying in this house?" Kai asked.

Thane waved off the danger. "It's one madman, not an army. I'll be fine."

"I meant...will you be all right being so close to Miss Ross?"

"You mean will I be tempted to kill her myself? Only time will tell." Kai offered no response, but Thane didn't like the way his friends smirked after that statement.

Chapter 7

CATRIONA ALWAYS CONSIDERED HER FAMILY home to be a sanctuary, and to have it invaded by the hulking, oppressive, always-alert Thane MacPhearson was nigh intolerable. It seemed that everywhere she went in the house, he was either already there, or he happened to walk by a few minutes later. Only in her own bedroom did she have some privacy, but one could not remain in one's bedroom all day and all night.

Whenever she encountered him, he had a way of either ostentatiously ignoring her presence, or of managing to make a simple statement sound just short of an insult, such as when she offered him tea the first afternoon.

"Is it from the same pot you're using?" he'd asked.

"Yes. Darjeeling."

He gave the humble brown-glazed teapot a suspicious glance. "Then I'd prefer not to."

"Do you have antipathy toward Darjeeling, or toward our dishes?"

"Neither, Miss Ross." He left before she could say anything more, but the implication was obvious to her. He objected not to the tea service, but the tea server.

"Well, that's the last time I have to be nice to him," she muttered into her raised teacup. The brew suddenly tasted bitter.

However, Thane was always smart enough to never do anything that might get him in trouble with Aunt Tacita. In the older lady's presence, he was mild-mannered, attentive, and charming—the perfect guest. It made it impossible for Cat to raise any specific objections to his being in the house.

Late in the evening on the second day, Cat was coming down the stairs, aiming for the parlor, where she thought she'd left the pamphlets she'd been reading earlier. She paused when she overheard men's voices in that very room. She peeked in, seeing Duncan and Kai speaking with Thane. Thane had removed his jacket, and was pacing in front of the fireplace. *Oh, make yourself at home, sir*, she thought sarcastically, before her gaze was ensnared by the outline of his body under the thin fabric of his shirt, shown clearly as he stood between the fire and her.

Cat had never dwelt much on the male form, considering herself above such flighty musings. But the glimpse of a shape normally hidden from ladies' view was enough to send her mind on unexpected paths. What was so special about the inward curve of his side from the broad part of his chest to the narrower waist? Not a thing. And certainly there was nothing remarkable about a man's forearms. Yet because Thane had rolled up the sleeves of his shirt to the elbows, she'd seen his for a split second, and now, her back pressed against the wall of the darkened hallway, she was somehow still seeing it, complete with the nimbus of firelight surrounding Thane's form.

Cat squeezed her temples with her fingertips. What nonsense. A *nimbus*, no less! As if Thane were some angelic being, rather than a flesh-and-blood annoyance.

Then she heard her name spoken, and refocused on the conversation in the next room.

"—to Miss Ross. I spoke to the Travellers who'd been on the street where the carriage lost its wheel," Duncan was saying. "They told me that a clergyman encouraged them to set up there, at the behest of the church across the street. He even gave them coin, and said there'd be more the next day if they stayed."

"A clergyman?" Thane sounded skeptical. "They're not usually keen to provide aid to such folk. They usually chase them off, calling them thieves or devils."

"I imagine that our charitable gentleman simply used the costume as way to distract attention from himself. When people see a clerical collar or other emblem of priestly rank, that's all they see. The man behind the cloth is invisible."

"Just to be certain, we went to the church," Duncan went on. "The man we spoke to there was quite adamant that no one there did the deed, and he was clear that Travellers—well, he called them something else—wouldn't be welcome inside, or within five miles."

"Not very Christian of him," Thane muttered, and Cat had to agree.

Kai chimed in, "If the clergyman was the shooter in disguise, the so-called charity was more or less a bribe. Thane, this means someone engineered the whole scenario! Using the caravans to block half the road, they were hoping that Miss Ross's carriage would skid out and fly over the edge there, killing her and anyone else inside."

Duncan agreed, saying, "Her aunt and the driver were considered quite expendable, yes. Not to mention passersby on the street, or the Travellers themselves. We're dealing with a person of no conscience."

"I know people get heated about some of the positions these enlightened women take," Kai added, sounding bewildered and upset. "But to murder a lady simply because you don't like what she's saying is hard to accept. Can't they just ignore her?"

"Perhaps they tried," Thane said. "But you've met Miss

Ross. She's not the sort of person one ignores."

Cat blushed. His words could have been a compliment, but his tone was hardly flattering. Feeling suddenly awkward and out of place in her own home, Cat fled back up the stairs rather than face the man who so despised her.

* * * *

The next few days were no better, though she tried to occupy her mind with perfecting the speech she intended to give at the next rally. While Cat had stood up and spoken at various events before, this was only her second legitimate speech, where she would be on a stage and the sole object of the audience's attention. Yes, the stage was little more than a raised wooden platform in the park, but it mattered to Cat to present her ideas just as if she'd been invited to speak before Parliament. Miss Fairchild had strongly argued for Cat to be included on the slate of speakers that afternoon, and Mrs Roberts had happily agreed, saying that Cat's combination of youthful vigor and dignified manner would be an excellent advertisement for any passing folk who might want to hear more. "Just keep your argument straightforward and use logic to bolster your points, dear," Mrs Roberts had said. "And the mourning garb will lend you a certain gravitas that might sway a listener or two. You know, the sort of people who might dismiss you if you wore frothy lace."

Cat chose to focus on the natural equality of women as her topic, and she spent hours writing drafts of her speech. She refined line after line, scribbled new phrases in the margins of her papers, and read other thinkers' books and pamphlets to see if she was missing anything.

She needed to actually practice the speech, though, and she wanted to do it outside. Since she wouldn't be allowed out to the neighborhood's own park, she'd have to make do with the family garden.

The French doors to the garden were in the parlor. Cat was just about to enter the room when she saw MacPhearson standing there, looking out. She halted and pulled back, regarding him warily from the hallway. Not that he was doing something worth regarding, unless one counted the act of standing around in a broodingly handsome fashion to be "doing something." Was he actually keeping an eye on something interesting in the garden? Or was it just a way to block *her* from stepping outside?

She kept her attention on him, trying to decide what he was up to. Her gaze slid to his profile, which was (as she'd been forced to notice countless times before) absolutely perfect if one needed a model for some noble-looking sculpture of a chilly ancient god. The high brow, the long sweep of the nose, the lips that could appear either cruel or sensual depending on his mood…

Her gaze drifted lower, past a simply tied cravat and the equally simple cut of a dark green jacket that skimmed his shoulders and emphasized their breadth. As for the rest of him, she could hardly look at his legs without blushing. The pantaloons were on the tight side, to judge by the fact that she could practically trace the outline of every muscle in his thighs. Thank God the falls were looser, or she'd have to faint like a decidedly non-enlightened woman.

It was almost with relief that she finally noticed his tall black leather boots. The look was appropriate for daywear in the city, though on him, it managed to convey a military readiness. Like he'd be able to break out in a dead sprint at a moment's notice.

"Did you require something?" he asked, looking back over his shoulder. "Or were you just lurking for your own amusement?"

With a start, Cat realized that he had noticed her, possibly a while ago. "I...I intended to walk in the garden." She did not want to tell him that she wanted to practice her speech. He'd probably laugh at her (and she also didn't want to remind him that there was a rally coming up).

"Then do so."

"You're blocking the way."

"I am capable of movement," he noted with his usual patronizing manner.

"You didn't appear to be," Cat snapped back, now striding into the room. "You looked as if you'd encountered Medusa."

He gave her a half smile. "A heroine of yours, I assume."

"Medusa?"

"Well, she lived all by herself and she could turn men to stone. Seems like a lady you'd admire."

Cat wished she could turn him to stone. "Oh, you are a wit. What a shame that you're denying Edinburgh your presence at all the parties, and loafing here instead! If you applied yourself to the endeavor, you could get as many invitations as you liked and be engaged by the end of the week."

A look of such disgust crossed his face that she almost laughed. "No, thank you," he said. "Anyway, as soon as we resolve your situation, I'll be returning home."

"Which is where?"

"My family estate of Kinlochlie is near Inverness. Well, near-ish."

She smiled sweetly. "I'll pray for your swift return."

"Your prayers will strengthen my own," he shot back.

By this time, Cat was nearly level with him at the doorway, and still he hadn't moved aside. "If you don't mind, sir."

Thane looked down at her and seemed about to say something. Cat instinctively raised her chin in preparation to argue whatever point she'd be forced to defend...and realized that they were practically standing chest to chest, close enough to kiss.

Not that she wanted to kiss him, of course. Just the thought of it sent her into a fit of anger, heralded by the heat in her chest and cheeks, a pounding heartbeat, and the urge to run…anywhere. That was anger, wasn't it? Or was it nervousness? She often felt lightheaded before speaking publicly. But this was hardly public. It was very, very private. Only her and Thane…

Who was still looking at her, his expression intent but his thoughts obscured. What was he looking at, his gaze practically down to her décolletage?

Oh. Of course. Her necklace. She nearly always wore a tiny pendant that was the twin of a charm Brodie always carried. Thane must have noticed the similarity.

She put her fingers to the pendant. "We got them on our thirteenth birthday. You know Brodie wore his on his watch chain. But I've always worn mine as a necklace."

Thane nodded wordlessly. Then, all at once, he stepped to the side and back into the room, leaving the doorway wide open. "Out you go. Enjoy the afternoon."

"That's it? No warnings to look for assassins? Or suspicious crows hired as co-conspirators, perhaps?"

"A group of crows is called a murder, so if you notice a large gathering, be alert."

Cat refused to laugh. "And what will you do now? Find another place to lurk?"

"I'll think of something, Miss Ross." He walked toward the door to the hallway, but then turned back. "Don't leave the garden."

"It's walled."

"Knowing you, you'd climb over. Promise me you'll stay on the property."

"All you demand is my promise?" Now she did laugh,

unable to believe he was relying on such a flimsy protection.

"I know you'll keep any promise you make. Brodie always did."

The words hit her hard, choking off her mirth. She nodded. "Very well. I'll stay here in the garden until tea, unless I come back inside the house for some reason."

"Good enough." Thane left her feeling more unsettled than ever.

The garden was green, even at this time of year, mostly thanks to the verdant emerald moss that flourished in the shady spots, and the lighter green of lichen clinging to the stone of the house. Her mother had instructed the staff to not disturb these often-maligned plants. *If they're strong enough to survive Scottish winters, they deserve their place*, she'd said.

Cat took a deep breath, glanced down at the papers in her hands, and then began to recite her speech.

* * * *

Thane allowed Catriona through to the garden, resolving to come back in a quarter hour just to make sure she didn't try to slip out like the little minx she was. Wait, did minxes slip? What actually was a minx anyway? Was it an animal? And if it was, were there any in Scotland?

Ever since he met Catriona, Thane found himself pondering such daft questions. The woman could turn any normal, logical man into a complete mess. Thane sometimes wondered if his brain had turned to oatmeal—arguing with her tended to make him feel like an idiot, and they argued *constantly*. Like the stupid discussion about whether he was blocking the door. He hadn't meant to block the way, and he surely hadn't meant to blather about murders of crows. The idea just popped out, because his damn mind was too focused on the expanse of enticingly soft skin above the edge of her gown. God, she was far too fair to be so cold.

Thank Christ she'd assumed his attention was snared by her necklace rather than the rise of her breasts. And the reminder of the necklace's twin charm did work to snap him out of his daze. Christ, Brodie's sister. This was not a woman he ought to be having such thoughts about.

He paced through the house aimlessly, but he was back in the parlor even before the quarter hour was up. He told himself he was just being careful. He was here to protect her, after all.

When Thane heard Cat's voice, he almost darted past the doors, certain she was talking to someone. But then he saw her walking alone, in a little circle, speaking to herself.

"…it is an essential fact of Nature that there is virtually no difference between the sexes in matters of survival. Male or female, all beings must eat, and find shelter, and defend themselves from attack. Why should we pretend that it is different in our so-called modern society?" Cat inhaled, then went on, "Women must be free to see to their own needs, whether that need is as minor as a meal, or as significant as the selection of a mate. Women are not appendages to men, but fully independent beings in their own right, and expecting of respect….wait, no, demanding of respect? No, damn and blast, what comes next?"

"A thrashing, if you'd said all that in my father's hearing," Thane said, now strolling out to the garden. "He never took it well when anyone upset his view of the world."

Cat looked up from the sheaf of notepapers in her hands, her eyes wide and her mouth falling open. "Excuse me, but I do not wish an audience!"

"Why the hell not? You're rehearsing a speech, aren't you? Not much point in speaking to an empty room…well, garden."

"I'm not ready yet," she protested, her cheeks pinking up. "I haven't even memorized the words."

"If you don't mind some advice, you might be able to concentrate on the words better if you're not treading a hole in the ground."

"Oh, you're here to help, are you?" Cat asked, her eyes narrowing as she put her hands on her hips. She looked annoyed, but also frankly somewhat panicked.

"You're nervous about it," he guessed. "You needn't be. The people who agree with you will think your speech is good, and those who don't agree with you wouldn't like your speech even if it were delivered by Saint Michael himself."

"Thank you for that vote of confidence."

"Considering your ultimate goals, you should be happy for any vote you can get."

Cat bit her lip to stop a laugh, and Thane felt a little thrum of victory.

"Go ahead," he encouraged her. "What's the worst thing that can happen? Afraid I'll puncture a hole in your impeccable logic?"

"You're truly hateful, you know that."

He just grinned, liking how Catriona's eyes sparkled when she got heated. "First piece of advice: don't insult your audience."

"You're not my audience, you're my jailer." She closed her eyes and took a deep breath. "Men cannot live without women," she said then, reading from her paper. "Yet they treat them as if they are completely expendable."

"Oh, please," he objected. "That is far too broad a statement to be supported by evidence."

"The evidence is all around you," Cat retorted. "Society's very structure is designed so that women can be hidden away as wives or mothers or nurses or governesses. Or if they prove difficult to control, men can simply replace them with a more biddable woman in the role. All the laws and customs of the nation favor men's choice in these matters."

"Well, if they do, it's surely because men are responsible for the women under their care."

"Women do not need to be under men's care," she said, adding harsh sarcasm to the last word.

"Miss Ross, you surely aren't suggesting that women could survive without men."

"Let's try it and find out," she said, her hands on her hips. "It wouldn't require too much for the experiment. Let's just take"—her eyes suddenly lit up with a wicked humor—"the Isle of Man. We'll ferry all the men off it and turn it into the Isle of Woman! After a few years, when we're settled in, we'll even send a delegation to Parliament to discuss our results."

Thane shook his head. "You're forgetting a few key details. Your womanly utopia will wither in a generation. It's difficult to sustain a nation without children."

Catriona frowned, as if this wrinkle in her plan truly just occurred to her. "Well, we'd accept newcomers, of course." She brightened. "Actually, it will be perfect, considering all the poor women who find themselves pregnant by scoundrels who've no intention of caring for the bairns they've fathered."

Thane nearly choked on his planned rejoinder. What the hell did Catriona Ross know about bastards and bairns? "You will *not* mention bastard children in your speech."

"Of course not," she agreed easily. "There will be plenty of listeners in the audience who'd faint dead away if I told the truth unvarnished. Mrs Roberts is very careful to not give any reason for the authorities to shut us down. We can't convince others of the rightness of our cause if we're not permitted to talk in public."

"Hold a moment." Thane just remembered something.

"Why are you rehearsing *any* speech? You know it's too dangerous to go out in public while some gunman is taking aim at you."

Catriona drew a breath, then locked eyes with him. "I have to practice my speech, sir. I have to do *some*thing. If I do nothing, I shall go mad."

Thane had too many memories of long days or nights waiting for an order to be given, any order. He sympathized with the desire for action when pinned into place by circumstance. Still, he couldn't let her go to some public place and *speechify*. "Do not think I'll relent on this matter, Miss Ross."

"I know you would not," she said loftily. "But you cannot stop me from hoping that by the time I would give this speech, this ordeal will be over. How foolish would I feel if I simply dithered until the day, only to learn that the man has been captured and I can go forth freely once again? I must prepare for the world I want, even if all I can foresee is the world I'm forced to live in."

She does have a way with words, Thane thought. *Just like Brodie did. Too damn persuasive, that lad. Especially at the end, when it led to...* Thane pulled himself back from contemplating his fatal mistake. He said to Cat, "Very well. Would you like to recite it to me, from the beginning? I won't interrupt."

Catriona just shook her head. The heaviness in her face was there again, and she looked unbearably tired. "I couldn't. If you will excuse me, Mr MacPhearson..."

She moved past him, and Thane almost reached out to touch her. But that would be folly. Hoping to regain control of his own emotions, he reminded her, "You're to stay within the house and garden till we tell you otherwise."

She sent him a withering glance. "I'm aware of what is expected of me. Honestly, Mr MacPhearson, you must think

I'm very dim."

"I didn't say that."

"You didn't have to." Catriona strode off before Thane could think of a suitable reply.

Chapter 8

DAYS PASSED, AND NOTHING CHANGED. Kai and Calan stopped by from time to time, but only to report a total lack of progress. Kai explained that they were going through the names on the signed letters one by one, though several men weren't at home or possibly had moved.

"We'll find them, though," Calan said. "It's just a matter of time."

Though he smiled as he spoke, Cat sensed a darkness in his tone, a relentlessness, a complete unwillingness to let even one of the names slide away. She would not want to be a target of Calan's hunt.

Duncan's visits were fewer, and even less hopeful. He told her, "Can't find any hints of similar aggression in the city, and when I explained what was happening—not using any names, of course—the magistrates all sided with the shooter. They didn't care at all that some madman was taking aim at Edinburgh's residents. One even said that it ought to teach you a lesson to keep your mouth shut."

Cat lifted her chin. "Now you see why we don't wait for men to change things."

Duncan rumbled an agreement. She'd always liked him, ever since Brodie first brought him over for a visit years ago. He was like a friendly bear, sometimes a bit grumpy, but in general a staunch ally and a steady presence.

Thane, who'd been standing nearby, said nothing to that, and she hated him a little more. The man seemed indifferent to her plight, except for how it reflected on his own responsibility to Brodie. That he never forgot, judging by how closely he kept an eye on her. Always Thane was there. And even when he left the room, he remained in her head, regardless of how hard she tried to think of anything else.

The day of the rally crept closer, and Cat despaired of the problem being solved in time to give her speech. She didn't dare speak to Thane or the other men about it—she knew what they would say, and it would be to stay home and skip the rally. But then the shooter would have won, silencing Cat by keeping her confined, even if he hadn't succeeded in killing her.

And anyway, would the man dare take a shot at her in the middle of a park? Surrounded by people, in broad daylight? The attack outside Lady Balfour's party had been at night, with only Thane next to her. This was a very different situation.

Plus she couldn't bear to disappoint Mrs Roberts and the other women. Miss Fairchild had championed her inclusion on the list of speakers—it seemed churlish to back out, citing a shadowy attack that might never be repeated.

So she would go.

The only question that remained was how.

Cat *had* to get outside unseen. If she closed the door to the small parlor, she could slip out the side entrance into the garden, and scale the wall by climbing the oak tree—a feat she and Brodie had done countless times as children when they wanted to go have adventures. Cat and Brodie made a pact to never tell *any*one about their escape route. So the secret remained theirs alone, meaning Thane and his men wouldn't think of it. After she got off the property, she'd go to the little park down at the end of the street, which was surrounded by a tall iron fence and gated to keep out random passersby. Residents held keys, and Cat reasoned that the crazed gunman probably wasn't a neighbor, or else he'd have shot at her closer to home. There she'd wait just long enough to make sure no one noticed her departure, and then she'd hail a hackney cab to take her to the site of the rally. She had coins for the fare, she could tuck her speech in her reticle, and she'd leave directly after her part in the rally was done. She'd be back in less than two hours. With luck, no one would miss her at all.

She dressed in her usual black, wishing that it wasn't quite so dramatically different than the spring surroundings of new green grasses and budding trees. Perhaps she was being a little capricious.

No. She had a duty and she intended to complete it. Just as Brodie carried out his duties as a soldier, regardless of risk. She touched the charm at her neck.

"Wish me luck, brother," she whispered.

* * * *

On Thursday, morning came and went, and Thane felt his eyelids dropping a bit. He hadn't been getting enough sleep since he started watching Catriona. And not just because of the late-night watch duties. The woman seemed to designed to rob a man of sleep—if he wasn't fuming over something she said, he was getting distracted by her face and figure. A woman so determined to eschew men shouldn't be so damned alluring. If he had to watch her nibble the end of her pencil while she stared out the window composing her next speech one more time…it was maddening. Especially because he knew that technically, he did not have to look. But he wanted to look. Something in him craved the torment Cat so unwittingly caused.

But now, no one was presently tormenting him. The whole house was covered in a hazy, sleepy quiet. Yes, he knew that the servants were moving around, especially in the kitchen and in the back of the house and the small yard—he could hear the splash of water as a few of the young women washed household linens. But the main rooms were totally empty. Tacita had gone up for an hourlong nap, which he'd learned was the lady's habit.

Catriona had been talking to the housekeeper earlier, but he hadn't seen her since midmorning.

A housemaid came by, a bucket of coal in each hand. She bobbed a curtsey to him.

"Excuse me, Jenny. Do you know where Miss Ross is?"

"The side parlor, sir. By the garden doors. At least, last time I saw her."

He let the maid go by and then made his way to the parlor, hoping to catch Catriona in a good mood. Maybe they could talk like civilized people for once.

"Miss Ross," he called, knocking on the closed door. "May I come in?"

There was no answer. He rolled his eyes. So much for civilized conversation. She must be determined to act like a brat today.

"Miss Ross, it's important."

Still nothing. He frowned. It wasn't like her to keep quiet—a wickedly barbed comment was far more her style.

"Catriona?" he asked, risking her given name. Unbidden, a familiar burn began to form in his gut. It was the feeling that accompanied him so often as a soldier. The feeling that something was wrong.

He opened the door and strode in, preparing for an indignant yelp from Catriona, or some censure for not respecting a lady's privacy.

But the parlor was empty.

"God damn it." He quickly crossed the room. The glass doors to the garden were closed, but not locked. Had someone got in and taken her? She would have screamed the house down at the sight of an intruder. Unless the intruder had the means to silence her.

Thane cast about, searching for some clue.

A half sheet of paper lay on the floor, pinned down by the leg of the chair. He bent and picked it up. Not a ransom note, he realized instantly. Just one of the announcements that Cat and her ladies' league always seemed to have in their reticules, ready to foist upon unsuspecting people. This one was for an upcoming event in the park promising speeches on the cause of women's rights.

Then he inhaled sharply. This wasn't an upcoming event. It was today. It was happening *now*.

And Cat had snuck out of the house to be there to give her damn speech.

Chapter 9

THE DAY WAS IDEAL FOR an outdoor gathering. White rags of clouds raced across a blue sky, even the lowest of them far above the summit of Arthur's Seat. Sunshine flooded the world as soon as each cloud passed, and the park was lushly green, with dark grass underfoot and the lighter green of young leaves dappling overhead.

A banner with the name of the League for the Advancement of Scottish Women had been hung up between two trees. Mrs Roberts had arranged for a small wooden platform to be set up in one of the sunny clearings near the main path through the park. It was just large enough for two people to stand upon, but not three.

"Perfect for an execution," Miss Fairchild quipped nervously. "I worry that half this crowd would like to see us all beheaded."

Catriona had to admit she had a point. There were plenty of onlookers. Many of the women had come expressly for the event to hear from the group and give support. But there were others—both men and women—who clearly thought this was more of a theatrical side show, a farce. And there were definitely a few men who were enraged by the day's topic. One had shouted obscenities until a guard employed to keep the peace steered him to the edge of the park. (Cat suspected the man's infraction was not intimidating her colleagues, but rather upsetting the park's passersby with coarse language.)

Cast also looked around anxiously to see if Thane or any of the other men had come. She was still hopeful that she'd be back home within the hour, and Thane wouldn't even notice her absence. She planned to sneak back into the garden and then through the glass doors to the parlor. Then she'd pretend to have been there all along.

She didn't see anyone, so she assumed her subterfuge was working. She felt a little smug. The threats against her life were quite overblown, after all.

Mrs Roberts had opened the proceedings and was just finishing a rousing speech, to the cheers of most fervent attendees in the front.

"Your cue!" Miss Fairchild said, pushing Cat toward the stage. "Knock 'em dead!"

Cat took a deep breath and stepped onto the little platform. Mrs Roberts took her hand, and raised their arms together, to some applause and a few catcalls.

Mrs Roberts announced Catriona as the next speaker and then climbed down. Clutching her copy of her speech, Cat looked over the crowd. It was more intimidating when she was elevated like this, where everyone could see her and judge her. For a moment, she wanted to turn and flee.

But no. That was not what she came here to do. She inhaled, smiled, and said, "Thank you all for coming to listen to the voices of your friends, your sisters, your daughters, your mothers. It takes great courage to listen to new ideas… but I hope that by the end of the day, you'll all recognize that what we ask is only what everyone here would ask for themselves. We wish to be treated fairly. We wish for our voices to be valued at the same level as the men of this country. That is all. For it is an essential fact of Nature that there is virtually no difference between the sexes when—"

Someone in the crowd shouted, a loud male voice. She thought it must have come from one of the angry men toward the back, so she tossed her head and tried to ignore it.

"Er, no difference when it comes to survival—" A sudden crack broke through the air, and Cat gasped as something whistled past her.

Then everything seemed to happen at once. Mrs Roberts screamed in alarm, a huge form knocked Cat down and pulled her off the platform, and the crowd shifted and pulsed and split apart all around her.

"What…"

"Stay down!" Thane's voice ordered, right by her ear.

Oh, God, he was the person who'd come flying at her! Cat could barely breathe with Thane's weight on top of her. This was far more intense than the first time, when they'd at least both been standing.

Perhaps Thane realized that too, because he rolled off her and grabbed her by the shoulders, helping her to her feet.

"Keep your head down," he muttered. Thane flung his light-colored coat around her and ran for the nearest gate. Another crack echoed behind them.

"Lord, they could hit somebody—" she said, shock making her mind slow.

"They're trying to hit you!" Thane sounded so angry that it silenced her, and she let him push her into a carriage for hire. He shouted the directions at the driver sitting above and hopped in as well, sliding next to her on the bench.

"Slouch, as low as you can," he ordered, pushing her downward.

"What, on the floor?"

"Yes! Duck your head."

She understood then that the hired carriage had no curtains to pull closed, not like her family's own well-appointed vehicle. She sank onto the floor, gathering her skirts tight around her legs, trying not to think of all the boots and shoes and bare feet that had stepped there. With her head down, she couldn't see where they were going, or if anyone was following them. Thane said nothing useful, only telling her to keep low every time she tried to ask what was happening.

The carriage took a hard right turn, knocking Cat from her precarious crouch, so that her knees hit the floor. *Well, that's the end for this dress*, she thought, hearing a seam rip somewhere. She let out a laugh, more from shock than amusement.

"What," Thane said, sounding distracted. He was peering out the window, not focused on her.

"Nothing," Cat muttered. "It's just that my clothing fares poorly around you."

She looked up, realizing that she was kneeling at his feet, and he was staring at her with an expression she'd never seen before.

* * * *

"Get up here. On the bench." Thane looked away, trying to catch his breath as she scrambled up. Christ, Cat on her knees was an image he'd never get out of his head.

"You said I should hide," she protested, fussing with her black dress.

"It's safe enough now. Whoever the shooter was, they couldn't have followed us fast enough."

"They don't need to follow, do they? They know where I live." She sounded scared and small and miserable. And he hated it.

"I can't believe you snuck out like that." Anger and the lingering hit of lust made his next words harsh. "You deserved to get shot."

It was a mean thing to say, and he waited for the retort, the furious protest. But Cat only gave a soft moan. He looked over to see her hunched over and crying, clutching at the little charm at her neck, the same one that Brodie always carried.

"I know," she whispered. "I was stupid. I should have died."

"Cat, don't—" Whatever he meant to say was forgotten when he saw something bright red on the back of her hand.

He pointed at the spot. "What the hell happened?"

"What?" She looked up, confused, and then down at the growing streaks of red dribbling onto her skin. "Is that blood?" she asked, as if from very far away.

"Were you hit?" he asked, reaching out to touch her, run his hands over her body.

The moment he grazed her upper arm, she winced and cried out.

"Christ, you're wounded." He whipped out the square from his pocket and held it to the spot.

Cat shrank away. "It hurts!"

"Of course it hurts! Stay still. When we get you home we'll see how bad it is. Just breathe slowly. Are you hurt anywhere else?"

"I don't know." Her face was ashen, but he couldn't tell if it was from an injury or just from the shock of what happened.

He very lightly ran his free hand over her torso and her other arm, then down her legs. She didn't even object, which he took as a bad sign.

"Do you think you were hit twice?" he asked. Hell, when would this carriage get to the house?

"I...I don't think so. It would hurt a lot, wouldn't it? Have you ever been shot?"

"Aye, few times," he said shortly. "Believe me, you notice."

"Then why didn't I?"

"Well, there's sometimes a delay. And you weren't expecting it."

"I wasn't expecting you to tackle me either. And I hurt from that."

He restrained his impulse to yell. In a strained tone, he explained, "I had to get you out of the shooter's sight line."

"Do you think anyone else was hurt?" she asked, worry clouding her eyes.

"I don't know. I hope not. Probably the man fled as soon as he realized he wasn't going to get another clear shot."

"Did you see him?"

"No. But maybe someone else did. We'll work on that later."

Just then, the carriage clattered to a halt. Thane helped Catriona out, thrust some coins at the driver, and then hurried up the walk. He felt acutely exposed with their backs to the street, so he put his arm around her shoulders and kept her as close to him as possible to make her a more difficult target. Though, he thought wryly, Cat's stalker probably would be happy to hit them both. Considering that he'd opened fire outside a busy party and then later amid a crowd in a park, the man clearly didn't care about collateral damage.

When Thomas the footman finally closed the front door after they got in, Thane heard himself give a sigh of relief.

"Were you out, miss?" Thomas asked, confused because all the servants had been told in no uncertain terms that Miss Ross was meant to stay at home.

"It's not important now, Thomas," Thane said. "Will you send for the family doctor? Miss Ross may need some medical care."

The footman's eyes went wide and he rushed out the

door.

Meanwhile, the housekeeper had come in, taking in Cat's appearance—including the blood—with an admirable calm.

"Bring her down the hall to my room. We'll want hot water, and the kitchen will be close."

Thane was evicted from the housekeeper's little office the moment after Cat sat down in a chair. (The removal of some of her clothing meant that no male could be let near her, with the notable exception of the doctor.)

So Thane sent word to the other men to come to the house for a meeting, and spent the next hour pacing in the parlor, waiting for news of Cat's condition.

Then the doctor walked in. "You're MacPhearson? The man who brought her back home?"

Thane snapped to attention and nodded. "Yes, sir."

The doctor was a man of about sixty years of age, with silver hair and crow's-feet at the corners of his pale blue eyes. He took one look at Thane and said, "France?"

Thane nodded. "And the peninsula, depending on the year."

"I was over there too for a while, treating the wounded. I still wake up nights, remembering what I saw. Turns men's minds, sometimes. Do you think that's what happened today? Some discharged soldier in the park just…forgot where and when he was?"

Thane shook his head. The doctor's question implied that Cat hadn't confided the full truth to him, so Thane wouldn't either. Aloud he said, "I'm afraid we don't know. My friends and I intend to find him if we can."

"Aye, I hope someone does. Absolute madness to fire upon innocent people in a park, of all places. It could have been fatal."

"But Cat—Miss Ross will recover?"

"Oh, yes. She suffered a graze to her upper arm from the

passing bullet. I cleaned it and bandaged it. She'll be right as rain in no time. In less than a fortnight, only a scar will be left."

"Thank God," Thane muttered, though he was angry that she'd still have a scar to haunt her.

"Wise of you to call me round, in any case. I suggested a wee dram for medicinal purposes. She's quite shaken. Poor lass. I've been treating the whole family since she and her brother were babes. Never imagined I've have to see her like that." The doctor looked more closely at Thane. "You're her…intended?"

"Just a friend of the family," Thane said hastily. "I served with Brodie."

"Ah. So that's it. Didn't really think she'd get engaged again anyway."

Thane's head nearly snapped around. "*Again?*"

"Er, yes," the doctor said, startled at the reaction. "Did you not know? Well, perhaps you wouldn't. She had a young man, oh, a few years ago now. Broke it off and he took it rather badly. I had to come to the house to patch up Brodie's nose—he and the other lad got into a fistfight about it."

"Brodie never said." *And neither had Cat.* Thane intended to question her about that as soon as he saw her.

The arrival of Calan and Kai gave him something to think about until he could talk to Cat. He gave the men all the information he had.

"Christ. I need a drink," Calan said after hearing the news.

"Ask the footman. He can direct you. And get one for me and Kai as well. We're going to need fortification."

Calan left and Kai asked, "Why fortification? The worst is over, isn't it?"

"The worst is never over, because the worst is Miss Ross herself."

"That's hardly complimentary." Kai crossed his arms, frowning.

Thane snorted. "You don't have to deal with her every day. She's an extraordinarily horrible person."

"She's an ordinary person going through a horrible time," said Kai. "It's different. Would you judge a man based on how he behaved the night after a battle when he'd lost half his squadron?"

"No." Thane sighed. "I hope I wouldn't."

"Besides, I can't picture Catriona Ross being horrible. Brodie always spoke of her as the sweetest thing on earth."

"He may have not been completely objective."

"Not like you," Kai said.

"I'm objective," Thane objected. "It doesn't matter to me if she's the Devil. I'm just fulfilling a promise."

"Oh, I see." Kai nodded, and his expression was completely innocent. But Thane felt the weight of meaning in those few words.

"A promise to Brodie," he clarified. "And once it's done, I don't need to or want to see Catriona Ross ever again."

"Mm-hmm."

"She's a vexing person. Argumentative."

"Indeed."

"She always thinks she knows best." Did Thane sound defensive? He felt defensive.

"Ah."

"And she doesn't listen. Or admit when she's wrong. Which is practically always."

"Sounds difficult to live with."

Calan returned with small tray holding three glasses, which distracted Kai from saying anything more. The men each took theirs, and Calan then raised his to the other men and said, as if he'd asked himself this several times before, "Why the *hell* did she go today?"

"Because she said she would," Kai replied.

Thane and Calan looked at him, Thane wondering if Kai had some insight to Cat's behavior.

"Don't look surprised," Kai told them. "Brodie was the same, and you both know it. If he said he'd do a thing, by God, he did it, even if he could have begged off with some excuse. Or even a good reason."

"That's true enough," Calan agreed. "Remember the whole Christmas pig fiasco?"

Thane laughed and groaned in equal measure. "I still can*not* believe he did that. The company will be telling tales about that night for decades."

Kai was laughing too. "That poor pig. Brodie never should have been let near a farmyard. Anyway, my point is that he wanted people to rely on him. So it's no surprise his twin believes that as well."

A knock at the front door signaled Duncan's arrival. The men quickly told him the latest developments.

"Ought to lock her in a tower," Duncan said. "I mean, if any of us had the authority to do so, which we don't."

"Oh, that reminds me," Thane said then. "I learned a fact from the family doctor, who just happened to mention it, even though Miss Ross didn't bother. She's got a jilted suitor."

"What?" Calan looked surprised, deservedly so.

"A few years ago, she was engaged and broke it off, and the man was so angry that Brodie got into a fight with him. It may possibly be relevant."

"Who's the man?" Kai asked, ready to write it down.

"Patrick Melrose," Thane said. "I found that out from the footman, after the doctor left. Apparently, his family lives not far from here. Would be good for someone to look him up."

Kai gave him a nod, accepting the order. "I'll find him."

"I'll come too," Calan added. "Just in case."

"Duncan's idea of locking her in a tower is perhaps a bit direct," Thane said, "but we do need to do something different to what we've been trying so far. Even if Miss Ross actually *stayed* in this house, there are too many ways to get to her. If they poisoned a dog, they can poison a person."

"Not to mention they could put a shot through a window at an opportune moment," Calan grunted. "It would be best to get her out of the city altogether."

Kai frowned. "Aye, we could split our forces. One or two of us could escort her and her aunt somewhere safe, while the others remain here and continue the search for the shooter."

"Who's on what detail?" Duncan asked. "I'm better at nosing around, I think. So's Kai. And Calan is a good man to have on hand if we need to get answers from someone who doesn't want to talk."

"Struan would be an excellent choice to escort the ladies," Kai said. "Along with you, Thane, since you're already familiar with them."

"But where do we escort them?" Thane asked. That was the difficult question. Where in the world would Catriona be safe?

The men discussed possible options, whittling them down, discarding one after the other due to various weaknesses or complications.

Thane didn't like the final option, and he knew Catriona would like it even less.

Just then, Catriona walked into the room, with Tacita close by. Cat had changed into a grey dress, and maybe that was why her skin looked a bit more healthy and pink. Then again, the doctor did say he gave her a dram of spirits, so maybe that explained the color.

"Gentlemen," she said, sitting down on the chair with the

hideous pillow. "Thank you for your patience. I am now willing to concede that someone is trying to kill me."

There was an apology in her tone, and even a little humor. Thane couldn't help but admire it, though he was still furious at her decision to go to the park in the first place.

"We're glad you're not dead," Kai said brightly.

"As am I. My actions today were unbelievably foolish," Cat went on, her eyes flicking to Thane. "I…I didn't want to believe the truth."

"It's not an easy truth, Miss Ross," Duncan said.

"Whether it is or not, I should have listened to you all. I am sorry."

"You didn't listen before," said Thane. "So perhaps you'll listen now. If you want to keep on living."

* * * *

Cat gave Thane a wary look. She didn't care for ultimatums, but he did have a point. "I'll listen to what you have to say."

"Very sensible," Tacita approved from her perch on her favorite chair by the fireplace. She'd been horrified to see Cat's wound earlier, though she'd calmed down since thanks to a splash of whisky in her tea, courtesy of the housekeeper.

Cat tried hard to hide her discomfort from the bandaged wound. The doctor assured her it was minor and she'd recover completely and quickly. But it burned now, throbbing painfully despite the hearty dose of medicinal brandy she'd drunk down herself.

"Are you all right, Miss Ross?" Duncan asked, evidently not fooled.

She nodded. "Aye. Well, let's have it done so you don't have to linger here all night." Not to mention that people might start to talk if four unmarried men were in Cat's home for hours on end. The one was bad enough! "What do you think of my situation now that I've made a bigger mess of it all?"

Kai waved a hand, dismissing the notion that she was at fault. Calan said, "Trust us, Miss Ross, we have no wish to make your life more difficult."

Thane, she noted, said nothing.

Cat urged them on. "Clearly, you have something particular to tell me. Pray be blunt if necessary. We seem to have left convention by the wayside long ago."

"Well said." Calan nodded.

"So what is the plan? Oh, I know. I change my name and wear Brodie's old clothes, enrolling in one of the medical schools to learn how to be a surgeon, so I can stitch up my next bullet hole myself." She was being sarcastic, but she suspected that the real plan would somehow be more ridiculous.

"Nothing so drastic, Miss Ross," Kai assured her. "We discarded several ideas simply because they would raise too many eyebrows around town. We don't want your attacker to know that he's being sought by us."

Cat breathed a sigh of relief. "I'm glad to hear it. So what ideas weren't discarded?"

"Only one," Calan said, though his handsome expression looked anything but pleased.

"One? Dear Lord, it had better be genius."

"It'll be unexpected," Kai said.

Cat gripped the arm of her chair, mentally bracing herself. "Tell me."

Duncan said, "We've got to get you out of Edinburgh, to a location where it's easier to control who's coming and going."

"Oh, that's very sensible," she agreed, relaxing. "My family has a house near Cardross on the river Clyde where we typically go in summer. I'll simply arrange to go earlier, and—"

"No, that won't do," Thane interjected. "We have to assume that the person trying to kill you is aware of all the houses your family owns, and could easily pursue you there. Or worse, that he's already got a plan for how to kill you at that house, which he might have visited beforehand."

"Then where can I go? Rent a house? You make it sound like this madman has some way of tricking me into renting his *own* house!"

"Thought of that," Kai said, nodding, as if pleased she caught on to this insane idea.

"The only locations we can trust are ones we control," Thane said.

Cat's jaw almost dropped to the floor. "One of *your* houses? Whose?" She looked at the men in turn, wondering which of them was going to produce a cottage out of nowhere.

They all looked to Thane, who ground out, "Mine."

Chapter 10

CAT WAS MISERABLE. NO, SHE wished she were merely miserable. Misery was a level to aspire to. She was somewhere far below misery, and if Death appeared at this moment and offered to take her away, she'd listen.

Worse than learning that of the five men from Brodie's company, it was Thane MacPhearson who she'd have to accept hospitality from, it turned out that she also had to get to this supposed safe haven by *sea*.

The men had decided that traveling by road was too predictable and therefore too dangerous. The many rest stops and changeovers meant more opportunities for Cat's enemy. So Thane decreed that they'd go most of the way by ship, leaving the harbor in Edinburgh in the dead of night, and arriving in a small port town fairly close to the MacPhearson family holdings in the Highlands. Cat hadn't asked what "close" meant, and now she assumed it merely meant "also in the northern hemisphere," because it felt like they'd been sailing for about one hundred years.

Cat thought back to yesterday (had it been just yesterday?) when Aunt Tacita not only failed to tell the men to all get out, she'd actually agreed that making Cat leave the city was a good and worthy idea. Cat had protested vociferously, but in the end Tacita simply said, "Go pack some things, dear. You're going, so you might as well go gracefully."

Thus Tacita had spoken, and Cat was powerless to deny her aunt's wish.

But, oh, how she wished she could! The ship rocked relentlessly on the sea, the pitch and roll of the deck mocking her pitiful attempts to keep her stomach's contents inside her body where they belonged. Bile rose, and she scrambled—again—for the bucket in the corner of the cabin. Lord, how could she *still* be sick? There was nothing left in her to be thrown up. And yet.

Gagging at the vile taste in her mouth, Cat still gave a sigh of relief. If the past experience of the several hours she'd been at this was reliable, she would have about five minutes of internal calm before she'd need to repeat the process.

The door to the cabin banged open, and Thane strode in, disgustingly hale and hearty. "Miss Ross! Didn't you hear me calling?" He looked around, and finally saw her huddled in the corner of the cabin. "What the hell are you doing down there?"

"What do you think?" she growled, gesturing to the bucket. Then a wave of nausea hit her again. Early! No doubt it was a reaction to *him*. She quickly bent her head over the bucket again.

Thane moved closer.

"No!" she said, holding one arm out to stop him. "I'm disgusting. Everything is disgusting."

"You didn't say you got seasick so easily."

"How would I know?" she spat, furious at him for existing. "I've never sailed before, you hideous…kidnapper!"

Thane knelt by her, but offered no words of comfort. Instead, he hooked his hands around her shoulders and hauled her up. "Come with me," he ordered, virtually dragging her along.

"Saints preserve me, where? Are you going to throw me overboard?"

"At this point, I'm considering it," he muttered, guiding her through the narrow passage and then up to the deck.

A spray of seawater hit her cheek the moment she emerged. Cat grimaced at the cold, though it was a salve to her overheated, sweaty skin.

Then the ship rolled again, and her stomach heaved along with it. Cat moaned and lurched toward the side. Thane practically pushed her to the rail, his hand on her back as she cast up what little remained in her stomach into the swirling waters below.

After a few dry heaves, she stood there, stiff-armed against the rail, her whole body shaking from the aftermath of her sickness.

"I want to die," she said, her elbows suddenly buckling.

"Don't say that." Thane grabbed her and pulled her away from the rail. Cat was unable to keep her feet, her muscles having turned watery. He swung them both around and slid down so that he was leaning against the gunwale's side and she was leaning against him.

It was inappropriate, to say the least. But how could she object when she couldn't even walk? Raindrops spattered over her, sticking strands of hair to her face. Weakly, she tried to pick them away. She *hated* hair on her face.

"Let me," Thane said gruffly. "You're done out."

His fingers smoothed back the loose strands, and then wiped away the wetness of the rain, or tried to. It was a losing battle.

"Is this punishment?" she asked. "You hate me so much that you chose to sail so I'd flip inside out on the journey."

"Today's a rather rough passage, though as you said, no one knew you'd have this reaction," he said. "But I chose it for speed and safety, not to punish you."

"What good is it to arrive faster if I die on the way?"

Thane, damn him to hell, chuckled. "You're not dying. A touch of seasickness never killed anyone. Once you're back on land, you'll feel just fine."

A *touch* of seasickness? "I hate you," she said.

"Aye, you've made that clear before."

"Oh, no. I disliked you before. Now that you've put me on a ship, I despise you. Oh, God." Her stomach heaved once more, and she tried to stand.

Thane instantly helped her up and kept her in one place as she vomited over the side again. His legs, steady as anything, pressed against her own, pinning her so she couldn't lose her footing…though at the moment, the ship was listing dangerously far to the side.

Cat saw the surface of the sea come closer, closer. In a panic, she gripped him hard, terrified she'd slip free and fall.

"I've got you," he told her, his voice as unwavering as his stance. "You won't fall, Cat. I've got you."

She took a breath. The ship was righting itself, and the sea pulled away. Cat's nauseousness was temporarily forgotten. "Oh, God," she whispered. "I hate the sea."

"I didn't know," he said in apology.

"I didn't hate it until today!" she snapped, turning her head to look back at him.

She caught those green eyes gazing at her with an emotion she'd never seen before. Not from Thane anyway. *Tenderness.*

"You can let me go now," she said, furious that he was so close, and that he might have just saved her life. Again.

"Perhaps you'd first let *me* go?" he inquired, amusement in his voice.

With a start, Cat realized that her hands were spread over his thighs, gripping tightly, and she could feel his muscles underneath the linen, hard and taut. She released her hold as if scorched. "I *didn't* intend that!" she warned him with a glare. God, he was…a very strong man. Did he develop those muscles from riding? Did his other muscles compare?

What are you thinking?! one part of her mind screeched in alarm.

The other part was registering that Thane had again helped her to sit down on the deck. He sat beside her, which ought to have felt safe, except she could only gaze at his thigh lying next to her own leg, the outline of which was clear due to the sopping-wet fabric of her gown. She plucked at the skirt to obscure the too-obvious shape of her legs underneath.

"Leave it," he said. "No one can see."

"You can see."

"So? You've told me again and again that my opinion is worth less than nothing."

"Well, that's true," she grumbled. She did not care *at all* what Thane thought of her legs.

He went on, "Though I must tell you, as fact and not opinion, that your complexion is a rather alarming shade of green. I've seen others get seasick, but I don't think I've ever seen it this bad."

"Imagine if you had to feel it instead of see it." She raised a hand to her cheek, wondering exactly what shade of green her skin was. "Do I look hideous? I feel hideous."

"You could never look hideous," he said with a little smile.

Dear Lord, was he being *kind*? She must resemble a corpse about to be dropped six feet down.

"Why are we out here instead of inside?" she asked, feeling the sting of the wind.

"The fresh air will help you. And some say that when you can see the ship move through the water, it makes the seasickness lessen."

"I feel no better."

"Give it a moment."

"The cabin did stink," she said, sniffing the mineral tang of the sea air. "At least it smells better out here."

"Aye, there's nothing like it."

"I always thought the ocean smelled bad."

"Near the shore, sometimes. But that's not the ocean. That's the seaweed and the fish and the shells and all the work that goes on near the shore. Out on the water, it's different. Purer."

She nodded, admitting to herself that he was right. Then the breeze swept across her, chilling her wet face and body. Cat fought off a shiver. "My cloak's in the cabin."

Thane immediately shrugged out of his heavy wool jacket and settled it over them both, like a blanket. He put his arm around her and drew her closer to him.

"Take long, slow breaths," he advised. "Keep your gaze on the horizon and just try to stay calm. We've hours to go, but the good news is that the ship's dinners are never very good. You won't miss a thing."

She bit back a gag at the mere thought of food. "I hate you."

"Yes, I know. Breathe. There you go. We'll go back below deck in a few minutes, once you feel better. That's fine. You're doing just fine, Cat."

She laid her head back, only to encounter his broad shoulder. She was too drained to resist, and in fact his body did make a rather excellent pillow. She'd relax just for a moment, until she opened her eyes again…

* * * *

Thane kept his arm tight around Cat as she finally gave in

to exhaustion. She must have been in absolute misery down there in the cramped, airless cabin, probably feeling ill from the moment the ship left the safety of the harbor.

A sailor passed them, and spared a look for Cat. Even sick as she was, her face held an undeniable beauty.

"She all right?" the sailor asked.

"Seasick is all. Fresh air is the best cure."

"Aye, so it is. But when your wife wakes, give her a touch of warm brandy too. Her throat'll be raw."

"She's not..." Thane instantly gave up on explaining. "Aye, I will. Thanks for the advice."

The sailor nodded and moved on.

His *wife*. If Catriona heard that, she would have jumped up and slapped him across the face for perpetrating such a foul notion. Poor Cat. First dragged aboard a ship, then heaving her guts off the side, and, worst of all, being mistaken for *his wife*.

Unexpectedly, Thane smiled. This would be a fun taunt for later.

Then Cat murmured something and nestled closer to him under the cover of the jacket, and all thoughts of teasing fled. She was so soft. It was difficult to believe, especially since her whole attitude was more barbed than a porcupine. But when she was asleep, her tart tongue couldn't come up with the deadly insults she seemed to have infinite stockpiles of. Christ, they should have had *her* at the front. Artillery? Why bother? The enemy would have fled in the face of her vitriol.

The image made him laugh, but then he recalled that she had not been at the front. Her twin brother had.

And he had died.

Putting Thane and Catriona in this very odd position.

Not that the position was all bad, not with Cat curled up next to him, her breathing gentle and her chest rising and falling peacefully. She was no longer shivering, and in fact felt quite warm. With the slightest shift of his hands, he could explore that warm flesh, find out if it was as silky to the touch as it was to the eye…

No. Christ. His body was responding to this errant, error-ridden thought with more enthusiasm than it should. This was Catriona Ross. The little sister of Brodie, who he'd vowed to protect, and then utterly failed to do so. And as if he forgot, a spitfire little hellion to boot.

So Thane didn't move an inch. He strove to think the coldest, most unsensual thoughts he could to calm his primal urges. And he sure as hell didn't enjoy the softness of Cat's limbs against his own, or her sweet mouth falling slightly open as she dozed, her lips pink and glistening.

He noticed that her hair had once again fallen onto her face, and he reached to push it off. His fingers trailed along her cheekbone, and then drifted to her jawline, relaxed now, rendering her expression into something much more vulnerable than how she presented herself to the world.

Maybe that brittle brilliance was more of a mask than he'd realized. It was how she protected herself against society after losing her twin, and then her mother too soon afterward.

Regret filled him. He'd lost Brodie, but Thane would go to hell and back to prevent Catriona from dying too.

"I've got you," he told her softly. "No matter what happens, I'm going to keep you safe."

Beside him, Cat's eyelids fluttered as she slid deeper into sleep.

Chapter 11

THE MACPHEARSON CLAN HAILED FROM deep in the Highlands, an arduous trek from the port on the north shore of a narrow corner of the Moray Firth, where the ship sailed in before dawn. Yet that second part of the journey was conducted entirely over land, and thus Cat would not make a single complaint about it. Yes, the carriage was bumpy (they were always bumpy). Yes, the road was horrible (was it even a road?). And yes, Thane was an absolute cold-hearted bastard.

If Cat thought he was growing kinder on the ship, she corrected that mistake now. Clearly his gentle behavior toward her was for the sole purpose of getting her off the ship in one piece, and not out of any regard for her as a person. He barely spoke to her once he'd secured her in the carriage, and propelled the small entourage of the carriage and a few attendant riders and a supply cart forward relentlessly. Lord, if she weren't the sister of Brodie Ross, Thane probably would have left her for dead on the pier. (Or more accurately, she amended, he never would have got involved in the first place.)

The ride lasted several hours, with at least one changeover of horses. The ship had arrived in port so early that they began the ride in the dark, and Cat had lost all sense of time or indeed location by this point. She slouched in the carriage—alone—and tried not to feel as though she was being driven to her doom. Every time the wheels hit a bump, she told herself that it was really a blessing, since it meant she was no longer at sea. Her stomach was still queasy and tender after the ship, and she eyed a hamper of food on the opposite bench seat with suspicion. Eventually, she fell into a fitful sleep, her dreams filled with towering waves, mountain crags, and voices telling her what to do, only to tell her she was wrong as soon as she heeded them.

A sudden lurch of the carriage jarred her awake. She blinked, seeing Thane riding alongside the open window. He surveyed her, his eyes dark.

"Comfortable?" he asked dryly.

She was sprawled on the bench, a woolen throw pulled up over her; it was a tartan weave featuring mostly blue, black, and burgundy overlaid with thin lines of white. He probably thought she was lounging in luxury while he rode in the weather. He looked rather unkempt. His hair was windblown and he hadn't shaved since leaving Edinburgh. Annoyingly, this did not detract from his appearance, and she had too-clear memories of him pressed against her on the deck of the ship, and the way his wet clothing made his physique impossible to ignore.

Realizing that she was taking too long to respond, she hoped that he'd chalk it up to grogginess. She said, "I lost count of the bumps, so I took a nap."

A smile tugged at the corner of his lips for a moment. "Very practical, Miss Ross."

"How far have we got to go?"

"We'll be there in a few more hours." He glanced at the food hamper. "Did you eat all the oatcakes?"

"I didn't eat anything," she said, still slightly queasy at the thought of food. "I couldn't look an oatcake in the face at the moment."

He nodded, then said, "Give me a few?"

Cat almost retorted that she wasn't a maid, but she guessed that he wanted to avoid stopping the carriage and adding time to the journey.

She rustled through the hamper and came up with the oatcakes, as well as some cheese. She placed the food in a napkin and folded it, handing it to Thane through the window.

"If anyone else needs to eat, tell them to ride up and I'll give them food," she said.

Thane nodded, and then rode further away. He did not thank her. Cat reconsidered her gift of the cheese. He didn't deserve it.

Now awake again, she stared at mountain after mountain, rising up over scattered forest and golden gorse-covered hills (at least, those sides not still covered with snow) as the carriage wound through the twisting roads, climbing subtly higher with every hour.

Beautiful, yes. In a lonely, desolate way. What had her mother said about mountains? She had said something about them, and it struck Cat as very profound. She hated to think that her mother's words had faded from her memory already. What had she told Cat about the mountains? It was in the way of a warning…

But Cat couldn't summon the memory, and her failure put her into a sour mood, despite the loveliness of the view.

At long last, the carriage slowed. One of the outriders came close to the window and informed Cat that she'd be able to see their destination now.

She peeked out the window and got a glimpse of a gloomy structure perched atop a gloomy crag. A very fitting home for the dour Thane MacPhearson. It had the look of a place that had been there for a long time and had no intention of disappearing anytime soon, which was also very fitting for a residence belonging to Thane MacPhearson.

Cat fully expected the interior to be dark, lifeless, and colder than the heart of winter. But when the carriage clattered to a halt in the courtyard, and she stepped onto ancient cobbles, she found herself in the middle of a bustling mass of people. These were the ones who lived and worked on the grounds, and they'd all managed to turn up in the courtyard at the exact moment that Thane returned. And they were attentive, eager, even happy to see the man.

Riding at the head of the group, Thane dismounted and walked among his people. Women of every age beamed at him as he passed, and men exchanged cheerful greetings and handclasps. Even the dogs prowled around his feet, gazing up at him as if he were the sun itself.

Lord, they all love him, she thought in astonishment, trailing along in his wake. How? Why? He was such a despicable, heartless man…well, not to them, evidently. Amid his people, Thane looked relaxed and easygoing. He had a smile for everyone, and it was a dazzling smile. Certainly, there were a few women who lived for it, throwing themselves into Thane's path as much as possible.

Cat's mouth tightened in annoyance. She just didn't like it when women behaved as if they were desperate for attention. That was all. It definitely had nothing to do with Thane particularly.

Then, he turned his attention back to her. "Miss Ross is a guest," he announced to the group immediately surrounding him, who seemed to be those responsible for running the place in his absence. "She'll be staying here for a short while. Mrs Ballard, I'm sorry I couldn't get word to you ahead of time. But you'll see that she's settled? Any chamber on the south side will do."

"Of course, sir," a grey-haired matron replied with a curtsey. Her curious gaze rested on Cat, and the woman beckoned her to come closer. Thane had already moved off, talking to a tall, gaunt man about sheep.

Well, I'm truly an afterthought, Cat decided. Thane hadn't even bothered to explain who she was. Or maybe he didn't think it mattered.

"Long journey from Edinburgh. I expect you're weary, lass?" Mrs Ballard asked her in tones that were kind but also plainly puzzled.

"Indeed," Cat said, giving her a nod. "I am Catriona Ross. Mr MacPhearson wishes me to stay here for the next few weeks. I'll shortly be joined by my aunt Tacita, and I think some of Mr MacPhearson's old army comrades as well. I'm sure he would have explained if he weren't…distracted. But I thought you'd like to know so that you may plan for who to put in what rooms. My aunt and I will share, naturally. When she arrives."

"Your aunt? Well, then." Mrs Ballard still looked puzzled, and Cat knew why. A gentleman generally did not bring home a previously unknown woman, unless he intended to marry her or make her a live-in mistress. Cat hoped that mention of her aunt arriving would squelch rumors of the second assumption, though she wasn't sure how she'd counter the first, other than by making it very clear through her behavior that she wasn't the slightest bit interested in Thane as a man.

Mrs Ballard led her through long stone passageways and up a twisting spiral staircase, until they ended up in a hallway where the housekeeper opened the last door to reveal a pleasant bedchamber with windows on the south and east sides. A four poster bed dominated one side of the room, but there was space enough for two chairs by the little fireplace, not to mention a small desk for writing letters set below the south window.

"Oh, it's very pretty," Cat said, pleased. "And so bright!" The inner halls of the castle-like home were so gloomy that it seemed she might never see sunlight again, until stepping in here.

"It's rather far from his rooms," Mrs Ballard noted hesitantly.

"Wonderful," Cat said, not bothering to hide her relief.

"Forgive my impertinence, miss, but is there then no… understanding…between you both?"

"Certainly not," Cat said with a forced smile. "His offer of hospitality is more in the way of a favor to a friend. I expect Mr MacPhearson will explain it to you when he is able. I don't mean to appear secretive, but it is his home, and his right to tell everyone what he wishes them to know."

"Aye, miss." Mrs Ballard appeared relieved at this intelligence, and Cat's evident understanding of how things worked here. "And when do you expect your aunt?"

"I hope within the week, but I am not precisely sure."

Just then, a pair of men brought in Cat's trunk, still smelling of salt and brine from the rough voyage.

"Do you require help unpacking, miss?" the woman asked after the men left.

"I can handle that, but if you don't mind showing me where to hang my gowns…"

The older lady pointed out a hidden alcove with hooks, and the two of them opened the trunk together. Cat was relieved that no seawater had penetrated the interior, ruining the items inside.

Mrs Ballard viewed all the black clothing within. "Who have you lost, miss?"

"My brother, Brodie, and then my mother not long after," Cat said. Tears pricked at her eyes, despite how often she'd had to explain this news over the past months.

"Does your father yet live?"

"No, he passed several years ago." She did not add that his passing didn't cause too much grief.

"Your brother and mother, though. Ach, either would be a hard loss for anyone, but coming so close together is more than a double blow. Why don't you rest, lass? I'll have hot water and some tea brought up to you."

"Thank you, Mrs Ballard. I would appreciate that very much."

The housekeeper left, and Cat sank down on the corner of the bed, suddenly overwhelmed with fatigue.

She was far from home. She had no one to talk to, other than a man who despised her, and she had no idea how long she'd be stuck in this admittedly pleasant prison.

What good was all her philosophy now? How could she direct her life when she couldn't even know when she'd be leaving this house?

Cat sagged to her side, curling up on the bed and closing her eyes. If she still had her brother, none of this would be happening. She whispered, "Oh, Brodie, why'd you leave me?"

* * * *

Thane was inordinately happy to be back at Kinlochlie. This was where he was always meant to be, and why he resented the need to go to the Continent, even while he appreciated the reason for it. Thank God the war was over for him.

In the next few days, he would make a point to get out and explore. It had been far too long since he'd ambled through the woods surrounding the house and up to the summit of the nearest mountain, where as a boy he'd pretended to be a king surveying his whole domain. Throughout his time as a soldier, he'd been given only occasional brief leaves to visit his family home, and each time had felt compressed into a moment, he was so intent on speaking to everyone he could and spending time with his father before he'd passed away, quietly and peacefully. His older sisters, Annella and Effie, had got married and gone to live else- where, though Thane was lucky that both were fairly close. In particular, he was grateful for Effie's proximity, because her respectable presence at Kinlochlie would be the shield to protect Catriona's reputation.

Speaking of which, he had to leave the welcome warmth of his estate in order to ride like hell to his sister's home and beg her indulgence for his mad scheme. Which was how it felt, after the first panic had abated and he had time to con- sider just how disruptive Catriona's presence would be, not merely to the daily operations of the house, but to his peace of mind.

Brodie Ross would rise from the grave and call Thane out if there had been any way for a ghost to know the sort of thoughts Thane was having about his twin sister.

Well, no help for it now. The die was cast, and Thane had to plan his next moves in a way that wouldn't dishonor him- self, his late friend, or the woman unexpectedly at the center of this problem.

Thankfully, Effie lived not far away—her new home was once part of the MacPhearson holdings. A few generations before, it had been sold to the MacDonnell family, close al- lies to the MacPhearsons for hundreds of years. Not surpris- ing, then, that one of the MacDonnell men had found a hap- py match with a MacPhearson woman. Thane was just glad his sister was close.

The idle thought caused another to come up unbidden: Catriona had no sibling close by anymore, and only Thane knew why that was. He felt a pull in his chest, the same hor- rific ache he always got when thinking of Brodie's last living day, and he quickly buried the feeling as he had so often be- fore.

Moments later, Thane crossed the top of a rise and saw

the house he was aiming for. He sped his horse up with a nudge. The horse seemed eager to comply, and they were there in almost no time.

A maid opened the door. "I'll tell your sister of your arrival, Mr MacPhearson," the woman said, all smiles. News of his return would be spread across practically the whole of the Highlands within a few days, he reflected as he waited in the parlor. But would that news be accompanied by the fact that he'd brought a dark-haired harridan with him? He hoped not. Perhaps he should have come up with a false name for Catriona.

Ha, as if the lass would deign to use one. Catriona was nothing if not forthright.

"Thane!"

He turned, smiling.

The woman who rushed into the room was a little older, a little stouter, but she glowed with joy to see him. "Thane, my heart, I'm so happy!" Effie flung her arms around his shoulders, and he swung her around as he used to do when they were younger. She let out a laugh like pure gold. "Home at last! My wee brother."

"Your wee brother has come to ask a not-so-wee favor," Thane told her. "Not that I'm not delighted to see you again, of course. But there's a matter I need your help with."

"Dear Lord, are you in love?" she gasped. "About to propose?"

"What? No! God help me, why would you think that?"

"Well, what else does a younger brother come to his big sister for advice with?" She heaved a sigh. "I was so hoping that you sought my wisdom on how to catch a lady's heart."

Thane rolled his eyes. "If I did, I'd go to Annella, who as I remember at least made her swains work a bit. You're so open and soft-hearted that you would have married a puppy if it knew how to propose."

"Oh, they always have such soulful eyes!" Effie said, clapping her hands. She had never seen a dog that she didn't want to pet. "But if I am not to offer sermons on how to win the esteem of a lady, then what do you need from me?"

"Chiefly, your presence," he confessed. "Circumstances have put me in an odd position, and there is at this moment a guest at Kinlochlie…an unmarried lady who certainly cannot remain at Kinlochlie without the company of a woman of suitable standing."

His sister's expression was so stunned he might have laughed, if the situation weren't so dire. "Who is she?"

"Brodie Ross's sister."

Effie's eyes widened in instant understanding. After all, she'd heard near a hundred stories about Thane's close friend over the past eight years. "Poor darling. They were twins, were they not?"

"Yes. And something happened in Edinburgh which…" He sighed, and looked to the comfortable armchairs Effie had placed near the fire. "Let's sit. I'd like to tell you the whole story, but it would take too much time. And Miss Ross is adamant that no one else hear the details, lest some rumor fly that could hurt someone."

Thane offered a very truncated version, emphasizing how many unknowns there were in the situation, and how Catriona needed to remain hidden and anonymous to stay safe. Throughout the story, he got several exclamations from his horrified sister, and at the end he said, "It would be a favor to me, but more to Miss Ross, if you would decamp to Kinlochlie for a short while—a week or so?—until Miss Ross's aunt joins her here, or I can safely return her to Edinburgh."

"Oh, Thane, you are a loyal friend," Effie said, though it wasn't quite clear whether she meant her words as a compliment or an admonishment. "I hope your impulse to do good by Brodie's memory won't harm anyone. You know what they say about the road to perdition."

"If you can come to the house, I am certain that we can deflect the only legitimate risk, which is to Miss Ross's reputation. All the rest will be easy to deal with," Thane said with a confidence that he didn't feel.

"I do hope so. You have not spoken much about the lady herself," his sister added with curiosity in her eyes.

"When you meet her, you'll have every opportunity to judge that on your own terms."

She hid a laugh behind her hand. "If that's not a warning, I don't know what is. Well, you could not have done better if you wanted to lead me along. Wait here but an hour, and I'll have things packed. Fortunately, I won't have to explain to my Robbie what's in the wind, since he's away for the next sennight or so."

Thane stood up. "Don't rush on my account. If you can make a late supper, that will be sufficient for propriety—I think it would be better if there was a suitable lady in the house overnight. It's not as if Miss Ross is alone—Kinlochlie houses dozens of people."

"People, yes, but not women of her station. She'll be lonely. I'll be there as soon as I can."

So Thane rode back with a lighter heart. Effie's reaction was in keeping with her nature, which rushed to help anyone in need. But what if she'd been away from home? Thane cursed himself for his hasty planning, and the morass he'd got himself into with Catriona Ross.

Why had he jumped into the fray? Yes, because she was Brodie's sister. Yes, because the moment Thane pulled her behind his body at the sound of the gunshot, he'd already committed to some degree. But he knew that others would whisper that it was because Catriona was beautiful.

Which she was, but that wasn't why someone was trying to kill her. At least, he hoped not, because that would mean they were dealing with a madman.

The other men were working on it, he told himself. He'd soon get word from them, and they'd no doubt be able to learn more about who was after Catriona. Thane reflected that the lass would welcome any news because it would mean she'd get away from him. Cat made her irritation with him clear—on board the ship, she'd practically been insensible before she'd accept any help from him.

So give her some whisky to get her to cooperate later, he thought with grim amusement. Then his mind leapt to the other reason a man plied a woman with drink, and he quickly determined that he'd never give her even a dram of anything. The mere idea of a tipsy, cooperative Cat was enough to send his blood straight to his groin. He closed his eyes and envisioned it all too well. Her hair down, her eyes soft, a curve to those pink, plush lips that would curl up further when she said his name, inviting him to explore all her curves and the luscious flesh hidden under her black gowns…

Black gowns. He knew, more than anyone, why she wore that color. Thane winced. Christ. Where was his head? Why was he lusting after this woman when she was the last one in the world he should think about in that way?

What he needed was something to distract him, to get all these ideas out of his mind.

Thane rode back to Kinlochlie. At least he'd have Effie here in a few hours to keep a gloss of respectability on things. It was up to him to keep his thoughts about Cat to himself. Luckily, Cat's utter disdain for him meant that she'd never be the one to start anything.

Pity.

Stop it, he told himself sharply. He left his horse with one of the stable lads and stalked into the main building, intending to wash and dress before the evening meal.

Mrs Ballard found him shortly after he returned. "I've

given the lass the corner room at the southeast. I hope that's satisfactory?"

He understood his housekeeper's hesitation. Cat's status had no precedence. She wasn't family, she wasn't a fiancée, she wasn't a paramour. She was a mystery.

Thus, the housekeeper had chosen a room that was not so close to Thane's to be scandalous, but not so far from the better guest rooms that it might demean her as a near-servant.

"Excellent choice, Mrs Ballard, as always. I expect Miss Ross was relieved to be able to rest after the journey."

"Indeed, sir. She did look rather peaked," Mrs Ballard noted, then added hastily, "but very polite and well-spoken. A true lady."

"She is the sister of a very good friend," Thane said, knowing that he'd have to make certain facts known, though he hoped to keep Cat's presence as unremarkable as possible. "And I hope that everyone will respect her privacy while she's here, and not pester her for details of her life."

"I'll see to it, sir. Poor lass in mourning as she is, no one will dare intrude. Not unless they want to deal with me, that is."

Thane smiled despite himself. Somehow, Cat had made an ally of Mrs Ballard within ten minutes of stepping foot into the building. She had a gift for words and persuasion, that was clear.

He walked toward the great hall, feeling slightly more optimistic about the odds of this mad plan to save Brodie Ross's sister. Here she would be surrounded by people he could trust.

Then he saw Andra.

Oh, hell.

He hadn't counted on Andra being here at Kinlochlie! In fact, until clapping eyes on her, he hadn't thought about her at all. He assumed that the lass would have married some man and moved away long before now. It seemed impossible for her to remain *un*married, given her voraciousness.

Andra was a flame-haired, blue-eyed beauty with a figure of a nymph…and the desires of one as well. Judging by the sultry, knowing look she gave him, she hadn't changed one bit. And he was going to have to explain that he *had* changed.

"Welcome home, Thane MacPhearson," she said with a little smile as she approached him.

"Andra, you're looking very…healthy," he said inanely.

"Aye, I've a healthy appetite," she responded. "But you know that, Thane. Will I see you tonight?"

He schooled his expression to remain composed. "That's a matter we'll have to talk about, Andra. Later."

"Of course," she said, looking down demurely, an act that only made her look more sensual. "Whenever you like."

The promise in those words was undeniable. Yes, Andra was going to be a problem.

Chapter 12

AS PROMISED, HOT WATER FOR washing and a tea tray appeared in her room, and Cat eagerly availed herself of both. Tea in the Highlands meant a malty brew of such fortitude that she could practically stand a spoon in it. She splashed milk into her cup and sipped it with pleasure. Heartened, she cautiously nibbled a thick oatcake. Her stomach seemed to have fully recovered from the sea voyage, for she ate the whole biscuit and its companion, spread with a soft sheep's cheese. Heaven.

Cat fell asleep after that, and woke up surprisingly refreshed. The light was failing outside—it must be nearing time for the evening meal. She hadn't remembered any instructions about it, so she decided to simply dress for dinner and go downstairs, hoping that she wouldn't be too early or too late.

Her choices for a dress were simple: black or black. With a grimace, she pulled on the black gown she'd worn the least, and then remembered why that was so—the tiny cap sleeves didn't provide any warmth, and the cut of the bodice was rather too low for a mourning gown. This dress had originally been a pale blue confection meant for long summer days; rather than buy all new gowns for mourning, Cat simply dumped her existing collection into a vat of dye in the backyard. The maids shrieked when she did it, exclaiming that she was ruining her finest gowns. Cat had been too distraught to care, saying that there was no need for her to dress to please anyone again, even after her mourning concluded. "I'm staying in this house forever!" she'd declared tearfully.

But of course she did need to leave the house, once the first, sharpest period of mourning passed. And by then she had only black to wear.

Frowning at her pale reflection in the mirror now, she pulled a wrap from her trunk. This item must have been packed by mistake in the chaos of her sudden departure. It was a soft cashmere in the lightest shade of shell pink, nearly white, and wildly inappropriate for mourning. But it was the only wrap she could find, so she put it around her shoulders and hoped for the best.

She walked down the spiral stairs and through a few twisting passages until she found the great hall, almost by mistake. Luckily, the sound of voices led her forward, until she saw Thane standing by a massive fireplace, with a woman a few years older than he was.

"I didn't know the hour for dinner," Cat said, knowing she was interrupting yet unsure how else to begin.

Thane turned to her, and seemed about to say something. But then his eyes widened slightly as he took in her appearance. Was the use of a non-black wrap that shocking? Something in his face suggested that he was surprised by something.

There was a beat of awkward silence, broken by the woman.

"Ah, you must be Miss Ross!" The woman immediately came forward, extending both hands to take Cat's own, as if they were long-lost friends. "I'm Effie. Euphemia MacDonnell, though I used to be Euphemia MacPhearson, as I'm sure you've guessed. Thane thought you'd appreciate having another woman around to speak to, for Thane and his ilk are not always the best of conversationalists! Talk of sheep and oats and who's gone to Inverness this month...nothing to amuse a fine lady from Edinburgh."

Cat wasn't sure how to respond to this onslaught of friendly chatter. "I am Catriona Ross, and I'm pleased to meet you. I hope I have not disturbed everyone's routine too much." Damn. That sounded far too formal.

Thane merely raised an eyebrow, since he already knew how much she'd disturbed everything.

But Effie actually enfolded her in an embrace. "Ach, never fear about that, poor darling! You're here now, and we're glad to have you. Aren't we, Thane?" She shot a look at her brother.

"Delighted," Thane muttered.

Effie had exactly the same color of eyes as Thane, but her gaze was kind and motherly, and she had a way of looking like she was always about to laugh, which was very disarming.

Throughout dinner—which began just after Cat appeared, making her think that she had indeed delayed the meal—Effie kept up the conversation with a level of skill that would have impressed Cat's most demanding teachers of etiquette. She told stories of things that had happened in the area while Thane had been gone, adding enough details for Cat to understand the import of certain names and events.

Effie also asked Cat more questions about herself, which Cat answered as politely as she could without telling too much...the result being that she sounded aloof and cagey to her own ears. Effie's smile never faded, but she must have known that Cat was hiding something. If only Cat knew how much Thane had told his sister! They hadn't a chance to talk privately since arriving, and Cat knew she'd have to speak with him tonight, if only to get their stories straight.

As the meal went on, Cat covertly watched the others in the hall. Everyone dined more or less together, with only the locations of the tables to distinguish the higher family and guests from those who worked at the estate. She couldn't help but notice a voluptuous woman her own age. She was wearing simple clothes, but her figure was stunning and she had the most amazing flaming hair. There was no question as to who the most beautiful woman in the area was. All the men kept looking at her, and she kept looking at Cat.

Cat didn't get the sense that the other woman was jealous, exactly. It was more the gaze of a lioness who was puzzled to find a sheep wandering so close to her den. Cat would have to find out who she was, and if she could make trouble for Cat. *For example, by telling a stranger I'm here. A stranger who might be trying to kill me.*

She shook her head and focused her attention on her meal. She was being silly. Thane and the other men moved her without any warning to a location that no one could possibly guess at, let alone reach very quickly. She was surely safe here for quite a while, especially if she kept to herself and didn't give anyone a reason to resent her presence.

So Cat nibbled dutifully at her food: mutton cooked to surprising tenderness and served in a rich brown gravy, a velvety mash of potatoes and turnips to sop up the extra gravy, and thick slices of rye bread that would have been a meal in itself. Cat was happy to discover that her appetite was fully restored, and she managed to put away most of what was on her plate, though she refused any more, fearing to tempt fate.

Unlike formal dinners in the city, here there was no separation between men and women for the second half of the evening. If any man wanted to indulge in a smoke, he merely stepped outside and did so, rather than all the men lingering at the table while the ladies went to the drawing room.

Of course, here there wasn't a drawing room, which also simplified things.

Hence Cat was able to walk up to Thane near the fireplace of the great hall, where padded benches and a few high-backed chairs were grouped.

"We should tell your sister the full truth," she whispered.

"I thought we agreed it wasn't a good idea to let anyone know."

"She's different. She'll keep circumspect about it, won't she?"

Thane looked uncertain. "Possibly, if I impress upon her the need for absolute discretion."

"Have you told her anything?"

"Only a little. Really, just that you're Brodie's sister, and in need of a refuge."

"I'm sure that only made her more curious."

"That is certain," Thane agreed. "Effie does like to know every little thing that happens in her domain. And I assure you that she definitely considers this place her domain, even though she no longer lives here."

"It's still her home," Cat said softly.

Just then Effie walked up to them, asking, "What's that?"

"Miss Ross was saying that you still think of this as your home."

"Oh, aye, where one is born is always home. And until Thane marries, there's not another lady to take up the mantle, so I shall play hostess when I need to."

At the mention of marriage, Thane looked distinctly uncomfortable. "Good thing you play hostess well, Effie," he muttered.

"Don't rely on me too much," Effie returned with a cheeky grin. "Once I'm surrounded by bairns and whatnot, I can't just up and leave because you call!"

She laughed, but neither Cat nor Thane did. Thane said,

"I appreciate your coming this time, Effie."

"As do I," Cat added hastily. "Without any warning, to boot. My aunt will be here soon, though, and you won't have to chaperone me anymore."

"Oh, it's hardly a chore," Effie said. "After all, I know Thane well, and you're a sensible lass with no silly ideas in your head."

"She's got plenty of those," Thane said. At Effie's raised eyebrow, he added, "That is, about politics. Just ask her."

Effie turned to Cat, who said, "What your brother is referring to is my belief that women should have a voice in politics, and the world at large. Which is *not* silly, but rather eminently fair and practical." She glared at Thane, who just rolled his eyes.

Effie gave a delighted laugh. "Oh, my, this shall be fun! You'll have to tell me all about your philosophy, Miss Ross."

"Please do…when I'm not around," Thane said.

"Then go," Cat told him. "It is your castle, is it not? Prowl around it as you please if you cannot abide a spirited conversation about a vital topic."

He seemed about to argue, but then visibly checked himself. "I've plenty of work to occupy me, so I'll take myself to my study, where there's plenty of whisky but no meddling women."

Cat waved goodbye, to Effie's amused laughter. Thane frowned at them both and then fled.

"Oh, my," Effie said. "A more complete rout I've never seen. Are you certain you won't consider him for a husband?"

"I wouldn't consider him for a scullion," Cat retorted. "And anyway, I refuse to marry at all. It disagrees with my philosophy."

"Tell me more of that, Miss Ross. Of course, I'm already married, but I'd love to know what to tell my future daughters."

So the ladies chatted, and Effie proved to be a much more sympathetic listener than Thane ever had. Good thing she shooed him out. Of course, Cat would have been more pleased with her victory if she hadn't noticed the flame-haired beauty following Thane down the same hallway a few moments later.

Chapter 13

THANE DID NOT LIKE BEING chased away from his own hearth, but the idea of facing Cat while she had Effie on her side was too much to bear. Not to mention that Cat's gown left little to the imagination. Yes, it was black. But it was also temptingly low-cut, with the bare hint of sleeves to keep it on, leaving an expanse of skin he couldn't stop staring at. And that soft thing she'd thrown around her shoulders only served to make her look more soft herself. He'd never seen a color besides black next to her skin. The pink brightened her complexion and made those snapping eyes stand out even more. The longer he remained near Cat, the more he wanted to reach out and touch her.

He should thank her for chasing him off.

He retired to the small room down the hall from his bedroom that served as a study. He was sitting at the desk, preparing to write to his comrades to let them know of their safe arrival (not referring to his home by name, just in case) and to share a few scraps of information he learned during the journey.

But before he could dip a pen in the inkwell, Andra strolled in without knocking.

"Why'd you bring that woman here?" she asked, frowning.

"I don't recall having to explain myself to you," he said in his coldest tone. Christ, Andra going to be a worse problem than he anticipated. He certainly hadn't thought about renewing their affair, which was years gone by this point. It had been a fun and harmless dalliance that any young man would have been fully up for—in more ways than one. But Andra was part of his life before the war. He didn't picture her being part of his life now that he was back.

She evidently thought otherwise. She put on a pouting expression that somehow conveyed *Come here* rather than *Go away*. "Thane, I'm only asking a question that's on everyone's minds. She's a stranger, and not even from the Highlands. What's she doing here?"

Thane sighed, and picked up his glass of whisky. "During the war, just late last year, actually, I lost one of my closest comrades. Brodie Ross. She's his sister. I met her in Edinburgh and learned that she's in some difficulty. So I brought her here for a while, until she's able to go back." He kept all details out of his explanation, since Andra had no right to learn Catriona's private struggles.

"So she's breeding?"

Thane almost choked on the whisky. "*What?*"

"Isn't that what people mean when they say a woman's in some difficulty?" Andra blinked, apparently completely sincere.

"She's not! Or, if she is, that's not the difficulty I mean. Christ, woman, why are you giving me *more* to worry about?" Because now Thane was picturing Cat pregnant, and the picture was both troubling and strangely appealing… which was troubling on its own.

"How long will she be here?" Andra pressed, moving to where he sat.

"God willing, not for more than a few weeks, a month at the outside. Then she can go back to the city and her own life and I don't have to ever think about her again."

Andra smiled, quite pleased with that answer. So pleased, in fact, that she leaned in to kiss him. "I'll give you something to think about."

Before he'd fully registered what she was doing, she straddled his lap, her hand reaching down to his falls. "I missed you, Thane," she purred. "I dreamed of the night you came back, and how we'd celebrate it on that big bed in your room."

"Keep dreaming," he said, pushing her hand away, though not before her eager strokes created a reaction. "I'll not be going to bed anytime soon."

"We don't have to go to bed," she said, not deterred. She began to kiss him more seriously, her plush lips seeking his. "Thane, I want you. And I can feel that you want me. Lord, it's been so *long* since we've been able to be together." As she spoke, she skillfully worked him to a state of arousal. It had been a long time, and she was clearly very willing to do whatever might please him.

Thane closed his eyes and momentarily gave in to the game Andra was playing, feeling the pulse of pleasure she was stirring up in his cock, and the heaviness in his balls. A night with Andra promised to be very enjoyable indeed, just what he needed after the exasperating, tension-filled journey with Cat.

Cat. At the thought of her name, her face and figure immediately followed. Thane groaned as he imagined Cat's hand working him so eagerly, Cat's sweet pink lips open and ready for a kiss...

"Enough," Thane said to Andra, more sharply than he intended. He pushed her off him, and she stood up, eyes stony.

"What's the matter?"

"I told you that I couldn't dally tonight. I've work to do

and it can't wait."

"I've not displeased you?" she asked, her eyebrows knitting together.

"No, of course not," he said, shaking his head. "It's nothing to do with you. I've got a lot on my mind."

She smiled, back to her usual charming self. "I'd never want to make you angry. I'll tell Cook to send up some food for you later, so that you can work uninterrupted."

"Aye, thank you," he said, grateful that this would not turn into a scene. "I'd appreciate that."

"And whenever you are ready for bed…" She sucked on her lower lip for a moment, and he felt the twinge in his cock as he remembered the many times she'd pleasured him with her mouth. "…do tell me so I can join you."

Thane said nothing, but she took his silence as a wordless promise and sashayed to the door, her hips moving in a way that didn't help calm his arousal at all. He swept his hand over his front, trying to restore the alignment of his clothing and to get his body back to a state of normalcy.

At the door, she turned for one moment, flashed him a wicked smile, and yanked her bodice to expose nearly all of her breasts to him. Then she spun back and walked out, adjusting her gown as she did. Thane focused on the papers scattered over his desk, telling himself to get back to business.

A yelp from the hall suggested that Andra had startled someone else with her antics. Thane sighed, thinking that if a maid saw that, she'd instantly report to every other servant that the master had renewed his affair with his mistress that very night he got back.

Then Cat's tart voice came from the doorway. "Excuse me. I didn't realize you had…company."

Thane looked up in alarm. The lady's face was expressionless, though her spine was held so straight and stiff that it was very clear she'd seen much of Andra's assets, and had drawn the natural conclusion about why the woman would have been pulling up her bodice on the way out of Thane's room.

"Nothing," he said quickly.

Cat looked confused. "Nothing what?"

"Nothing happened," he clarified, before remembering that he didn't have to clarify a damn thing to Catriona Ross. "We weren't doing anything."

Cat merely rolled her eyes and let out a tiny sigh of irritation. "As if I care what you do or do not."

She cared a *little*, to judge by the faint tightening of her jaw. Or maybe she was just offended by encountering a man's mistress—*presumed* mistress—in the hallway. Thane doubted if finishing schools covered that potential social event.

"I thought you were chatting about revolutions with Effie."

"I was, but she suddenly felt rather tired and we agreed to discuss it all tomorrow. She's gone to bed."

"And you came here. Is there something I can help you with?" Thane asked, keeping his tone cold…mostly to help cool his body.

"You said you had business. I thought it might have to do with my situation."

"It does, actually."

"Good. I thought it might save you some time if I was on hand, for who better to know my situation than myself?"

"Aye, that's sense."

"You seem surprised to find the quality of sense in a woman, Mr MacPhearson."

"I'm surprised to find it in anybody, Miss Ross," he said honestly.

His words earned him a slight smile, which he found

gratifying. "Too true," she agreed. "The world would run a great deal more smoothly if people didn't let their feelings rule their actions." Though the words were airy, Thane sensed something more serious behind them. This was a woman who avoided *feelings*. Why?

But he had no time to ponder it, since she reached out and tapped the blank paper in front of him. "You were about to start a letter, yes? To whom? What are you asking for, and why are you asking it of them? Do you have any new theories about why someone might want to kill me? Do you think it could be a mistake after all?"

He couldn't answer any of her questions, for she plowed ahead. "I confess I've racked my brains since you first announced your theory, and I've got a new idea: it was a mistake. Surely whoever shot at me had another victim in mind, and I was simply wearing a similar outfit that evening, causing the person to fire at me instead of the woman they truly meant to kill."

"You forget the incident of the carriage. And the dog."

She frowned, clearly upset. "I wish I could forget it. Who hurts an innocent animal, Mr MacPhearson?"

"Someone very dangerous, since, as you say, the animal is innocent. That lessens the chance that whoever it is feels that they are avenging some injustice. It suggests that they are motivated by anger, resentment, or even hate."

"Feelings," she said with clear distaste.

"You may not like feelings, but you shouldn't doubt their power," he said.

Catriona looked at him, her expression unreadable. "Is that something you learned during the war?"

"The war reinforced the lesson," he allowed.

"How so? I should have thought that battle doesn't allow for much other than instant physical reaction."

"During battle, yes, that's true," Thane said, recalling too many times that a soldier beside him had turned too slowly, or simply failed to raise his weapon in time, and fell wounded or worse. "It's the times between the battles when men's thoughts begin to weigh. When there's time to think, there's time to think the worst."

"Brodie was always careful to keep his letters full of cheer, but I could tell when he was worried, or thought the command had done something foolish, or when he was simply sick of fighting," Catriona said quietly. "I felt it my duty to relate only frivolous gossip, or confide good news and avoid the sad events that occurred at home. But perhaps I did him an injustice, to avoid the more melancholy side of life."

Thane shook his head. "Never think that. Brodie lived for news from home, and it bolstered him. He read aloud a lot of what you wrote, especially the stories of life in Edinburgh. We didn't have to know the people you mentioned to appreciate the tales. It lightened many a dull day, I promise you."

"Brodie read my words to everyone?" she asked, cheeks coloring. God, she was so pretty when her natural tones came out. The black really didn't suit her.

"Nothing untoward," he assured her, then added in a teasing tone, "Why, did you confide anything in those letters?"

"Certainly not! As if I *had* anything untoward to confide. A woman's life is bound on all sides, Mr MacPhearson. There is little hope for scandal."

"Would you like some scandal?" Too late, he realized how that sounded.

Catriona's eyes widened slightly, but all she said was "I suppose it's already found me. Here I am, would-be gunshot victim twice over, now swept away to a strange place, imprisoned by a man I hardly know."

"You are not a prisoner."

"Oh, no? What would you do if I left this place?"

I'd drag you back and lock you up where you're safe, he

thought. Aloud, he limited himself to, "You would not, Miss Ross. As you noted before, you're a person of great sense, and therefore would never do something irrational or dangerous when you've got a better option. And anyway, with luck we'll find out who's behind these incidents very soon."

"And if you don't?" she asked. "Would I stay here indefinitely?"

Thane didn't allow himself to examine his instant physical reaction to that bombshell. "We'd find a suitable solution."

"Why should I believe you? You haven't thus far."

Thane stood up. "Cat, you're beginning to irritate me."

She gave him an arch look. "Just beginning to?"

"All right, then. You're driving me mad." *In more ways than one.*

"Sounds very much like you want me to leave."

Don't you dare. Thane moved around the desk and stepped up to her, chest to chest, using his bulk to block her way out the door. "You'll be staying. Until I say otherwise."

Chapter 14

WITH HIM JUST INCHES FROM her, Cat got an eyeful of Thane's chest. Even though his flesh was covered in the fine wool weave of his shirt, the drape of the fabric didn't conceal that he was well muscled, and quite capable of picking her up and hauling her off anywhere he wanted.

Typical male, she thought, ignoring the heat rising in her body, as if she'd stepped near smoldering coals. *Using brute strength to dominate.*

As if that would work! Cat looked up at him, ready to tell him that no man was going to win her silence through bullying…and caught his gaze.

Years ago, she once touched a scorching-hot andiron when she got too close to a fire in her home. This was hotter. Thane's eyes roved over her face. He didn't say anything more, and all Cat could think of was warning words ringing over and over again in her mind.

"What is it?" he asked softly, but with no less heat.

Cat shook her head. "I was only thinking of something Mother once told me."

"And that was?"

"I can't remember quite how she phrased it."

But Cat remembered every word now, etched onto the slate of her memory as designs are etched onto crystal. *Men, like mountains, can be stunning to behold. Impressive, even inspiring. But they are best admired from a vantage point far distant, and the wise woman does not venture forth upon them.*

It was the sort of advice mothers gave daughters in an effort to warn them, without fully explicating all the true dangers that lay ahead. Cat dearly wished her mother had been less poetic and more blunt, for what she needed to know was why something inside her craved more attention from Thane MacPhearson, when the prudent course was to ignore him completely.

She cleared her throat. "I…I believe that my staying here would not be very wise." Not the way he was looking at her now, and the way her body was reacting to his attention. Not the way she wanted to feel more of whatever he was stirring up inside her, just by standing there.

He lifted one hand to her face, his fingers barely grazing her cheek. For such a gentle touch, it sent shock waves down her spine. His eyes seemed to soften, as if he too was surprised by what was happening between them.

"Cat," he said, her pet name sweet on his lips and tongue. "I'm not making you stay. I'm asking you to stay."

"Because you respect my autonomy to make decisions as an independent woman?"

"Because you need to be kept safe."

"Oh."

"And…" He hesitated, and his gaze dropped to her mouth. "And because I want to taste you."

Oh. *Oh.*

Cat tilted her head, even as she lifted her hands slightly, hesitating between pushing him away and dragging him closer. She also very much wanted to taste him, but did she dare take that step off the precipice?

He held still, and she realized he was also waiting for that decision, putting himself quite literally in her hands. One corner of his mouth quirked, a tiny movement that nonetheless quickened her heartbeat. "At your leisure," he murmured. "You see, I respect your autonomy to make decisions as an independent woman."

She ignored the mockery in his voice. She understood now. This was a *dare*. And she wanted to meet it. She had to meet it.

Oh, she didn't know what she was doing, and he was going to tease her for doing it poorly. *To hell with it.* Cat rose up on her toes to bring her lips to his.

After a split second of surprise— *aha, I* knew *he didn't think I'd have the courage*—she felt his fingers curling lightly around the back of her neck, his touch strong enough to guide her in how to tilt her head to better kiss him, and gentle enough so she didn't feel steered.

So warm. Warm and vital and rich and sweet. The kiss sent her better sense flying away, and all she wanted was to taste him and find out just what else she could dare him into doing.

Finally, after far too long and also too short a time, Cat took a breath.

"I still hate you," she informed him, because she didn't want him to think that she was so easily won over, like a silly woman in love with love.

"Aye, I know," he said. He sounded quite calm about it, and then kissed her again, teasing her mouth open, running the tip of his tongue over her lower lip until Cat let out a tiny cry that was half satisfaction, half desire.

Hearing her, Thane deepened the kiss. Cat tried to match his actions, but it was difficult to think about what to do next when heat was blooming all over her skin and she felt like lightning was about to strike nearby.

When had she twined one arm around his left shoulder, or hitched herself up on his thigh? Why did she feel the intense need to claw at his clothes till she could shred them right off, and how did she still need more kisses from a man she didn't even tolerate?

"Thane," she said, his name lost between her lips and his.

Still, he heard her, and pulled away so she could see the pleasure welling up in his half-lidded eyes. "Yes, Cat. Are you going to tell me to stop?"

"If I did, would you listen?" She wanted to sound acid about it, but it came out breathy and soft, as if she were a butterfly confronting a lion.

He brushed his lips against hers lightly. "All you have to do is tell me no. And you do still hate me, after all."

"I do." But she didn't hate his *kisses*, which was a problem. "And you've been very clear that I irritate you."

"Constantly." He ran a fingertip along her jaw, and then traced her earlobe, like he'd never seen it before. "There are a dozen times a day I wish I'd never met you." He tipped her head to the side and laid a soft kiss on her neck. Cat trembled at the promise there.

"Then why are you kissing me?" she asked.

He smiled a bit, his expression more relaxed than she'd ever seen it. "For the same reason you're kissing me. We want what we want."

"It seems a very bad idea."

"Terrible." He pressed his mouth lightly on her forehead, between her eyebrows. It was less sensual and yet far more intimate than the previous ones, and for some reason Cat felt exposed in a way she hadn't before.

"Especially in light of the situation," she said, striving hard to reach a familiar shore—the sedate intellectual country where she preferred to spend her time. "That is, I must guard my conduct more than usual, being so often in the company of an unmarried man. That is, we surely don't want to find ourselves in a situation we cannot get out of." Goodness, she was babbling. "I mean, that is, you want to maintain your freedom, and I want to maintain my freedom, and we don't even like each other, so anything that would result in being shackled together for the rest of our lives is to be avoided, yes? Don't you agree?"

"You talk a *lot*, Cat," Thane murmured, his hands slipping through her hair, half combing, half massaging. She wanted to close her eyes and let his touch soothe her jangled nerves. But wait, wasn't his touch the very thing jangling her nerves in the first place?

"You probably think women shouldn't talk at all," she accused him.

"I don't mind talking," he said in a languid, even lazy tone. Then he laid a series of little kisses along her collarbone. "But there's so much more a mouth can do when not… talking."

Kiss.

"What lips can do."

Kiss.

"What a tongue can do."

Kiss.

"What teeth can do."

Kiss.

"I want to show you all the ways to *not* talk, kitty cat."

Kiss.

"Do you want that too?" he invited, his breath warm and tantalizing on her skin. Her body clamored for her to continue, to say yes, yes, yes to his enticement, to throw caution to the wind and indulge in wickedness she never dreamed of.

A quarter hour ago, she'd have laughed in his face at such a proposition. Now she was melting to hear him call her a kitty cat.

What has he done to me to make me so unlike myself, so quickly?

"Cat got your tongue at last?" he asked, something warm

and dark and dry in his tone, something that made her heart thud in anticipation. He murmured, "Just a few kisses, kitty cat. You deserve it."

Why does he think I deserve to feel this way? Why do I think I deserve to feel this way?

Cat went still. She pushed away all the wonderful, rapturous feelings he offered. She could not endure them any longer.

"I don't deserve it. And I don't want it," she told him, harsh and cold. "Not from any man, and certainly not from you!"

Chapter 15

CAT FLED TO HER ROOM, furious with herself for allowing such a thing to happen, for allowing Thane to make such a fool of her. She'd been so certain that Effie's oversight was a needless sop to convention. And then, not ten minutes after Effie left, Cat found her way into Thane's presence *and* let him humiliate her with that display of passion.

She must be losing her mind.

Yes, she was curious. Curiosity wasn't a crime. Well, it shouldn't be. Women ought to be allowed to be curious, instead of be punished for it. There was surely some essay on exactly that topic among her readings…

Then she huffed out a breath. As if she'd find the answer to her turmoil in an *essay*. Lord, she was completely upside down, all thanks to that horrible man and his horrible, teasing kisses. What good was her philosophy now?

After all that she tried to learn and how much she attempted to live a life of independence, here she was…a virtual prisoner in a remote castle, at the mercy of a cruel man who she hated…and yet couldn't seem to resist.

She ought to resign her place in the ladies' league and take up the writing of gothic novels. She was practically living her own: *The Swooning Virgin of Kinlochlie*!

Cat laughed at her own ridiculousness, and felt slightly

better. She got up and looked out the south window. The moon spilled a ghostly light over the landscape below her. Silver trees covered silver hills, and the charcoal-sketched mountains were still topped with pure white snow, even this late in spring. She took a deep breath, inhaling the cold Highland air. It felt so much more pure than the air of the city—of course, the city was filled with coal smoke and the fetid stench of too many people and animals sharing too tight a space. Even in the wealthy neighborhood she called home, it was an ordeal to walk through the back alley on a summer day. In contrast, this place seemed to be perched in the clouds, surrounded by winds still icy-clean from the mountain peaks. If she were a bird, she'd fly all the way over the range she could see outlined in moonlight—no one would ever tell her where to go or what to do.

But she wasn't a bird. She was a woman of the nineteenth century, bound to the earth as every other woman was.

Cat turned away from the window, disenchanted with the view. What good were dreams when one had to wake up?

* * * *

The next morning, Cat rose in a more even mood. She scoffed at her silly emotions from the night before—both her weakness with Thane, and then her despair at the window. Too much travel and the discomfort of finding oneself in an unfamiliar place. That was all!

Being in a place other than her own home might be somewhat helpful, she realized. For that morning was the first time that she'd woken up without hearing Brodie's voice echoing in her head, his words indescribable, but with the sense that he'd just been telling her something important before she was pushed out of her dream. She held the charm on her pendant and thought about her brother. The ache was still there, but it also felt different this morning. The edges smoothed, somehow.

"You'll not believe where I am just now," she murmured. "Your friend's home in the Highlands. In all your stories and letters, you failed to mention that Thane lives in a castle."

Didn't want you to start dreaming of being the princess there, Brodie's answer came back.

"Small chance of that if the castle comes with an ogre," she replied, quite pleased with the comeback. Too bad she was the only one around to hear it.

Cat dressed in her black wool gown just as someone knocked on her door.

"Breakfast, miss," a maid announced, bringing in a massive tray. She set it on the small table by the fireplace, which had gone out during the night. "Shall I stoke the fire for you, miss?"

"There's no need. After I eat I should like to explore," Cat said. "Does Mr MacPhearson...I mean, do the family take breakfast together?"

"The master eats in his chambers, miss. Well, he did today. He hasn't been back for years—not for very long anyway—so we don't know his habits."

"And Mrs MacDonnell? Has she eaten?"

"Oh, aye, she's been up for hours. You'll find her in the hall when you're ready."

Cat felt some judgment in the words—no doubt they all thought her a soft and lazy lowlander. Perhaps they were correct. "Thank you...what's your name?"

"I'm Janet, miss." The maid gave her a little bob and left.

Cat sat at the table and uncovered a bowl of thick oat porridge. There was a little pitcher of cream next to it, and Cat poured the whole thing in, stirring happily. She ate every speck, and washed it down with the strong, malty brew in her teapot. Afterward, she felt much more ready to face whatever the day might bring. Gothic dreams were no match against oatmeal.

She found Effie in a sunny nook of the great hall, where this part of the building had been altered from its medieval origins to feature a few tall glass windows low enough that a person could look outside. The top of the window frame was much too high to touch, even for the tallest man. Effie was knitting, her needles clicking pleasantly as she turned a skein of red yarn into a shape that Cat guessed would eventually be a shawl.

"Am I interrupting?" Cat asked her.

"Not at all!" Effie gave her a smile. "Perhaps you have something of your own to work on? I've got some spare needles."

"I am not very skilled at knitting," Cat confessed. (In reality, she was terrible at it.) "When Aunt Tacita arrives, she will surely want to know everything about every stitch. Although I suppose that when she arrives, you'll want to return to your own home."

"Ach, it's more interesting here," Effie said. "With my man away, it's too quiet. I confess I get lonely when he's gone very long."

Cat remembered her own mother sighing in relief when Cat's father left on a journey—a more frequent event in later years, since the two of them could hardly stand to be in the same house. She said, "You must be lucky."

"I married my dearest friend," Effie said, smiling. She pointed to a plate of biscuits on the bench next to her. "Have a ginger biscuit. Good to calm the stomach. I heard it was a rough passage."

Cat groaned at the memory. "You have no idea. I always thought I had a strong constitution, but that journey nearly killed me." She felt much better this morning, but she still took a bite of the biscuit, which was just as spicy as she hoped.

"You know, Thane was very susceptible to seasickness when he was a child, but he eventually outgrew it."

"Really? Perhaps there's hope for me, then. Not that I plan much ocean voyaging in my future. I am happy where I am. I mean, where I usually am. I mean, not that I'm not happy here—"

"I know what you meant," Effie said with a laugh. "It must be difficult to uproot yourself, especially with so little notice?" The larger question was in her voice—*why* was Cat here, and how was she connected to Thane?

Cat sympathized with the woman's curiosity. Lord knew she'd be pestering everyone for answers if she were in Effie's place. She didn't want to speak here in the hall, though, where someone might overhear information meant to be kept close. She offered, "Perhaps we could walk outside for a bit?"

Effie's eyes narrowed as she glanced around the hall. She seemed to understand exactly what Cat was afraid of. She put her knitting aside. "I think that with the sun being out, I ought to show you more of this place. You've barely had a chance to see where you are."

"True," said Cat. "All I know is that I'm in the Highlands. But I couldn't name a single mountain or river or lake in my sight."

"Then come with me," Effie said. "I'll name them all, till you're sick of knowing."

"I can't imagine being sick of your company," Cat said, to Effie's laughter.

"Aren't you a charmer," she said. "No wonder Thane smuggled you home."

"Oh, he didn't smuggle me." Cat frowned, thinking. "Actually, I suppose that is what he did!"

As the two women walked along the long green edge of

land before the mountainside fell away to the valley below, they talked. Grateful to have a kind ear, Cat told Effie very nearly the whole story, from the near-miss gunshot at the party to the men of Brodie's company suddenly acting as protectors, with Thane in the lead.

"So like him," Effie murmured. "Though he surely finds it a pleasant duty to protect *you*."

Cat shook her head. "I assure you, there's no…personal interest. Thane is merely upholding a promise."

Effie's mouth quirked. "He may be keeping a promise he made. He always does that. But I've seen the way he looks at you, and there's certainly some interest."

Cat bit her lip. "Well, perhaps. He's a man, after all."

"That's true enough." Effie's amusement was clear, but Cat sensed that it wasn't at her expense. "I expect that you've received quite a lot of attention from men. You're very striking. And yet, you must not be engaged, or else some fiancé would have sheltered you."

"I am definitely not engaged," Cat said fervently. "As I mentioned last evening, I don't wish to marry."

"Do tell."

Cat gave her the reasons, though with less verve than usual. She finished with, "Not that I say no one should marry. After all, you are married."

"Very happily so," Effie agreed. "But I admit that not all unions are so fortunate. It would be a better world if people could make their choices based on their own hearts. But I suppose we must make the best of what we have."

"I hope to make the best of what we have better," Cat said stubbornly.

"I can see why he likes you so."

"He doesn't. Thane barely tolerates me, even if he did…" Cat stopped before she blurted out the embarrassing truth.

But Effie caught her, and raised an eyebrow. "He did…

what?"

Should she tell Effie? It was mortifying. But then again, maybe it would feel less frightening if she explained it out loud, instead of letting the memory dominate her brain the way it had since last night.

"Well, it's just…it's that last night, he, um. He kissed me."

Effie's brows rose further. "Did he now."

"I think it was mostly to upset me. He enjoys putting me on my back foot."

"On your back…foot," Effie echoed thoughtfully with amusement still in her eyes but now something else as well. "Yes, I can see how he might want to do that."

"It's really very mean," Cat said. "Did he do that when he was young? Taunt people, I mean?"

"You think his kiss was a taunt?" Effie asked.

Well, it was more than one kiss, Cat thought. But she didn't dare say that, lest Effie decide that it was so close to being compromised that Cat would get marched right to the altar so as to prevent damaging the MacPhearson family honor. "I believe he did it to test me. Or to make fun of me."

Effie seemed genuinely surprised at what Cat said. "You can't possibly think that Thane would have done it for a jest. That's not his way."

Cat sighed. "I misunderstood, then. Is that what you're saying?" Of course his sister should take his side.

"In part. Though it sounds as though he didn't explain himself either. He doesn't, you know. It's part of being the lord of manor and all that. Plus, the war made him different."

"Different how?"

Effie gazed out at the vista for a long moment, gathering her thoughts before putting them into words. She began slowly, explaining, "He was always the sort of person who saw danger before anyone else. I remember one time we were climbing up the mountain—that one there, see? With the peak that looks like a lion's tooth." She pointed until Cat could identify the peak in question. Effie went on, "I was about thirteen then, which would have made Thane almost twelve. Mama had put me in charge of him, of course, as I was older. But he never needed minding after the age of seven or eight. That's, what, twenty-five years ago now?" She sighed. "He's thirty-two, you know. Seems older with all the cares he took on after our father's passing, and then the war. How old are you, if you don't mind me asking?"

"I'll be twenty-five come Saturday," Cat said, rather surprised to think of it—she'd forgotten her birthday until that moment.

"My goodness!" Effie said. "You've got the air of an older lady. By which I mean you've got your head about you, not that you're a crone."

"Why thank you," Cat said, laughing. "I believe I have a few years before I am officially a crone. Though I might as well be one, for refusing to play the marriage game. But tell me about the danger Thane kept you from."

"Oh, yes!" Effie nodded. "That day, I was scrambling up a rock face ahead of him, and I was excited because I'd just glimpsed a wildcat above. I dearly wanted to see it better, and I must not have been paying as much attention as I ought. Suddenly Thane *ran* up from behind, and pulled me sideways. Scared me half to death and I was yelling at him for being so reckless. I near lost my footing on the slope!"

"You could have died!"

"I could have, but not how you think. I'd been about to step into a gap, a crevasse that had opened up at some point in the winter. And who knows how I'd have been hurt? A sprained ankle at best, but perhaps a leg broken? Or worse. We were far enough away from help that I could have easily been stranded on the mountain all night, if not longer."

"But he saved you," Cat said.

"He saved me because he's always paying attention. That's my point. Thane's always been like that."

"He did the same thing to me," Cat said, "but in my case it was a bullet he'd noticed."

"The war amplified his alertness," Effie decided. "But that's merely a matter of degree. The war changed him in other ways too. He's more reserved than ever."

Cat made a sound that was very nearly a snort. "I say dour."

"He used to be more open. He made jokes all the time."

"Jokes? Are you still talking about Thane?" Cat asked, raising an eyebrow.

Effie smiled. "He can be very funny when he's in the mood. But he hasn't been in such a mood for years. And it has to be the war that did it."

"Well, a war is hardly a jovial undertaking."

"I think he saw worse things than some other soldiers did," Effie said softly. "I can't be sure because he won't talk about his experiences to me. Or anyone."

"Perhaps he talks with the other men in his company?" Cat offered. "I saw three of them that night I was shot at: Duncan MacKenzie, Calan Shaw, and Kai Buchanan. They all seemed very close."

"Men put into battle together must form a bond we women can't imagine," Effie agreed. "I invite some ladies for a day of knitting about once a month. It helps pass the time when we can talk, but I can't say I'd expect one of them to give her life for me."

"Knitting circles don't offer much chance for danger," said Cat. "Though if there was some intruder, at least you'd all be armed with two sharp needles."

Effie laughed at the image. "The Highland Defenders! We look like ladies, but we fight like lions," she said as she continued to giggle. "Oh, if only."

"Why not propose the name at your next meeting? You can have a crest as well: crossed needles before a skein."

"Wouldn't that be marvelous? Alas that women cannot go into battle as they used to in bygone days!" Effie laughed again. "I'm glad you're here, Catriona Ross. Though it will only be for a short time, you've brightened all our lives already. Within a week, you'll be on speaking terms with every soul in this castle."

"You're kind to say so." Privately, Cat didn't believe it. She'd caught looks from half the people in the house, wary and skeptical. And Thane still barely spoke to her. He couldn't wait for her to be gone, she was sure.

If not for the time when he kissed her, she would have thought he forgot her existence. But that moment—it was seared into her memory, and part of her hoped that he'd at least remember *some*thing about her when she left.

Chapter 16

THANE COULDN'T GET THE ENCOUNTER with Cat out of his mind, no matter how much he tried to think of other things. Any other things. But the reports of the last wool harvest lacked the urgency needed to distract him from the memory of Cat's lips on his, the way she briefly—so briefly—seemed to be in perfect resonance with him. Until the moment he pushed things too far, when she snapped back to her former frostiness and left.

What had he said? Probably the phrase *kitty cat*, which was, granted, much too soft and sweet and familiar for her. He didn't even know why it came out, other than that he was so fully occupied with the idea of Cat in his arms that there was no room left in his brain for intelligent thought. Clearly, it wasn't his brain that had been in control just then. But Christ, for one minute, it had felt perfect.

But it was an illusion. And he needed to stop letting the illusion rule his actions. In short, he needed to give his body what it was craving, so the cravings would fade.

He immediately thought of Andra. She'd be delighted to indulge every wild notion he voiced, plus a few more he'd probably not even imagined. Yes, taking Andra to bed would keep him occupied. But he had a hunch that he'd still be thinking of Cat afterward. Not to mention that he didn't want to get involved with Andra again. It would feel like stepping backward into the past. And the past was a place he did not want to go.

By midday, he admitted he was useless to do anything that required thought. So he rode to the village closest to the estate to visit with people he'd not seen in years. The residents greeted him with smiles, but some of those smiles were strained.

"God bless your return, MacPhearson," one woman said, two small children clutching at her skirts. "We prayed for you while you were away. If you hadn't come back, who knows who would have taken over."

"My sisters, well, probably mostly Euphemia, would have seen to everything," Thane reassured the woman.

"Is he here to send us away?" one of the children asked his mother in a small, nervous voice.

"Hush," she warned her child. Then she said to Thane, "We've heard tales. So many folks are being cleared off the land. They say there's opportunity in the cities, but we don't want to leave."

"No one's leaving while I'm here," Thane said. He'd also heard stories of landowners declaring that tenants who'd farmed the land for generations suddenly had no rights to do so. Apparently, there was some new breed of sheep that had proven more profitable for the owners. Thane knew that much of the land in the Highlands was difficult to farm, but he didn't see the reason in driving people away. The people *were* the Highlands. And he'd be damned if he fought a war to keep his people safe, only to send them away in favor of some cud-chewing animals. "You may tell everyone that Thane MacPhearson said so."

Her expression melted into one of relief. She offered Thane a glass of home-brewed ale and food, which he politely declined, knowing that every sip and bite the kitchen produced would be better used for the family. He promised to send some the men from the castle to help patch up the roofs damaged by the winter winds, and rode on. The village showed some disrepair, but that's how it always was after winter. At least, he remembered it that way. Was it worse than before? Thane hated to think that his absence meant the people under his care suffered, but it had been a long absence, and he'd frankly pushed off the idea of settling down to do all the everyday duties that his father had done. It had seemed so dull, and as a young man, he'd craved excitement. Joining the army was the perfect solution for his restless soul.

But now he had to admit that perhaps he'd taken it too far, stayed away longer than he ought to, and relied too heavily on Effie to be the caretaker he should have been. Especially with her married now and no longer living at their family home, it was high time for him to take the reins.

It was in this gloomy frame of mind that he rode back to the castle. When he strode into the great hall, he saw Catriona sitting with Effie. He walked over to them, and Effie stood to embrace him.

"There you are," she said. "Now you can keep our guest company," she added with a significant look. "I'm off to take a wee nap. I'm so tired lately!"

"Oh, I'd hoped to talk about the estate with you," he said, feeling that it was a weak excuse, even if it was true.

"A fine idea, but later," Effie said. "I'll see you both this evening."

She left, carrying her knitting with her. Thane faced Cat, who regarded him steadily from her spot near the hearth. *A cat indeed*, he thought. Even her eyes held the same aloof and superior attitude.

"Where've you been all day?" he asked.

"Where have I been all day? Here, with Effie for company. She told me about the castle and the land, and pointed out all the things I ought to know." At that moment, Cat glanced across the hall, and Thane saw how she was tracking Andra's progress with narrowed eyes. Oh, hell, had Effie told Cat that he and Andra had a history?

Then he winced. Effie wouldn't have to. After all, Cat had seen Andra leave his study last night, her dress conspicuously askew.

"I hoped to find you earlier, but I had some tasks to attend to." Despite his best efforts, he still sounded upset. "I wanted to speak to you."

She frowned. "Why? Did you learn something from the men? Did you get news of Tacita? She's all right, isn't she? Oh, if anything happens to her—"

"Calm down, Cat. As far as I know, she's fine, and the men are checking in with her every day until she sets sail. I have no more news than I did yesterday."

"Then what did you want to talk about?"

He tilted his head, trying to decide if she was really that naive. No, Catriona was far too intelligent for that. So he said bluntly, "Us."

"There is no us." She actually looked horrified at the thought, which got him riled.

"Cat, will you pretend that last night didn't happen?"

"I'm sure I could, if you agree to as well. No one ever needs to know about the kiss. It was obviously a mistake."

How could she sound so unmoved by it?

He frowned. "I don't intend to shout it from the rooftops, but I also don't want to ignore what's happening."

"*Nothing* is happening."

Ah, wait. He saw the color rise in her cheeks. She was not nearly as cool about this as she was pretending. He said, "You can deny it with your words, but I know you felt something."

Cat set her jaw. "What I felt was annoyance."

"What you felt was want." He wouldn't let this go until she admitted the truth. "And I felt it too. Stupid to lie about it to each other. So the question is, what do we do about it?"

She frowned. "I propose we do absolutely nothing. Or did you think that my presence here came with additional services?" Her tone dripped with disdain.

"I'm not suggesting anything like that. Christ. I'm just saying that we should avoid the chance of it happening again."

"Ah. In that case, I fully agree. You seem to have your hands full anyway, what with all the demands of your…estate." She nodded slightly toward Andra, who had just burst out into a flirtatious laugh as she bantered with one of the men in the hall.

"I've known Andra a very long time."

"How nice for you," Cat said with a false smile.

"I mean, there's nothing between her and me. Besides… just knowing each other. Anyway, I don't want to talk about Andra. I want to talk about us, and how to…maintain a proper distance."

"Don't kiss me," she suggested.

"Fine. Don't come into my study at night, alone."

"Oh, so what happened is my fault? I'm Eve and I'm Delilah?"

"You're maddening, is what you are. I'm trying to keep you safe, Cat. Your reputation as well as your life."

"You're talking as if anyone cares about my reputation," she said, sneering. "Please remember that I am utterly unconcerned with the idea of being a pure and perfect virgin for some man to buy at the marriage mart."

"Who would pay to live with a fury?" he retorted. "You're not the only person in the world, Cat. If something happens, it affects me too."

Her eyes widened.

"I don't mean that you'll be marched to the altar," he said hastily. "I just mean that…I don't want to break my own promise."

"Your promise? Wait, have you got an understanding with some woman up here?" Cat looked truly alarmed now.

"No! I meant my promise to protect you. Which includes protecting you from…me." He sighed. "What happened last night was my fault, Cat. I know it and I swear to you I didn't plan it. I don't know what the hell I was thinking."

"Nor I," she admitted, her cheeks pink as she dropped her gaze. "It was so foolish. I thought you were making fun of me."

"I wasn't," he assured her. "But it was monumentally daft, and I won't do it again."

"That would be for the best," she murmured, still looking anywhere but at him. "But the fault wasn't yours alone. I was…susceptible. And curious, I suppose. I've never kissed anyone before. Not like that."

He swallowed. Cat had never kissed a man before him? Not even her one-time fiancé? Not once? He knew she was innocent, but not quite that innocent. "I'm sorry."

"At least now I know," she said, finally looking at him. "Perhaps I should thank you."

"You're welcome," he said, smiling despite himself.

A slow answering smile warmed her expression. "Perhaps *you're* welcome. I do hope it wasn't too boring for you."

He shook his head, unable to say any of the words that sprang to mind. *Boring* wasn't one of them.

"I don't want to fight anymore, Thane," she said quietly, growing serious again. "I know you don't like me, but you have…" She stopped, and seemed to struggle for words—Cat, who lived with words. She went on, "You've done more for me than I could ever ask, and I know you did it for

Brodie, not me. But I'm still grateful."

"It's…" He also fought for what to say. "I'll see it through." Damn it, that wasn't what he wanted to tell her, but he was feeling so muddled now.

"I know. And I hope it won't be too long before the other men discover something, and Tacita gets here, and all will be as it was before."

"Yes," he said. Though how the hell could everything ever return to how it was before? Before, he hadn't known Cat at all. Before, Brodie had been alive. Before, Thane was a different man.

Chapter 17

FOR THE NEXT FEW DAYS, the détente between Cat and Thane seemed to hold. It was true that she did not want to fight with him. What was the point? If she was going to be at Kinlochlie for the next few weeks, she ought to make the best of it.

So she rode out with Effie during the mornings, and learned more about this corner of the Highlands than she ever expected to. She found the slopes and slants of the mountains in the nearest range becoming familiar to her, and she loved seeing storm clouds forming around the peaks, until in the early afternoon they crashed against the mountain stone and unleashed a distant fury of thunder and rain. The advancing spring made the hillsides impossibly colorful, giving the appearance of an Eden. Though she learned it was something of an illusion—the seemingly lush landscape wasn't very fertile, and only sheep and goats had much success in finding food there. The valleys held a patchwork of fields and garden plots tilled and planted by tenant farmers who called the MacPhearson family their landlords. But these areas were dwarfed by the wilds of the upland meadows and the rugged rock faces of the mountains. Forests grew up in the pockets of land too difficult to clear for farms, and this was where the deer and birds and the occasional bear dwelt. Once, she heard the distinctive howl of a wildcat, and felt an answering thrill in her heart. Something inside her was growing to love this part of the world, so untamed and ancient. It was too bad that she was here only a short while.

On the fourth day, Effie announced that her nose was so stuffed she couldn't go outside. "But Thane is riding, and you ought to join him."

"I'm visiting farms to check on the crops and the state of the fields," he objected. "It's not a sight-seeing trip."

"I don't need to be entertained," Cat said. "I can ride on my own."

"Like hell you will." Thane frowned at her. "Anything could happen."

"So I should remain here, like a caged bird?"

He sighed. "Fine, come along. Just don't expect a grand tour."

She suppressed an eye roll, and went to get ready. One of the reasons she enjoyed riding here so much was the simple fact that she had had to borrow the proper garments from Effie, and thus they were not black (though her own boots still were). Cat enjoyed the soft green jacket and the modified wool skirt for their color as much as for the comfort they offered.

Fortunately, Thane seemed to be in a better mood when they met at the stables, or maybe he'd forgotten how to be dour for a little while. They rode out and headed east, aiming to visit several tenant homesteads so that Thane could speak with everyone following his return to Kinlochlie.

Thane rode well, which shouldn't be surprising, considering that he must have been riding since he was little boy—there was no other good way to get around this whole area, which was too wild and rugged for roads, other than a single track that led to the castle from the village. She glanced over the fields and noticed a man sitting on a rise. He lifted a hand in acknowledgment of their passing, and Thane returned the gesture.

"Who is that? He doesn't look much like a shepherd," Cat noted. The man was too big and bulky for that.

"He's not," Thane said shortly, looking sidelong at her. "He's watching."

It took her a moment to understand, then it hit her. "You've got guards out, even here?"

"Of course. Any stranger appears, anything odd at all happens, and he'll get word to me. All the men have their orders."

"How many?" she asked.

"Enough," he grunted. "They don't know the details for why they're being asked to do this, but they know to be alert."

"Wait, you can't have a garrison of soldiers at the ready. So these men ought to be working elsewhere."

He shook his head. "There's less work around here than anyone would like. Trust me, they can be spared, and they're glad of the extra pay. And anyway, I didn't drag you all the way up here just to let your killer slip in afterward and finish the job. Not here, on MacPhearson land."

She nodded, feeling suddenly chastised. Thane had never stopped thinking of his promise to keep her safe, even when she had. Though he didn't always appear to be, Thane was a soldier through and through.

"I didn't realize all the actions you've taken to protect me."

He shrugged. "I gave my word."

Why did his voice sound so hollow?

"Do you really think that whoever is after me could find me here?"

Thane's lips thinned. "Ordinarily, I'd say not. There's

little to connect us, and we left the city with no warning. But even up here, people talk. And you are a very unusual figure." He looked her over. "Black hair, black clothing… usually anyway. It's striking. People will remember seeing you. And people gossip because there's nothing else to do."

"But gossip up here in the Highlands won't make it back to Edinburgh," she said.

"Gossip goes everywhere, especially when someone is seeking it out. It just depends on whether the man trying to kill you is content to wait you out, assuming you'll return to your home at some point, or if he's determined enough to trace your departure. He could ask at the harbors. He could find out that a ship left for Inverness the night you disappeared from town, and that a woman was among the passengers."

"But that's nothing to go on! Many women travel. I wore a cloak, with the hood up," she reminded him.

"It's enough for a lead. I'd follow it, if I were looking for you."

"If you were looking for me, I assume you'd find me," she admitted. She couldn't imagine Thane giving up on any goal he set for himself.

"Aye, whether I wanted to or not," he muttered, though with a fleeting grin.

Something in Cat answered that slight hint of humor, and she smiled at him. "You're happy to be back home, aren't you?"

"I am," he said simply. "I was away far too long. But it's funny. When we first arrived, everything felt strange. Have you ever put on someone else's shoe by mistake? It looks all right, but then you take a step. You wonder if you're mad. And then you wonder how you could ever make such a daft mistake."

"I'm of a size with Aunt Tacita. The maids are forever

putting our shoes in the wrong rooms and I've done exactly that."

"Well, coming back here felt like being shoved into the wrong shoe: almost what I remembered, but not exactly. And then, this morning, I woke up and realized that I *did* fit back in. Everything moved back into place. Or I just stopped feeling like a stranger."

"I hope I won't feel that when I get back home," she said. "Not that I'll be years gone. With luck, you'll be rid of me in a few weeks. Or less."

Thane shook his head, not looking at her. "We'll see."

"You don't have faith in your compatriots?" she asked.

"Of course I do. But in the army, I learned that it's wise to plan for the worst."

"Well, the worst would be that I stay here forever."

He gave a theatrical shudder, and Cat laughed. "I share your horror of the notion. Imagine: seeing each other every morning, every evening. Having to share meals and chat with neighbors at church, and ride the same paths, and keep Christmas together..." She trailed off, because none of those things actually sounded so terrible. She could envision seeing Thane each day, seeing him smile at her, and reaching to touch him...

She shook herself. Madness. They loathed each other. And even if they didn't, she craved an independent life. Not a life shackled to Thane. Why was she dreaming of such silliness?

Thane looked a little odd too, and he rode forward a few lengths, scanning the horizon.

"That's Ben Abhras," he said, pointing to the mountain ahead of them. "It's nearly as tall as Ben Nevis, they say."

"I've not heard of it. What does the name mean?"

"Um, it might translate as *the spinning mountain*. Like a spindle, or a distaff. We tell the children a story that there's an old, old woman who lives on the top and she spins and spins and spins clouds out of the air, and that's why a storm can spin up so fast on a fine day. Really, it's just that the peak catches the passing winds and throws everything down the slope to where we live down here."

The solitary mountain dominated their sight from this location. Cat craned her neck to catch the peak, which seemed both close and impossibly far—some trick of the light or the air.

"Have you ever climbed to the summit?" she asked.

He nodded, following her gaze. "Got caught in a storm at the top, naturally. It's a rough climb. You have to start before dawn. And even then, it's a challenge."

"And you love a challenge," she murmured.

He gave her a sudden smile—he looked so different when he smiled. "Aye, I do. And it is the best way to see all the MacPhearson land. All the men in the family, and most of the women too, have climbed that mountain at one point. I did it just before I left for France."

There was a melancholy note in his voice, and she guessed he'd made that climb in order to say goodbye, in case he never saw his home again.

"I'd like to do it," she said.

"Climb the mountain?" He sounded surprised.

"Oh, are you implying I'd fail?"

Thane shook his head. "No. You're stubborn enough to climb twelve mountains in a day. But why do you want to?"

"The view?" she suggested.

"The view is amazing from everywhere around here," he retorted, both defensive and obviously proud of his home. "I suspect that you can't let a mountain go unclimbed because you know that it's mostly done only by men."

"And sheep," she added sweetly. "So how challenging could it be?"

Thane shot her a dark look, but then laughed. "I'd love to see you try."

"Depends how long I'm here. You say one must start before dawn. On the summer solstice, that's early, but the day will be the longest."

"If you're still here at solstice, I'll be in Bedlam," he muttered.

"You appear to be weathering the storm very well, Mr MacPhearson," she replied loftily.

"Appearances can be deceiving."

She glanced at him, wondering, but he was looking up at the sky again, now with his brow wrinkling up.

"Speaking of storms, those clouds are gathering faster than I'd expected," he said. "We should head back home."

Cat considered the grey masses pillowing up near the peak. "There weren't so many even a quarter hour ago, were there?"

"No. That's a storm, for certain."

They circled back around, but didn't make it far before fat drops of rain began to spatter on the grasses around them, and hit Cat's face and the horse's glossy coat.

"How far are we from Kinlochlie?" she asked, turning her head to see Thane, who was grimly assessing the sky.

"Too far. And we can't ride home through what's coming. See the green of those clouds? That's a bad sign," he called. "We have to wait it out in shelter."

He pulled his horse hard to the side, and gestured for her to follow suit. "There's a bothy nearby. If we hurry, we can make it before the worst of the storm meets us."

Cat wheeled about, but her horse was already shying, uneasy. Thane reached out and took the reins.

"I'll guide us. Just hold on," he told her.

Cat clung to her saddle as Thane directed both horses toward a smudged line of trees, their leaves tossing in the wind, alternating between silver and dark velvet green. Cat wiped raindrops from her face, trying to see their destination as they rode closer and closer to the edge of the woods. What shelter did Thane see that she could not?

They rode into the woods, slowing as the path narrowed. Then Thane pulled the horses to a stop. He leapt down, and hurried to help her. Cat was grateful for his strong grip as he lowered her to the slick ground.

"Where are we going?" she asked, staring up into his green eyes.

"Just past those trees," he said, nodding his head to the right. "Let me secure the horses."

He did so, then took Cat's hand to lead her on a narrow track between shaking oaks.

Then she saw it.

The bothy was a tiny structure, but solid, made of stone walls and a well-thatched roof. Cat stepped in with a sense of relief. "It's dry," she said, inordinately pleased to discover it was true.

"Aye, it's designed to keep all weather out. Anyone stuck on the mountains can use it."

"So we might have company?" she asked.

"Doubt it," he said with a snort. "Only fools let a storm sneak up on them."

"But it will pass quickly?"

"I hope so," he muttered.

"I'm sorry you're stuck with me. Again."

He looked slightly abashed. "I didn't mean it like that."

"Why not? We don't have a good record when we're thrust on top of one another," she pointed out.

"*You* weren't watching when you barreled down that hallway with that silly bird," he said defensively.

"*You* practically tossed me into that carriage in the park, like I was a sack of potatoes."

"A sack of potatoes would know better than to leave a protected location to give a damned speech for women's rights!"

"Potatoes don't give speeches for *anyone's* rights!" Cat retorted.

Thane stared at her. She stared back, realizing the absolutely inanity of their words.

Before she knew it, a giggle escaped her. And another. And then she was laughing helplessly at her own silliness. Thane smiled, then he laughed as well.

"You're going to be the death of me, Catriona Ross," he said at last.

"I am sorry," she confessed. "Maybe you should vow to protect potatoes instead of me."

"It would be infinitely easier."

"Until you get hungry."

He shook his head, grinning. "You look like a drowned kitten. Like on the ship."

"Ugh, don't remind me." She looked down at her soaked hair and clothes. He had a point. She shivered, feeling the clinging wool against her skin.

He shrugged out of his coat. "Here. You need it more than I do."

"But you'll be cold. There's no place for a fire here." The bothy was truly minuscule, making a croft look palatial in comparison.

"I'll live. I've been through worse."

"I imagine."

She peeled off the jacket of her riding habit, and found that her cotton shift was still relatively dry. She pulled his coat on and warmed immediately as the leather enveloped her. If only it didn't smell distractingly of him as well.

He took her habit and gingerly draped it over the rough-hewn bench set against one wall. "Sorry there's not a fire. At least it could drive some of the damp out of your clothing."

"We'd have to set the whole bothy on fire to do that," Cat said with a laugh. "And only fools burn their own roof."

"Aye, well, I'm already proved a fool for not watching the weather. I've been gone too long," he added, cursing under his breath. "I forgot how fast the weather turns in the Highlands."

"You'll remember next time," she assured him.

"What good does that do you?" Thane reached out and squeezed her plait, which had come unpinned. Water dripped onto the floor. "I'll be accused of drowning you."

"I've seen your people and how they view you. You'll be hailed as a hero for saving my life."

He lifted the plait, and tried to wind it about the top of her head again, to no avail. Cat tugged at his arm, saying, "Leave it. It's ruined anyway."

"I'm sorry," he said, his voice lower. "I don't want to ruin you."

"You haven't ruined me. Just my hair…"

Thane's hand let go of her plait and instead cupped her neck. Cat went still, her skin tingling at his touch.

He slid his hand to her shoulder, under the coat and above the thin fabric of her shift. His eyes were hooded, his mouth slightly open as he grazed the curve of her shoulder.

"Cat," he said, the word barely more than a moan. "Say you're cold."

"I'm cold," she told him, her temperature soaring as she took in his expression. Now he was looking at her, his eyes drinking her in. He pushed aside his coat, letting it fall so she couldn't claim it as protection.

Her cheeks flushed. "I'm so cold," she whispered, her hands reaching up to his chest. His shirt was damp enough to cling to his body, and she thought he should take it off.

Thane gave her a wry smile, and she realized she'd said

those words out loud. He pulled the shirt over his head, and dropped it over her habit on the bench.

"Now nothing will dry," she muttered.

"Stop thinking about things, Cat," he ordered.

He pulled her closer, and she went willingly. If there was any chance that she might have taken a chill before, it was gone. There was just too much Thane around her to let any cold in. The sight of his bare chest also made her blush in a way that would surely create steam if it went on much longer.

Then Thane bent his head, and kissed her just past the neckline of her shift.

Cat closed her eyes, feeling his mouth against her skin there, and shivered for entirely different reasons.

"Are you still cold?" he asked, his breath in her ear.

"No. I mean, yes. I mean, whatever you need to hear to keep doing this."

His laugh was a wave of warmth breaking over her, unlocking a need she'd kept inside for a very long time.

She turned her head and kissed him back, her mouth skimming his neck, feeling the scrape of stubble as she went. When she reached the smoother skin under his ear, she bit down.

He swore, and one arm circled her waist and pulled her closer to him. Cat's breasts pressed against his chest, her nipples hardened from the previous chill. Now, with exactly one layer of fine cotton lawn between them, Cat knew he felt everything. And he seemed to like it.

Still kissing her, Thane shifted slightly to angle one leg between her own, and the way he held her meant she was practically riding his thigh, and there was something so good about it.

She rolled her hips, seeking more of the pleasure spreading through her body, into her belly and up into her chest.

The first time he'd kissed her, in his study the night they arrived in Kinlochlie, Cat thought she'd finally understood what it truly meant to feel desire.

That had been nothing.

Now she wanted so much more. She lifted her mouth until she found his. Tongues tangled in a fight no one needed to win, and Cat sighed as Thane's hands kept finding new ways to soften her and mold her closer to him.

There was something so rewarding about making him moan whenever she flicked her tongue against his skin. She was glad he wasn't wearing his shirt anymore. She ducked her head and pulled back enough to lick his chest, curling her tongue at his nipple, wondering what that would do.

It made him swear. She thought it was a swear—it was in a language she didn't know.

He slid one hand into her hair and pulled her head back so he could see her face.

"You're torturing me."

"Does it hurt?" she asked, knowing that wasn't what he meant.

"An ache like you wouldn't believe."

He shifted again, and she felt the hard length of him pressed against the apex of her thighs. Her eyes widened as she realized just how aroused he was.

"Oh. Does it…does it really ache?"

"In a way that makes me mad for you." He moved enough to let her body glide over the ridge, and couldn't stop a groan of pleasure. "You telling me you don't feel an ache too, kitty cat?"

She was aware of…not an ache, exactly, but a need to soothe, to press and roll and massage until something broke through. "I liked it better when we weren't talking," she whispered, feeling too shy to explain what he was doing to her.

"But my kitty cat *loves* talking," he said with a teasing grin. He moved again, his leg pressing into her, his hand sliding to her bottom and lifting her higher onto his thigh. Cat rolled her hips once more, seeking that momentary rise as his muscled thigh and the hardened length slid against her tender core.

"Thane," she gasped, aware of, yes, a growing ache that was impossible to deny.

Then a bright shaft of sunlight cut through the space, thanks to the gap made by the slightly open door.

"The storm has passed," Cat murmured, still half-dazed with the pleasure coursing through her body.

"We should go," he said, showing no inclination to stop doing what he was doing to her.

"Yes," she breathed, stroking her hands along his chest. "I wish you weren't so handsome. Especially now that I know what you feel like."

His hands tightened around her hips. "If you were any other woman, I could keep you here. I could take you against this wall, and you'd love every minute," he growled. "I would fucking love to show you. Ask me to show you."

Cat's heart thudded in response to his words. It should feel like a threat. But it felt like an invitation to a world she'd otherwise never ever get to see.

Part of her ached to say *Yes, show me.*

Thane's gaze caught hers and he inhaled, perhaps seeing the thought in her eyes, the words on the tip of her tongue.

Then his jaw clenched. "What are we doing?" He propelled himself back, as if she were poison. He took a few steps back (any more and he'd hit the other wall of the bothy), and reached for his shirt, pulling it on. It clung to his skin, and she tried not to notice. Tried and failed.

"It's no one's fault," she said. She took the wet riding habit he handed over next. She didn't try to put it on—it was so sodden that it weighed three times as much as usual. She reached for his coat instead, and pulled it over her shoulders once more. "Really, it's very natural for my curiosity to take over when I was in a new situation. And you were just accommodating that."

He belted out a laugh. "You are not just innocent, Cat, you're insane as well."

"There's no need to be rude about it."

"I'm just saying that I wasn't doing you a favor."

"Well, no, why would you? You don't even like me."

"It's not that," he ground out. "But we are going to forget this happened." He opened the door, and peered outside. Cat glimpsed water dripping from brilliantly green leaves, looking as if they were adorned with crystals.

"I tried to forget the kiss from before," she admitted. "It's difficult."

"I know." He stepped out and she followed him. Thankfully, the horses were exactly where he'd left them, now chewing contentedly on grass, the storm a forgotten memory.

Thane loosed the reins where he'd tied them around a low branch. He did his best to wipe the saddle dry with his sleeve. Both his effort and the result were middling, which should have told her how distracted he was.

"Do you think about Andra when you're not with her?" Cat asked.

Thane nearly choked at her question. "I'm not with her, ever. Not since before I left."

"Really? That's not how it looks."

"She's a flirt."

"It's more than that."

"Christ, why do you want to know about Andra?"

"I don't know. Maybe because she's everything I'm not. She...plays the game."

Thane shot her a look. "Aye, she does. But you hate the

game."

"I do. Women shouldn't have to pretend to like men to get what they need. Or even if they're not pretending…it would be nicer if they could flirt because it was fun, or take a lover because they wanted to. Not because it's a way to find safety from other men."

"Cat, you've got a way of seeing the worst in everyone." Without asking, he lifted her onto his horse, then mounted up behind her.

"It's how the world works," she said, trying to focus on the conversation and not the feel of his body next to her. "Why am I not riding my own horse?"

"She's been known to spook easily, and so soon after the thunder, I don't want to risk her throwing you. Plus you'll be warmer if you ride with me."

"Oh. Thank you." She found it difficult to reconcile Thane's acerbic attitude with his thoughtfulness. He was always thinking of every side of a situation.

Thane's arms were around her, but only to hold the reins—her own horse trotted alongside, quite happy to follow. He said, "You don't think anyone feels love for someone else? Or affection? You think it's all like an exchange at the market?"

"Of course I believe love exists."

"You don't say that with confidence."

"I loved my family," she said.

"That's a very different sort of love. You know what I'm talking about." His hand gripped her waist in a reminder of what they'd done moments ago.

Cat refused to rise to that. "I think people feel passion and then mistake it for love. Take what just happened between you and me. It was merely the result of our reactions in a situation we didn't choose. And yet there are so many people in the world who would say that those few minutes of physical closeness was enough to compromise my virtue, despite my being just as much of a virgin after as before. And because a woman is only valued if she can prove to a man that any baby she bears is his, I'd be married off immediately. And to make it even worse, people would like me to then behave as if I loved my new owner, as if I'd do anything for him just because he kissed me. The whole idea of romantic love is a farce, designed to convince women that their captors have their best interests at heart. But the truth is that women are seen only for the wealth they bring or the babies they birth. Never for who they truly are."

Thane hadn't said a word, and she thought for a moment that she either shocked or shamed him enough to keep him silent.

But then he shook his head, and said very quietly, "Poor Cat."

"Poor me?"

"Aye. You wrap so many words around your feelings. But words won't keep you safe. And words won't keep you from feeling more, and soon you're going to burst with all the feelings that you're trying to wall up."

"I'm not walling up anything! I'm the most clear-eyed person there is—I see how the world is, not how I'm told it is."

"Aye, you're clever, and you're right about a lot of how society is tilted. But you pretend that you're above it all, and you're not."

"Don't pretend to understand me, Thane MacPhearson."

"Hell, I couldn't understand you if I had a hundred years to try."

Chapter 18

RIDING BACK TO KINLOCHLIE WAS—to say the least—challenging for Thane. Holding Cat close on horseback was bad enough. Holding her after losing his mind, and kissing her in the bothy, was maddening. Well, he'd done more than kiss her. He'd offered to rid her of her virginity, which was the stupidest thing he could possibly have done. And yet it felt so natural to have her in his arms, and she had reacted with such absolute candor and enthusiasm that it had quickly spiraled out of control.

He hadn't thought she'd even let him kiss her again. He hadn't thought at all, actually. He certainly didn't count on her allowing him to be as bold as he was.

But he should have guessed, because when did Cat *ever* do what was expected?

And now he'd gone and made everything more difficult for them both. All because he'd let his cock do the thinking.

It was still working against him. He wasn't quite hard anymore, but Cat's hip was rolling into his lap with every stride the horse made, and yes, it felt good.

He shifted slightly, trying to lessen the contact. No help.

Cat turned her head to look at him. "Is something wrong?"

What was wrong was the way her clear blue eyes made

him want to tell her things, things he could never ever tell anyone, least of all her. Only the way the tiny charm on the chain around her neck glinted in the sunlight stopped him.

"I'll be fine," he grunted.

"Are you cold?"

"No." If anything, he was too damn hot. In more ways than one.

"Should we stop for a moment?"

"No!" he snapped, then added, "We've got to get back. That last thing I need is for you to take ill because I was riding you all over the Highlands in a rainstorm."

"You couldn't have predicted the weather."

But he was from here. Thane knew the risks, and he still allowed it all to happen.

"I should have! I should have planned for the possibility. And I never should have let *you* go instead of m—" He broke off, appalled at his near slip. He reminded himself where he was, who he was talking to. Cat, not Brodie.

"Instead of who?" Cat frowned.

Thane scrambled for a suitable explanation. "Instead of what," he said. "Instead of staying at the house, where you'll be safe."

"Ah, back to my gilded cage." Her face grew tight, angry. The same face she wore the night he met her. This was the Cat he needed her to be, because the open and soft and giving Cat was far too dangerous.

"Don't flatter me. Kinlochlie is many things, but gilded isn't one of them."

"It's a very grand place," Cat said defensively. "It just needs a little attention. No surprise, since the master of it has been gone for so long."

"It's falling apart." Thane didn't know why he was being so petulant about his own home, other than talking with Cat always made him contrary.

"Only some of it! The oldest bits anyway. And it's not as if you need the archers' towers anymore. You're not making war on your neighbors, are you?"

"My nearest neighbor is Effie, so no."

"Well, then. You've nothing to worry about. Repair the structure as you can, and eventually no one will mistake it for a ruin."

"Easier said than done, kitty cat."

She stiffened at the pet name, but didn't make a fuss about it. Thane liked to think it was because she secretly enjoyed it, but it was more likely that she was merely too wet and cold to argue anymore. He pulled her a little closer, and felt the moment that she softened against him.

"I still hate you," she mumbled. "Don't forget that. I'm just chilly. I don't want to be near you at all."

"I know, kitty cat," he told her, smiling despite himself.

They returned to Kinlochlie, and Thane barely had to start explaining what happened (leaving out the time in the bothy) when Effie swept into the courtyard and threw a blanket over Cat's shoulders, cooing over her like a mother hen. No one questioned why the two of them had been alone —apparently, the storm had been even worse at the castle and the consensus was that the lord and his guest were lucky to be alive.

Thane took that small mercy as a sign, and decided not to push his luck. He let Effie take charge of Catriona while he went up to his own bedchamber. He changed quickly out of his wet clothes, but told the servant not to bother with a bath. Thane needed to stay cool after that ride with Cat.

Which reminded him. There was something he wanted to find. Where had he put them all? After looking all around his desk, he remembered that he'd stashed it in a small campaign dresser that he'd sent home ahead, as soon as he knew he'd be resigning his commission at last. It was meant to be portable while moving from camp to camp, but now he hoped it would never see another battle. Still uncomfortable with the memories that anything from the war stirred, Thane had put it behind a heavy curtain that covered an alcove in the room, and used it for storing items that he never used but for one reason or another needed to keep.

It was a beautiful object of fine-grained oak, with engraved patterns all around the outside. Two doors at the front opened to reveal several small drawers for paper, pens, ink, and other little necessities. The insides of the doors were painted with the images of two angels, one bearing a letter and the other holding a quill. Above the first angel was the word *veritas*, and above the second *caritas*. *Truth and love.*

Oh, yes. That was the real reason why he'd hidden it. Thane didn't want to be reminded of his lack of both those things just now.

Thane wrenched open the drawer, cursing the damp weather that always made the wood stick, even on a carefully constructed piece of furniture like this. As soon as the drawer opened, several folded-up letters flew out and scattered over the floor.

He turned and quickly gathered them, then halted when he saw his name scrawled over the front of each one in the painfully familiar handwriting. Brodie's letters. He'd saved them, as he saved most of his letters. But he'd put them out of his mind after Brodie's death.

Slowly, he unfolded the first one, and read again the news and musings of his friend.

By the time you receive this, I expect leave will be over and I'll be on a ship back to the Continent, but as I write now I have just come home. It's glorious in Edinburgh in summer, and Cat and Mama are like two bees, always buzzing about me. I make an unlikely flower, but I shall play the part for them. Cat asked after all my comrades, and I again remembered that you've not yet met her. You really ought to come with me on the next leave. I think you would find Cat highly amusing. She loves a good fight, and so do you.

Well, that was true, Thane thought.

He opened another, dated a few months before Brodie's death. He'd been with a detachment helping to secure supplies for the army's next planned advance.

...think we're almost done here and I should be en route back to the company within a few days. Not that I should tempt fate by writing this! I suppose it's just as likely that I'll be here another six months, or dead. *Sorry, old man. Ignore that. No chance of dying on this detail—I'm so far behind the battle lines I may as well be back home in Edinburgh. Lord, it's hot here. What I wouldn't give for a proper Scottish summer, wool scarves and all.*

Brodie

PS: If anything does happen, which it won't, you'll look after my mother and Cat, won't you? I know you will. I asked the others as well, of course. But I think you're the only one who might hold his own against them.

Thane folded the letter back up, his eyes pricking with unshed tears. Brodie's voice was so strong, his personality shining through every word he wrote. His joking manner, his easy way of putting up with boring, yet still dangerous duty.

"Shouldn't have been you," Thane said quietly.

Before he could do anything else with the letters, a servant entered with a small tray. He took several letters off the tray and handed them to Thane.

"Just arrived, sir. The rider must have been held back at the village due to the storm."

Thane thanked him and sorted through the various letters. Most were typical correspondence from his family solicitors and his man of business in town, but there were also a few from the men.

Thane opened Duncan's first, and read a thorough but depressing report which ticked several names off their list, but found no positive leads. Calan wrote that he and Struan had spent time in the park where the killer attempted to shoot Cat during the rally in an attempt to find witnesses, but without any real luck. Calan had also gone to the ladies' league to ask about other threats made against the members; most of them had received cruel letters, but no one else had reported anything like what Cat had suffered. Calan added that several ladies, including Miss Fairchild and Mrs Roberts, had inquired about Cat's whereabouts. (*I told them nothing, of course. But we'll have to decide on a plausible story for when we return her to her home. Gossip is the real killer for a lady.*) Thane laughed at Calan's typically wry insight. Struan wrote merely to say that by the time Thane received the letter he was holding, all the men would be on a ship heading north, escorting Tacita to rejoin Catriona.

"Thank Christ," Thane breathed. He needed the distraction of the others to keep him from losing his mind over Cat.

There was one letter left, from Kai. Thane opened it and read.

It's not much, but I wanted to report that I located that jilted suitor you mentioned earlier: Patrick Melrose. It wasn't difficult, but I don't think he's our man. He married about a year ago, and they're expecting their first child. He sounds utterly content with life. Unless he's completely fooled both me and Calan during our interview, he is not a man who'd pick up a gun and begin firing it at anyone, let alone more than once, or into a crowd.

Thane pondered that. Kai sometimes seemed naive, but he also had a knack for discovering things. And Calan...very few people fooled Calan. Fewer lived to tell about it.

He read on.

Melrose laughed when I asked about her. Admitted he'd been completely in love with her. "Head over heels," in his words. A youthful infatuation that led to a quick proposal, which Miss Ross accepted. But he said that less than two months later, she broke it off. He said he was shocked by it, and did get into a confrontation with Brodie when he went over to the house to argue his case. But in hindsight, he realized she was right. The engagement was his idea, and it was really just his pride that suffered when she told him that it was over.

Thane was still surprised that she ever accepted, considering her views. He'd ask her, because something about the whole betrothal, brief as it was, irked him.

He went in search of her, and was told that she was on the western lawn. It was safe enough to go to her there. It was a common area, and they'd be in full view of anyone the whole time.

He stepped outside. The clouds had mostly blown over to the east by now, and the sun had sunk beyond the furthest hills, leaving the sky a riot of color—reds, oranges, blues, purples. Cat stood at the stone wall, staring out, looking as if she wanted to take wing.

Chapter 19

SHE WORE A BLACK GOWN once again. Thane missed the riding habit's lighter shade.

"I trust you're recovered from our excursion?" he asked.

"Effie saw to it that I was steamed, boiled, and baked," she replied with a little smile.

"Aye, she's always been thorough. But she cares."

"I know. She's very sweet."

"Here." Thane offered her the bunch of folded letters. "These were from Brodie. I thought you might like to read them."

Cat reached for them, then paused. "But aren't they private?"

He smiled. "Don't worry, I've held back any that you couldn't see."

"How many of *those* were there?"

"Not a one. Brodie's correspondence was nothing out of the ordinary."

Cat read over each letter, smiling. She laughed out loud a few times, and wiped away a few tears. On the last letter, she looked up. "He asked you to take care of us—my mother and me."

"Aye, he asked each of the men to do that. We all promised to do the same for each other. When you're on campaign, you need some kind of hope. And knowing that there was at least one reliable man who could look in on those you left behind, that helps you sleep at night."

Cat bit her lip. "I wonder how many of those promises had to be kept."

Thane nodded at her wording. It was easier than asking how many soldiers died, and how many people grieved them. "All I know is that I kept mine, and I know Brodie would have too, if it had been the other way around."

"Thank you for showing them to me," she said, handing the letters back.

"Keep them while you're here," he urged. "You might want to read them again."

"Very well," Cat said, holding them to her chest.

"I got a few other letters today, of more recent vintage. The men are likely on a ship this moment, bringing Tacita to you."

"Oh." Cat didn't seem as relieved, or elated, as he thought she'd be.

"Isn't that good news?"

"Yes, of course it is. Does that mean…do they know who's behind the…who tried to kill me, that is?"

"Not that I've heard. But they may have learned something since then. That's the problem with letters…you can only hear from the past."

She nodded, gripping Brodie's letters more tightly.

Thane swallowed. "Speaking of the past, tell me about Patrick Melrose."

"Goodness, why?"

"Kai wrote about him, said he inquired about you. Melrose denied any involvement."

"Kai needn't have wasted his time. And believe me, Melrose is a waste of anyone's time." She rolled her eyes.

"Why did you ever get engaged to him?"

"I don't know," Cat said. She gave a shrug that somehow

made her look even more melancholy. "I was younger then. He paid attention to me. It was nice to have someone who called on me and took me out for a ride around the park, or escorted me to a party. And when he proposed...I...I didn't know how to say no. I was flattered, I suppose, but I also didn't want to hurt him by telling him I didn't really want to get married. All my school friends were getting proposals and planning their weddings. It seemed I should do it too."

"So you did want to marry," Thane said, envisioning a younger, more whimsical and hopeful Cat.

"I *tried* to want it," she said, "but after a few weeks I knew I couldn't fool myself into thinking I'd be happy. My mother noticed, and we talked. She waited for me to come to her about it, but I think she already knew what would happen. So I told Patrick I couldn't marry him. And he did not take it well. Said I lied to him and strung him along and I was a turncoat, all sorts of cruel things. Brodie happened to be home on leave at the time, and he came in and heard it, and they just...turned into *boys*, brawling in the parlor. And all I could think was *I am so lucky I stopped this now*. I would have been miserable as Patrick's wife. As any man's wife."

"But you don't believe Melrose would hold a grudge."

She shook her head. "Why would he? He already has exactly what he wants."

"And you? You got what you wanted too, didn't you? A life free of all men. Melrose probably told all his circle, and everyone else was afraid to go near you."

"You make me sound like one of *Macbeth*'s witches," she snapped. "And honestly, if this is what you say when you hear why I didn't marry, it only strengthens my resolve to avoid a husband."

"You weren't avoiding me in the bothy."

Cat's eyes widened, and he regretted his words.

But then she hissed, "How could I, when I had all of three steps before I hit a wall?"

"That's not what I meant."

"I know exactly what you meant, and I'll avoid you from now on, Thane MacPhearson."

Cat stormed off, and he let her, because she was correct and he was an idiot. He just hoped no one saw Cat and him fight. It would lead to questions.

So he stayed there and brooded, not appreciating the brilliant stained-glass sky one whit.

Why did Cat always make him lose his temper? He thought of their conversation again, his mind pulling back to the earlier part, before she got angry. When she was talking about Melrose. What had she said?

He already has exactly what he wants. Cat's phrasing was simple, but it illuminated something Thane had been missing. People rarely took action—whether violent or not—unless they had a reason to. Thus, most men who objected to Cat's political views would grouse and grumble, but nothing more. Why would they? They already had a superior position in society, and even if Cat and her compatriots managed some small change, those men were not in any danger of losing their comfortable lives.

But someone *had* shot at Cat, which implied that they were not comfortable or content with their situation. And they'd identified Cat as the reason. Not Mrs Roberts, the leader of the League. Or any of the other members. They picked Cat.

Why?

Thane gazed out at the landscape, lost in thought. An idea was coming to him, but far too slowly. Something about Cat's attacker…

Just then, Andra sauntered toward him, a sunny yet seductive smile on her face. He groaned inwardly—he'd much prefer to be solitary while puzzling out this thought, and Andra never heralded calm introspection.

"You're out here all alone," she said, now offering a pretty pout. Her skirt seemed to hitch up of its own volition. How the hell did she manage that?

"I *was*," he told her, not bothering to hide the edge of irritation that he felt.

"I saw Miss Ross leaving. I thought you two might have had a tiff."

He shook his head. "I never have tiffs." Well, with Cat that was mostly an aspiration.

She laughed. "Then why'd she storm off?"

"Who knows?"

"I'm glad I found you anyhow." A touch of her hand along his arm signaled her line of thought.

He didn't feel the least bit interested, especially since he sensed that she was performing a role she expected that *he* expected her to play. Time to end it. So instead, he asked, "Andra, what do you want in life?"

She raised an eyebrow. "Have I not made it clear that I want you?"

"Don't flirt. I'm dead serious. When you were growing up—no, strike that. If a stranger came up to you today, and said, 'Andra lass, describe the sort of life you'd be happy to live,' what would you tell them?"

Andra sank onto the stone wall. "Hmmm. I suppose…a tidy croft somewhere, with my man off to work in the morning and back every evening. Children playing…and all the food we ever needed. And a pretty dress I save just for holidays."

He nodded at her words. It was a familiar image to anyone in the Highlands. Even though Thane had grown up in finer surroundings, thanks to his family's wealth and ancestry, he wasn't that far removed from the common Scotsman.

He lived among them. And he knew that the average Scot didn't require much to be content (and indeed, often made a point on thriving with far less than others would consider adequate). Andra's wishes were very close to what most women her age would say.

"You do not want," he said, rather deliberately, "to be the lady of a great house."

"Lord, I'd be no good at that! Fine hostess, dressed like a princess and not able to sit down without a brigade of help!" She didn't quite sneer…but almost did.

"A fine house offers some advantages."

"Stephen says we don't need more than three rooms—" She broke off, embarrassed at the slip, and what it revealed.

"So that's the man you picture? Stephen Reid."

"Aye, then. Stephen Reid. He's got a farm over the hill, north of here."

"I know it. Has he asked you to marry him?"

"Not yet." She frowned. "He says he wants to build up his savings before he gets a wife and children to take care of. But with the last few harvests not so good, and so many workers being moved off the land, there's less call for what he's been growing, and so he's barely able to keep his head up. And I don't know when it'll change." She sighed.

"Do you care for him?"

"Aye. Very much." She wasn't looking at Thane as she spoke, lost in a dream she might never attain. After a moment, though, she suddenly lifted her head, realizing what she'd admitted. "Oh! I mean, I care for him. But not like *you…*"

"Hush, Andra," he told her, chuckling. "You don't have to lie to me. Even if you had fancied yourself in love with me before I left, it was a long time ago."

"I kept waiting for some horrible news," she said. "Everyone did, I think. No one ever said anything, but if

Thane MacPhearson died over there...what did that mean for everyone here? With your parents gone and no brothers to take charge."

"Effie would have managed."

"I suppose. But it's not the same. You're not going back, are you?"

"To fight? Christ, no." He was done with that life.

"Good. You're needed here." She said that with simple matter-of-factness. No longer the mistress aiming to keep her place, but just a local who knew what was expected of everyone.

"Andra, let me ask you something else. Suppose you saw a way to get what you wanted—the croft, the wedding, everything—but to do it, you'd have to commit a crime. Would you?"

"What sort of crime?" she asked, her eyes narrowing speculatively.

"Murder."

"Thane MacPhearson!" Her voice horrified. "No one would do such a thing!"

"Oh, people have and people do. Not you, though," he added with a reassuring nod. "You're not the type. Do you think your Stephen would do it?"

"Never! He's a good man, and he'd not hurt a flea. A person would have to be hollow inside to do that sort of thing. Think of living in a house and looking at the walls and the roof every day and knowing that it was bought with death. I'd never sleep a wink in such a place."

"Aye. It takes a certain type of person to be able to kill when it's not necessary."

She looked at him, worry on her face. "Is this about the war? Are you upset about something you had to do then? You shouldn't be. The soldiers on the other side didn't worry about you, I'll wager. Everyone just wants to make it to the next day still alive."

"I'm not ashamed of anything I did on the battlefield…" He halted. True—it was what happened *away* from the battlefield that kept him up nights. "War is war. We all knew what we were meant to do when we took the king's coin."

"Then what are you asking about?"

"I'm trying to understand the sort of man who kills for reasons other than self-preservation."

"Well, he'd have to be daft, wouldn't he? Just someone who's crazed and lashes out, like a beast."

"That's one kind of killer. But what about a man who's a little more…measured. Someone who takes the time to stalk his prey, plans things out."

"That's pure hate, then," Andra said, shuddering. "Or greed, maybe. But you have to live with everything you do. Can't imagine there are many men who can truly live with killing someone to get what they want. Unless they can tell themselves a story that makes it feel right."

He drew in a breath, struck by her words. That made sense. Perhaps someone was using Cat's politics to justify his own violence—telling himself it was the right thing to do.

Thane despised true believers. He hated them while in the army. He hated them outside it. True believers would destroy anything and everything as long as they didn't have to confront any suggestion that their own view wasn't completely correct. True believers were the sort of men who ordered whole brigades to march into certain death because the plan looked good on a map.

Was that the sort of man who wanted to kill Cat?

"Excuse me, Andra. I have to write a letter. It's probably too late, but I have to try to let them know…"

"Thane?" Andra was looking at him curiously. "Does this have something to do with Miss Ross?"

He paused, gave a slight nod, but said, "I can't talk about it."

"Does someone want to hurt her? That's why she's here, isn't it?"

"I just said—"

"Thane, you don't have to tell me," Andra said, holding up one hand. "But please don't think I'm stupid."

"I've never thought that."

"You're trying to help her, aren't you? I hope you can. She seems like she needs help—she's so sad."

He was surprised at Andra's sympathy for Cat, but then again, it wasn't as if Andra had any tender feelings for Thane anymore. He said, "Of course she's sad. She's in mourning."

Andra shrugged that explanation off. "When you solve her problem, are you going to ask her to marry you?"

"No!"

"Why not? She'd be a fine mistress here. *She's* got the proper touch, all elegant and smooth."

"She doesn't wish to marry."

"Hmm. I always found you persuasive when you want something."

He was alarmed. "I'm not going to…it's not going to happen."

"Very well, no need to make a fuss about it. Shame, though."

Andra got up off the wall and sashayed off, as if she hadn't a care in the world. That left Thane all alone, temporarily forgetting about the letter he needed to send. He stood there, imagining Catriona Ross as the lady of the house. The lady of *his* house.

He knew what it felt like to want something you couldn't have.

And, yes, he could picture doing something drastic to get it.

Chapter 20

CAT SPENT THE NEXT DAY largely on her own, since Effie had some task that required all her attention, yet none of Cat's assistance. Cat knew better than to press—she could tell when she wasn't needed. So she walked near the estate, clambering up a hill mostly for the sake of doing so. At the top, she found a small ring of stones, the center of which was occupied by one white sheep.

Figuring that if a sheep was allowed inside, so was she, Cat took a step, waited for some admonishment from the faeries, got none, and sighed.

"You might at least try to kidnap me," she announced. "Though I've already been kidnapped once this month."

The only reply was the wind.

"I suppose he didn't actually kidnap me," she admitted. "It was more of a desperate choice to save my own life. But I don't know if my life is worth saving. I don't know what I'll do with it in any case. I'll not get married, or be a useful woman in the house of some relative. I don't have any relatives who'd need those services of me. I'm no good at minding children, and I don't sew well, and I am hardly a pleasant conversationalist when people come to tea. I talk about the rights of women, and I quote the thinkers I admire, but I've done almost nothing to further the cause I profess to believe in. I shall be a spinster, and everyone shall say it's sour grapes when I explain that women should not have to depend on a man for her daily bread."

The faeries did not respond. The sheep was also unmoved by this speech, and continued to pull on the tender green grass.

"It's all right for you," she told the sheep. "Your meals are available on every hillside. Women are not so lucky. I shall probably starve at some point. What work am I suited for, and who would hire me to it? No one pays a woman to dream of a better world."

The sheep bleated in what Cat chose to believe was sympathy.

What would she do? Her time at Kinlochlie had shown her one ugly truth at least—she'd been sheltered and coddled before, at her own home. Even though she had joined the League and gone to rallies and given speeches (well, the beginning of a speech), Cat faced no real challenges to her own survival...until someone tried to kill her, that is. She was well provided for by the trust her mother set up for her. Aunt Tacita was a kind and wise guardian. And she had a lovely home with a full complement of servants. Who was she to complain?

"It's not a complaint to see a flaw in the world and ask that it be fixed," she told herself, echoing words Mrs Roberts often used at meetings. But the words felt hollow now. She must seem like a strange and laughable figure to Thane and his friends. They were helping her for Brodie's sake, not because of any particular connection to her.

At that, the thought of Thane's kisses the day before came to her unbidden. She wished she could say that they didn't affect her, but that would be a lie, and Cat didn't like lies.

The few moments in Thane's arms had been wickedly, wildly exciting, and she wasn't going to pretend that she'd forget them anytime soon. And in fact, she was conscious of wanting to find out more, what would happen if she found herself alone with Thane again.

No. That was how women ended up trapped, following a few moments of pleasure and earning a lifetime of regret. Cat had enough regrets.

And anyway, Thane and she didn't even like each other.

Cat sat at the top of the hill for a while, but not a single faerie appeared to steal her away, and eventually the sheep wandered off too. When the sun sank enough to make the stones' shadows grow long, Cat returned to the castle. She barely took note of the burly guard who'd stood on a hill about halfway back, at a vantage point where he would have been able to watch Cat the whole afternoon and report to Thane if anything suspicious occurred.

When it was time to dress for dinner, she pulled on her black evening gown, loathing it. She had the sudden notion that mourning wear was perhaps designed to hasten the progress of grief by making the wearer so utterly despise their wardrobe that they *had* to cast it aside, along with the memory of those they lost. What she wouldn't give to wear anything else. Even puce!

But black was what she had, though she did keep the shell-pink wrap that had somehow ended up in her trunk the day her maid so hastily packed for her.

Cat wound the wrap about her shoulders, feeling that summer might never truly come to this part of the world. Long days were one thing, but the breeze was still full of northern chill.

She walked into the hall and stopped short on seeing the preparations for a festivity. Was there some Highland holiday she didn't know about?

The high table was draped with a new cloth, and tall candles flickered in their brass holders, brightening the scene.

Spring flowers had been put in small vases and jars and tiny pots, dozens of them. Even the surprisingly pretty white flowers of the wild onion had been included. The overall effect was that of a lush glen having magically been transported to inside the hall.

"What's all this?" she asked, looking around. Why were people smiling at her?

"It's for your birthday, lassie!" Effie said, beaming with pride. "I thought you needed a celebration."

Cat's heart thudded once and dropped into her stomach. "Oh. Oh. Thank you," she added faintly, having forgotten it was her birthday. The polite response was rote—her brain was too overwhelmed with memory to fully focus on the present.

The memories of birthdays past: Brodie giving her a beautifully wrapped box that contained a live frog; her and Brodie getting sick on cake; Brodie and her whispering their wishes to each other before bedtime.

She made her way to her seat, and caught Thane's green gaze, but couldn't sense the emotion behind it, if there was any. Did he tell Effie to do this? Did it matter?

Dinner was awkward, for all that the whole room seemed intent on celebrating something, and here Cat was in the middle of it all, shocked and somber. She could tell that Effie was trying so, so hard to keep the mood light. But how could anyone do that when Cat was unable to even smile for more than a moment? She pulled out everything from her reserves, all the admonishments and advice given to her by her grandmother, her mother, her tutors, her aunt…all the words about behavior and grace and never letting your own poor mood ruin others', especially when they had good intentions.

And what was Effie but five feet and a few inches of good intentions?

As for Thane, Cat didn't dare look at him. She could

maintain a facade of politeness around others. But him? Never. He had such a gift for needling her with just the wrong word or phrase, and she would not lose her composure to fight him. Not now.

She couldn't even imagine what he was thinking of all this. And he didn't try to speak to her, which was probably the one reason she was able to endure the dinner so far.

There was roast beef, whipped potatoes, a leek soup, and more. It was so much more elegant than the usual fare, which was always good, but simple. The kitchen staff must have worked since dawn to prepare all the dishes. Cat wished that everything didn't taste like ash on her tongue.

When the last course was served, Cat could have wept with relief. Now she could escape. She nibbled a piece of cheese, and took a final sip of wine. She turned to her hostess. "Everything was delicious. Thank you, Effie. I believe I'll retire now."

"Oh, you can't yet!" Effie said, holding her hands out to prevent Cat from fleeing. "We've made you a cake!"

And there it was, on a tray borne in by one of the kitchen servants. It was a confection worthy of a Paris patisserie: a lovely round cake covered in buttercream, with real blossoms tucked all along the lower edge and scattered over the top.

"That's not big enough for everyone," one of the men at the table objected, the man next to Andra, who giggled.

"It's Catriona's cake, because it's Catriona's birthday, silly!" Effie replied with a laugh.

But Cat couldn't join in the joking.

Catriona's birthday.

It was never just *her* birthday, it was always *their* birthday. Hers and Brodie's.

Cat pushed back from the table, muttering, "Please excuse me." She turned and walked out of the hall, her gaze fixed on the floor lest she see the puzzled glances and questioning faces, these people who had no idea how Cat's heart was breaking over and over, every time she looked at anything meant to celebrate her own existence while Brodie couldn't share it. The candlelight, the cake, the food, the fire.

God help her, she had to get away from all this joy before she screamed like a howling ghost, unleashing fury at all these innocent people.

She didn't even know where she was going. She ran, one foot in front of the other, turning when the castle walls steered her this way or that. She was perfectly willing to get lost in a labyrinth if it meant she wouldn't have to face the pain.

Finally, she emerged outside, exiting the tower that formed one end of the western walk, parallel but high above the lawn. The sky was dark, and rags of clouds obscured most of the stars. If there was a moon, it hadn't risen yet.

Cat sank down against the stone well, black fabric puffing outward in a cloud. She wrapped her arms around her knees and tucked her head down to better hide from the world. It was quiet here, with only the whistle of wind coming through the gaps in the wall. Cat tried to stifle her sobs, hoping that no one overheard.

But of course someone had.

Thane found her where she was huddled, and simply sank down next to her. "Cat, what's wrong?"

"I don't know. I can't tell you. I can't tell anyone. It's too hard to describe." Her voice broke as she tried to use the right words to put Thane off. But there weren't enough words in the world to keep Thane away when he decided something involved him.

"Did someone say something to you in the dining hall? I'll set them straight. You're a guest, and I won't tolerate—"

"Thane, everyone here has been wonderful. I'm the only

rude person, running out like that. Effie will never forgive me."

"Of course she will. Why are you crying?"

"It's my birthday."

"Yes, I believe that was the point of the celebration."

"I don't know how to have a birthday now that Brodie's gone. I've never had a birthday without him! I've *never* been older than him, do you understand? Brodie will never have a twenty-fifth birthday. Or a twenty-sixth! Or a—"

"Cat, stop." Thane pulled her into his arms. "I'm sorry. I never would have let Effie do this if I'd known what it would do to you. When she told me about the surprise, I just assumed that it would cheer you up. You looked normal enough all evening, but then, you always do, don't you? I should have realized that it's not so simple."

She felt more sobs in her chest, threatening to jump out. She choked them down, willing herself to master the wave of emotions. "I'll apologize to Effie," she said, wiping tears from her eyes. "I'll go now."

"Christ, woman. You're in no state to go back in there, and you don't need to apologize to anyone. Just stay here until you've recovered a bit. I'll stay with you."

And he stayed with her, just as he had on the ship when she thought she was going to die of seasickness. Lord, how she'd prefer to be feeling that instead of this misery.

Thane said nothing more, but he remained there, close, his thigh touching hers, a contact that she should object to but craved too much to do so. She needed to be near someone who could understand.

"Can I tell you something?" she asked in a low voice.

"Yes." He didn't hesitate, which both heartened and terrified her.

"I've never told anyone this, not even Tacita," she said. "I...I felt the moment when Brodie died."

Thane put a hand out and then stopped, hovering near her drawn-up knee. "What?"

"I was sleeping, and I suddenly woke up. It wasn't as if from a nightmare, you know, when waking is the only way out of the horror. There was no reason for me to wake—it was in the middle of the night."

"Yes, it was," he said softly.

"I sat up in bed, my back so stiff I thought I'd suffered some kind of spasm. And that was when I felt it…"

"Felt what, Cat?"

"Brodie. His spirit. His soul, maybe. So close to me I could reach out and grab him in my arms. And then there was this horrible…wrenching, like something being ripped out of me. And I realized it was my connection to Brodie, my brother, my twin being…*severed*. Half of my own being yanked away out of this world by some callous hand. I screamed. I screamed and I screamed…." She choked back another sob.

"Cat, I'm sorry. I'm so sorry." Thane's arms were tight around her, holding her close and safe against the world.

She shifted, turning toward him, looking up into the only eyes that might see her as she was. "Why can't we ever keep what we love?"

"Kitty cat, I wish I knew." His shoulders curled inward, and his forehead touched hers. "And I wish I knew how to take your pain away."

Cat's breath caught in her throat.

"I know how." And then she lifted her mouth to his.

Cat could sense Thane's surprise at her kiss, but he didn't pull away. Instead, his hands rose to cup her face as he drank her in, the kiss growing honeyed as they explored each other with breath and tongue. Her body seemed to soften and thaw, her bunched muscles relaxing and then tensing again, but in a very different way. Her skin prickled with sensation—

Thane's breath, his lips against hers, the night wind teasing the fine hairs on her arms.

Then he pulled back. "Wait, Cat. You're not yourself, you're upset—"

"How do you know whether I'm myself or not?" she asked, need making her voice harsh. "If you want to find out what it means for me to be myself, you'd need to strip me bare, wouldn't you?"

He drew in a ragged breath. "Christ, Cat. Are you trying to tempt me?"

"Yes. When you kiss me, I feel...*some*thing. And for months I've felt just this...icy nothing. Thane, please help me feel again."

"Not like this," he said, shaking his head, even as his hands caressed her waist in an instinctive plea to continue. He did want her. She knew he did.

"Why not like this? Are you afraid of me?"

"I'm goddamned terrified of you, Cat. You break all the rules and I never know what you'll do or say next."

"Take me somewhere private and you'll find out." She leaned forward, and kissed him again, not with any great skill, but with all the honesty she could muster. Then she said, not looking at him, "I think you're the only man I could ever ask for this. Don't deny me, Thane."

Then he had her in his arms, and he said, "I'll deny you nothing tonight. Until tomorrow, Catriona, you own me."

Chapter 21

CAT HAD NO IDEA HOW they reached this room. She had no idea where this room even was located within the castle. All she knew was that Thane promised it was secluded and safe, and it had a bed.

Thane settled her on the bed and then turned away, but only to stride to the door so he could close it and bolt it. He cast a look at her over his shoulder. "Will you be cold? Do you want a fire?"

She shook her head. "I won't need it." Not the way she was burning up now.

Thane walked back to the bed and, surprising her, knelt down on both knees before her, reaching for her hands. He kissed her palms, slowly, then her wrists, his soft kisses turning to little bites as he worked his way up her arms, shifting to the left and then the right as if he'd be accused of favoritism if he lingered too long on one.

Then he looked up at her, and she saw the most wicked promise in his green eyes. "Lie back now," he ordered her.

"Why? I thought I owned you tonight."

"You do," Thane assured her. "But you've also got no idea what you're doing. So let me take the lead."

Cat stuck out her tongue, annoyed that he was right. He stuck out his own tongue, and then with both hands, slid her skirt up above her knees, exposing her stocking-covered legs.

"Black," he said, sighing.

"It's all or nothing," she reminded him.

"They'll have to go."

He found the ribbons that secured them and within moments had them loosened. He rolled one black stocking down, while Cat handled the other, determined to be fully involved.

He smiled as he ran his hands over her newly bare legs, his fingers hot on her skin. "Very nice," he murmured, pushing her skirts up further toward her hips.

And ducked his head right under the bunched fabric.

She did not quite scream, but she definitely made some sort of noise as she felt his tongue gliding along her inner thigh. He put his hands on her knees and nudged her legs further apart.

Cat did not ever think about being kissed on her legs. But now it was all she could think about.

"Thane, what are you doing?"

"Guess." That was the only word he spared. And then he licked her core with one long stroke. It felt so good that Cat thought she would faint.

He pulled his wicked tongue away, and sat up again. "I told you to lie back, Cat. This may take a while."

"How long?"

"Possibly forever. You are the sweetest thing I've ever tasted. Lie *back*."

Thane's gaze was so heavy, pressing her back on the mattress without his laying a finger on her. There was so much lust in his regard that she thought she might melt right there.

She let herself wilt onto the bed, pulling up her skirts even more as she did so. Her head was spinning. If this was how Thane *started* sexual relations, how did he intend to finish?

Maybe he'd never finish. Maybe this divine feeling would last forever. Cat moaned shamelessly as he lavished her with his tongue, drawing out a desire she'd been keeping at bay for far too long. Yes, this was what she needed. The raw pleasures of the body pushing away all the awful thoughts and cold, harsh words that had set up house in her soul.

Thane was destroying the old feelings, and she loved every minute of it.

Cat hazily became aware that she'd dropped a hand down onto his head, and was combing her fingers through his thick hair, unconsciously mimicking his rhythms. Likewise, she just realized that she kept emitting the most needy-sounding gasps as he pleasured her, gasps that sounded like *More, more, more.*

Well, she did want more. She wanted this warm, aching glow all through her limbs as Thane licked and sucked, and did lovely unspeakable things to her.

Perhaps men weren't completely useless after all.

Cat smiled at the thought, but then her back arched as an orgasm crashed over her. She cried out before belatedly turning her head into the pillow to muffle the sound.

Thane teased her into an aftershock before finally lifting his head, looking utterly disheveled and very pleased with himself.

"You like my tongue," he said. "I thought you would."

He crawled onto the bed and over her, surveying his work. "You look a little flushed, kitty cat. Maybe I should take you back to your room."

"No," she protested.

His expression shifted, and she saw that his light manner masked something deeper. "It's not that I don't want... Christ, Cat, you have no idea what you do to me. But I can't let you do something you'll regret the rest of your life."

"You think I'll regret not being a virgin tomorrow?" She scoffed. "I know what regret feels like, Thane. I'm alive and he's not. I'm here, but I'm alone—"

Thane silenced her with a kiss. A deep, open-mouthed kiss that wiped away any more words she might have spoken, and instead filled her with need all over again.

"You're not alone," he told her, his mouth hot on hers. He used his teeth as much as his lips to tease her, and she found herself craving the tiny twinges of pain amid the pleasure.

"It's warm," she muttered between kisses. "Too warm." He shifted away enough so that Cat could wrest her gown off, so hard the fabric scraped along her skin in places, leaving a pink trail. She didn't care. In fact, she liked the burn. It felt like being alive.

Thane tossed the remnants of her gown aside, did the same to her stays and chemise, and then pulled his shirt over his head. He rolled off the bed just long enough to remove the rest of his clothing, till he stood naked in front of her, his arousal commanding her attention.

She inhaled, taking him in. She often disparaged men as being too concerned with women's physical appearance, but she couldn't deny that here was a man she wanted because he was physically magnificent.

"This is what you asked for," he said, as if she might regret it.

Cat regretted nothing in this room so far, and told him so. "Get back in this bed," she ordered then. "You say I own you, but you're very bad at being owned."

"Aye, I am. But I'll do my best." He stretched his body next to hers, and reached to pull her over so she was sitting astride him, her slick folds riding along the length of his cock. It was shockingly intimate and arousing for Cat, yet clearly his way of telling her that she could stop here if she wanted, that he wouldn't press her.

Well, Cat would press him. She rocked her hips to test how it felt to have him between her legs. It felt magical. She let out a low moan and leaned forward, bracing her arms with her hands on either side of his head.

He seemed to like it as well, to judge by the lust on his face. He grabbed her hips and started a slow, strong rhythm as he drew her tight against him. Cat loved the push and pull, the slide up and down the hard length of him, how she felt the heat building between them.

"This is good," she whispered, even as her body clamored for more. "I like riding you."

He bit his lip at her words, and his cock twitched under her. A low laugh burst out of Cat. "Oh, I see. You like being ridden by me." Strange how she could feel so confident when this was all new to her. But maybe that was because Thane wasn't insisting on being in charge. It felt more like… playing together.

"I'd like it more if you leaned down lower," he said, that gleam in his eyes again, the gleam that promised some shocking pleasure to come.

She guessed what he planned, but when he bent his head to get his mouth on her breast, she was still unprepared. Cat bucked when she felt his tongue teasing her nipple to a hardened bud, heat surging not just in her chest, but in her core as well.

"Thane, more," she begged.

She wanted more of this, because every kiss and touch and stroke he offered pushed out the dark thoughts and replaced them with new sensations as bright as flame. She needed to keep him near her, over her, *in* her. That was the only way she could make it through this night.

He growled, and suddenly she was under him, so fast she wasn't sure how it happened. Thane grabbed her wrists and pinned them over her head with one hand, then reached lower with his other hand.

"I want to make you come again, Cat, and I want to see your face while I do it."

"Yes," she breathed, willing to go anywhere he took her tonight.

He dipped his hand between her legs and slid one finger inside her while covering her with his thumb. He knew exactly how to play her, and within seconds Cat was panting with need as her body reacted to his touch inside and out. His thumb circled the sensitive bud until she could barely stand the waves of pleasure he was creating. She strained against his grip, wanting to touch him, grab him, destroy him like he was doing to her. But he was immovable, and highly amused by her efforts.

"The only way you get free is to come undone for me, Cat. Let me hear you when it happens. Don't be shy."

He stroked her from the inside, and Cat could only moan with need. "More," she managed.

"More? Like this?"

He withdrew his finger, then slipped two in, stretching her. Cat arched her back, loving it. "More. Please more."

"Come for me, and you'll get what you want," he said.

Like a key, his promise unlocked all the tension inside her. Cat gave a wild cry and let the bliss course through her.

A moment, or a thousand moments, later, Cat opened her eyes. She found Thane watching her with the proprietary gaze of a lion. "Still more, kitty cat?" he asked. "Or have you had enough?"

"I'll tell you when I've had enough," she whispered. "And it won't be enough until you *take* me."

She knew what she wanted and what she needed, and that was Thane's body entangled with hers so that they could drive each other to such passion that there was no room left for pain.

"Hold me," she begged, even as she positioned herself so his cock brushed against her opening.

Thane raised his upper body and took her in his arms, folding her into an embrace. Then he guided her downward. Did she slide down onto him, or did he push into her body? Did it matter?

Cat let out a low cry as he filled her, and tightened her arms around his torso as they melted into one thing. Thane's thrusts into her drove waves of pleasure all through her body, expelling all other thoughts and feelings besides what he was creating.

"Yes," she moaned into his ear. "Yes, Thane. This is what I want."

"Take it," he growled, as far gone with need as she was.

Their congress became heavy and frantic, as Cat chased more of the feelings she'd caught before, those shattering bursts of peace she craved so much.

Thane was saying something, but it was low and harsh and only half for her. Cat was too lost in her own pursuit to pay attention—all she knew was that Thane was the only person in the world who was willing and able to take her where she needed to go.

"Now, Thane," she whimpered. "Now. Don't leave me behind."

"Never."

He gripped her hard and angled his body to push once more, and then Cat's body gave in, and she cried out as the bliss overtook her. Every nerve, every pore, every ounce of her glowed with pure physical release, and for a perfect moment, she had no thoughts at all.

Chapter 22

THANE HELD CAT IN HIS arms, still stunned. Had Cat actually just given her whole self to him? Did she actually trust him that much? Or was her mind just so fraught that any release would do, even with a man she despised?

Except that she didn't seem to despise him now. She lay half on him, her body supple and soft in the aftermath of sex. She breathed slowly, her mouth slightly open.

Her lips were a lush pink, swollen from their kisses. Her cheeks also had a glow that came only from intense love-making. He reached to sweep her hair away from her face, marveling at its silky texture. He couldn't seem to stop running his fingers through it.

"You could buy me a comb, if it bothers you that much," Cat said, her tone soft and drowsy.

"It doesn't bother me at all. I just like to play with your hair. Do you mind?"

"No. It feels nice." She cuddled into him, and something in Thane's chest unfurled, responding to the sweetness of the gesture.

Oh, God. I can't afford to be sweet about Cat, he thought, though part of him knew it was far too late for that.

He said, "You wanted it rough, Cat. Rougher than I ever would have guessed a woman would, for her first time."

"It felt right."

He gave one low laugh of agreement. "No argument here." Then he frowned. "But I hope you aren't hurt. I know you'll feel sore later."

She tilted her face to his, and gave him a wicked smile. "There must be something else we can do, something less rough, if you think I need to be…managed."

His brain immediately caught fire. There were many things he could picture doing with Cat. "I wouldn't want to shock you."

Cat chuckled low in her throat, a sound that aroused him like no other. "Please shock me. Tell me something we could do that would send a proper young lady into a faint."

He licked his lips, and growled, "I'd have you suck my cock."

A quick intake of breath and widened eyes showed him that he did shock her, but for only a moment. "Would that… you'd want that?"

"Every man wants that. You liked it when I put my mouth on you, didn't you?"

"I did," she said, desire flaring in her face again. "But I might not be good at it."

He laughed. "It's a risk I'm willing to take."

"What other shocking acts do you know about?" she asked, clearly determined to take advantage of the situation.

"Several. Taking you from behind, for example."

"Behind?"

"You on your knees, me at your back. Like animals fuck." He ran a hand over her bottom, and slipped one finger along the crack, teasing her there. "And there's always the option of fucking you there," he said, pressing on her arsehole. Cat whimpered, half excited and half scared. He could see it. "But I wouldn't do that until you're ready. Which you're not." He moved his hand to the small of her back, making little circles over her skin, soothing her.

"No," she breathed. "I don't think I could do that my first night."

"Hell, no. Most women never do."

"What do most women do?" she asked. "I don't want to be…typical."

"You're never that." He pressed her closer to him.

"Shock me some more. I probably won't get a chance to ask anyone else about this sort of thing."

She'd better not, he thought, instantly inflamed at the idea of her asking another man to tell her what to do in bed. *She's mine.*

"I could tie you up. Lots of people get pleasure out of games like that."

Cat frowned as she seemed to picture it, then said, "No. I wouldn't like that. It would be too…restraining."

"That's sort of the point," he said, laughing again. He ran his hand along her torso and stopped just under her breast, mimicking stays. He squeezed. "But I suppose you equate any restraint with oppression."

"I'd tie *you* up," she said. "Then you'd understand. You'd be helpless, completely in my power…" She trailed off, and bit her lower lip. The unconscious move created a stirring in his cock.

"You get it," he said. "The idea of me tied up and in your power…you like it."

"It has a certain appeal." She smiled slowly. "There would have to be rules."

"Always. It's meant to be pleasurable for both."

Cat chewed her lip thoughtfully, and Thane groaned. "If you're going to be biting something, bite me, kitty cat."

She responded by biting his shoulder, just a nip. But he felt it all down his body.

"More," he ordered.

Cat narrowed her eyes, but then rose up on all fours and crawled over him. *Oh, yes*.

She bent her head and nipped and nibbled her way across his chest. The bites were interspersed with licks and kisses, and he realized she was testing him, figuring out what he liked.

He liked it all, and told her so. He reached to cup the back of her head, guiding her very gently as she explored. When she paused at his nipple and sucked hard, he groaned.

"You sweet dirty girl," he said, his voice hot with desire. He was hard again, ready for more. He couldn't take her again, not so soon. But she could take *him*.

"Shock me, kitty cat," he begged.

She hesitated, watching him, her big blue eyes widening when she understood what he wanted, needed from her. Then she gave him the sweetest and most sultry look he'd ever seen. "Say please."

"*Please.*"

Cat continued to kiss and bite her way all down his torso, seeming to inch along so slowly that he'd go mad. At last she laid a hand on his cock, circling him delicately as if afraid she'd hurt him.

"You can be rough," he told her. "I know you like it."

"I don't really know what I like. Yet," she said.

Before he could say anything to that, she took him in her mouth, and Thane's mind went white. She licked and sucked as if he were her first meal in days, and through it all he wanted to howl her name. He'd grabbed a pillow to stifle the sounds he made, and Cat was determined to make sure he needed it.

How the hell did she know just what he liked? Then Thane wanted to laugh. He'd like anything she did to him. And her lips around him now…paradise.

When he was close, he told her to stop. She didn't listen,

and he had to grab her hair and pull her head back.

"Why?" She pouted.

"Use your hands to finish me," he ordered, feverish with need.

She did, and a moment later he spilled, covering his stomach with seed. "I couldn't make you swallow," he gasped.

"I could have," Cat objected, somehow *annoyed* at his decision.

"God damn it, kitty cat. You don't know everything."

"How do I learn if you don't let me?"

"You've learned quite a lot in one night." He used a corner of the bedsheet to wipe himself clean, and let go of her hair. "Lie down, Cat."

"Why should I?"

"Because I'd like to feel you."

"Oh." She stretched out next to him, and he reached to hold her. She was so good in his arms, her curves melding into his body.

"Did I shock you?" she asked softly, and after a second he realized she was nervous. She wanted to *please* him.

"Magnificently."

"I suppose I ought to go to my room now."

"In a while. We'll wait till everyone is asleep." It sounded practical, but the truth was that Thane couldn't bear to part from her just yet. He pulled the blanket up over them both.

He ran his hands over her slowly, savoring the feel of her skin under his fingers. He sensed the moment Cat started to doze. He couldn't fall asleep himself. He needed to stay alert so he could return Cat to her room safely.

And he needed to sort out what the hell just happened.

* * * *

About an hour later, when all was silent, Thane woke Cat and helped her dress. He made sure Cat got back to her own bedroom without anyone seeing her—or him—as they made their way from the room in the tower back to the main part of the building. He should have then gone to his room, considering it was well after three in the morning. But he couldn't sleep. He might never sleep again.

He instead returned outside, where he found Cat a lifetime ago. He paced from one end of the old walk, wondering what he just did. And if he would do it again.

He would.

But hell, he shouldn't have. It didn't matter that it was Cat who reached for him this time. It was Cat who was torn up inside, and he let her believe that what they did together would make her forget her pain.

Nothing could do that. He knew, because he knew exactly what that pain felt like. And he still hadn't dulled it.

Never mind that she told him it was what she wanted, and he wanted to believe it. He shouldn't have given in. Even if it felt so good to have her. To know exactly how she felt when he touched her, and how she sounded when she let go, and how she looked like a queen when she left the room at the end. No regret, no remorse.

That's what she said anyway. But she might feel very differently tomorrow, in the cold light of day. And then it would be his fault that he took advantage of her grief, even if in the moment she told him it was her decision to make.

He still shouldn't have let her make that decision. Catriona thought she knew enough to make her own mistakes. He knew the world didn't forgive many mistakes.

Thane would never be forgiven for his.

And Cat would never know what his mistake was. He'd die before he'd tell her. If only he could keep that resolve, because every moment he spent with her, Thane wanted to tell her everything. It was cruel to keep it from her.

But if he told her, he'd lose her. And that was more pain than he could face.

Because Thane knew why he'd really let Cat persuade him last night.

He loved her.

When did his irritation with her, his resentment of her attitude, his frustration with her refusal to listen to a damn thing he said to keep her alive…when did that all cascade over the edge and become love? He had no idea.

Possibly when she first kissed him.

Possibly when he threw himself in front of a bullet to protect her.

Possibly the moment he saw her, rushing toward him like a storm.

It didn't really matter when, because he was lost now. He was hopelessly in love with Catriona Ross, the one woman he couldn't have and the one woman who would hate him if she knew the truth about what he did during the war. The truth about why he was the one who came home when her brother didn't.

Thane flinched at a wave of memories, unprepared for the onslaught of wartime images after having spent half the night in the pursuit of pleasure. He'd pay in gold if someone, anyone, could extinguish the bitter thoughts of the war and replace them all with just the feeling of Cat's mouth on his.

But no one could, and Thane either had to shake off his mood, or get raging drunk to dull the bad recollections.

He didn't want to use whisky as medicine, though he held the idea in reserve. What he needed was to restore his sanity. What he been doing before the evening birthday party, when his tenuous hold on sanity collapsed?

Suddenly, he remembered that he'd never written to Kai about his new idea. The thought was enough to jar him out of his brooding, and he turned to go back to the tower stairs. Were the men still in Edinburgh? He was probably too late for a letter to intercept them. Damn it, why was there not a faster way? It was maddening to be so hobbled and chained, when thoughts couldn't fly, and words would be carried only as quickly as a vehicle or ship could take them.

He needed a bird. Or a messenger, ordered to lose no time. That could work.

But what if Thane's idea was wrong? It was a long shot in any case, a wild notion that might not have any bearing on reality. What if he actually pulled the others from their current investigations to go off on this tangent?

In his study, Thane lit a candle and reached for a pen and paper. The ink dripped and smeared in his haste, but Thane scrawled his message to Kai. Kai would know what to do. Despite his youth, Kai possessed a rare ability to strategize and make the most of his resources. He'd assess Thane's proposal and parcel out the duties among the men. That is, assuming the letter reached them before they left the city for Kinlochlie.

He sealed the letter and went down to the ground floor in search of someone he could use as a messenger. Luckily, he spotted a good man in no time.

Angus was a short, slender man over forty but not yet fifty. His hair was grey and he wore a short beard. Thane had known him his whole life; he'd also served in the army, though long before Thane did.

"Angus, care to take a journey?"

"Where, sir?" Angus asked with appropriate wariness.

"Edinburgh."

Angus relaxed. "Ah, that's all right, then. What am I to do there?"

"Deliver this letter. As quickly as possible."

"Shall I take a ship? Or meet a mail coach?" Angus's

questions were good ones—he was a sharp man who understood the task, which was one of the reasons Thane believed he'd be a good choice.

Thane pondered, then said, "Head for Inverness. Take a ship if one is leaving the same day. Otherwise, there will be mail coaches. Ride with one—don't just pay for the letter." He handed Angus a small pouch of coins, which should still be enough to cover any potential issue.

"Aye, sir. I'll leave at dawn." Angus took the letter and the pouch and tucked them away. Then he paused. "Is it about the young lady?"

"In a way. Why?"

"Nothing, sir. Not my business. But…it's known that someone's after her. Because of the men you've put on duty watching for strangers. No one wants anything to hurt the lass."

"Well, I hope that the letter might prove helpful in that regard. The sooner you get it to Edinburgh, the sooner my friends can act on it."

That fired Angus up, and he strode off to pack his things. Thane had no idea that Catriona was so instantly beloved at Kinlochlie. But then again, he shouldn't be surprised. Not with the way she'd twined shoots all around his own heart.

Christ, what was he going to do about her?

Chapter 23

CAT WOKE AT SOME TIME during the very late night. She blinked, confused for a long moment as she hovered between worlds. She wasn't sure where she was—this was not her bedroom, and the night bird outside wasn't any she'd heard in the city.

Then the memory of the previous evening rushed back. All the things Thane had done to her, for her. And all the things he'd allowed her to do to him.

Cat recalled the intensity of her body's reactions, and wondered why virginity was considered important at all when deciding on a match. What should matter was how absolutely blissful one could feel when being touched so intimately. Cat had tried to deny her attraction to Thane ever since she met him. But last night burned away all the lies she told herself. She wanted Thane as she hadn't wanted anything else in her life.

She waited for a sense of shame to come over her. After all, hadn't she just committed the one single act that an unmarried lady of her class must never ever do? And while Cat might have made the argument that she ought to have done it long before, as a matter of principle, just to ruin herself for marriage and therefore remove her name from contention for the rest of her life, the fact was that she'd always harbored a secret belief that to actually cross that line would damn her in a different way. Not that she believed it was an unforgivable sin—Cat had been taught that any sin could be forgiven if the sinner felt true remorse and contrition. But to transgress like that would…lessen her. Make her into a creature that valued physical desire more than the intellectual and moral pursuits she'd always admired.

Still, no shame. Only the pleasantly hazed memory of all the ways she'd discovered her body could bring joy, not just to her but to Thane as well. She recalled more than one time that he had reached for her and kissed just one part of her—her earlobe, her shoulder, her collarbone—when he thought she wasn't paying attention. His mouth always held such heat, and he always inhaled as if he were about to say something of tremendous importance…but then he just laid a kiss on her, brief but searing. And Cat realized that *was* the important message. This need to touch and connect.

In the dark, it was easier. Since losing her bother and then mother, Cat never liked to look people in the eye too long, even those people she held great affection for. It invited too much scrutiny. They might ask questions. They might pull Cat out of her own little world and back into theirs.

Which was exactly what Thane had done, even though he'd done it for Brodie's sake and not her own. He'd brought her into his world. Though he surely never meant for them to grow intimate when he whisked her up to the Highlands on that cursed ship.

But it happened, and now Cat was ruined as far as any traditional, respectable gentleman was concerned. *Good*, she thought. *There's one problem solved.*

It did bring up a new problem, which was how she was going to face Thane in the full light of day, among other people, and behave normally. How could she sit across from him at dinner and ask him to pass the salt after he'd licked salty sweat off her stomach while telling her to spread her legs?

No part of her education had covered this eventuality. She imagined bringing it up as a hypothetical during the next meeting of the ladies' league, and laughed as she pictured the shocked faces around the table.

It was too early to stir, so she remained in the bed. Not to sleep—her mind was too full. All she could think of was the absolute magic that happened when Thane overwhelmed her with so much pleasure that she forgot to think. It was marvelous and blissful and she couldn't wait to feel it again. Something told her that it wasn't just the physical act. If she touched herself now, she'd feel good for a glimmering moment, but it wouldn't reach her mind.

Thane had somehow pulled all the dismal emptiness out of her, just for a while. Maybe it was the novelty. Maybe if she spent another night with him, it wouldn't be as…transcendent.

There was only one way to be sure. She smiled to herself, thinking that Thane should be easy enough to persuade to continue the experiment. He seemed to be quite enthusiastic about helping her last night.

She slid her hand down her belly, then lower. She thought of Thane, but not so much what he'd done to her as how he felt under her hands, and how he smelled, and the way she heard the rumble as he spoke while her head lay on his chest. It was a pity he was so unreasonable about literally everything else. It would be rather nice if they didn't end up fighting all the time, because he did have some good qualities…

Cat stifled a moan as she reached her peak. Her body relaxed, but the glow lingered only a moment. Yes, as expected. There was something different about being with him, as opposed to being alone.

With a start, Cat realized that being alone was a thing

she'd never really been before, not till a few months ago, when the invisible cord between her and her twin snapped, and the cord that tied her to her mother suddenly unraveled, and she was adrift. And she was terrified that she'd remain adrift, and that the darkness she was always turning away from was the sea she'd be drifting in forever.

As she mused, dawn crept in and turned charcoal shadows to blue, and then outlined all the furniture and the walls and the ceiling until at some point that no one could ever quite capture, night gave way to day.

Even in this light, the shame never arrived. Cat waited a bit longer, and then decided she might as well get on with her day. She went to the window. At the far edge of her vision, she saw a single rider moving fast, away from Kinlochlie. She frowned, hoping it wasn't some herald of disaster.

* * * *

It was midmorning and Thane was in his study, pretending to go through the endless correspondence that came with administering any estate, and which had piled up during his absence. But really, he just stared at nothing, lost in thoughts about Cat. Some were pleasant—very pleasant—and others were downright alarming. He'd made a grand mess of things, for certain.

He wasn't entirely surprised when Cat entered the room. He was practically screaming her name in his mind.

"Are you busy?" she asked.

He shook his head.

Cat closed the door behind her and stepped into the room. "I had to talk with you," Cat said, looking—well, not shy, but uncertain. Which was unusual enough that he couldn't ignore her.

"Cat, what happened last night…I'm sorry."

She frowned. "You are? I thought you…enjoyed it?"

"It's not that." He'd happily sign his soul away to guarantee a few more nights as enjoyable as that one. "I took advantage of you."

"You certainly did not. I made the choice for myself." Her frown changed to a more familiar one, the frown of the furious emancipated woman. For some reason, this time it didn't raise his hackles. Now it made him want to laugh. How adorable Cat was when she got salty.

Carefully hiding any hint of delight at her anger, Thane said, "All I meant was that I hope you don't regret anything."

"I regret nothing." She raised her chin. "In fact, I consider myself remiss for not seeking out the experience years ago."

Like hell. "With who?" Thane demanded. "Your quickly discarded fiancé?"

"Oh, no, not *him*." Cat looked disgusted. "I suppose I would have had to…sort through some potential partners. It would have been a bother."

"Damn right, it would have been a bother. You'd have been ostracized if you tried."

"It's not fair. Women don't get to take charge of their own pleasure. One must simply hope for the best."

He couldn't stop a grin now. "You're welcome."

"I didn't say you *were* the best!" She made a face. "Lord, you must think I'm ready to fall at your feet just because you relieved me of my virginity."

"Wouldn't mind you falling at my feet," he said, knowing that it was a dirty thing to say and saying it anyway. He wanted to see her reaction. Something in him loved getting Cat's blood up.

Her mouth opened in surprise as she registered the innuendo. "You're not serious."

"I can be if you are," he told her, his voice dropping as he pictured Cat kneeling in front of him. "Or you can tell me what you'd like to do. I'm very willing to compromise."

Perhaps not the best word in this situation, but then, Cat was already compromised.

Her head still lowered, Cat looked at him through her eyelashes, a move that would have seemed cheap if it were calculated. But he knew it wasn't.

"Now? Here?" she whispered. Her voice was tight…with excitement, he realized.

"Yes. Anything you like, kitty cat. Come over here," he ordered. She stepped around the desk, and Thane pulled her atop him, her skirts tangling around his thighs as he ran his hands up her torso, skimming the silky fabric as he sensed the heat of her skin underneath.

"It's daytime," she whispered, even as she slid her hands under his jacket and gripped his shoulders.

"This is daft," he agreed. "Tell me if you want to stop."

"I don't. What will we do?" Hunger flashed in Cat's eyes, along with something darker, something that felt familiar and also too frightening for Thane to name right now. Instead, he kissed her deeply.

Cat's eyes slid closed, and her lips parted as she released a soft *oh* of pleasure at his touch. Thane didn't need more of an invitation than that. He palmed her breasts, rolling his hands over them, reveling in the fact that she leaned into it, pressing her breasts into his hands.

"I can think of a few things you might enjoy," he told her. There were so many things he wanted to show her that he would have to make a list.

He was kissing his way down her chest, intending to free her breasts from the gown, when a knock on the door froze them.

Cat's eyes flew open and she started to scramble off him.

"Steady," he murmured, helping her off his lap and onto her feet. He let go of her waist with a sense of regret. "No one will come in till I say."

"There's only one door. They'll know I'm in here. They'll guess what we were—"

"Trust me, Cat. No one will say anything. If you like, you can insult me while our visitor is present. I know how you like that."

"Go to hell," she said sweetly.

"Ah, that's my kitty cat."

She rolled her eyes and strode over to the narrow window, looking out.

Thane made sure his clothes were more or less in place. He couldn't do anything about his obvious erection other than stay seated behind the desk.

"Enter!" he called out, grabbing a piece of paper to uphold the pretense that he was merely working in his study, and not about to ravish Cat at ten in the morning.

It was one of the men who stood on guard duty, an older, grim-faced ex-sailor. If he wondered why Cat was in the room, he said nothing about it.

"Beg pardon, sir," the man said, carefully not looking at Catriona at all. "There are strangers approaching the castle."

Thane dropped the paper he'd been holding, the news alarming enough to shove all thoughts of lust from his mind. "From where?"

"Village road. Two men, both on horseback. One of the guards signaled earlier, and I just saw them a moment ago."

"I'll be up to look for myself in a moment. Resume your post."

"Aye, sir." The man left at double speed.

"Could they be here for me?" Cat asked nervously, looking over at Thane. "Maybe there's not just one man trying to kill me, but two?"

"We'll find out soon enough." Thane took her hand, escorting her to the door. "The tower walk will have the best view. And I've got a spyglass."

They hurried there, Cat keeping pace behind him on the winding stairs. At the top, another guard merely pointed to a couple of specks on the landscape. The castle had such a commanding view that the riders were miles away from the gate…but they could be seen. It was one of the reasons Kinlochlie had been built where it was.

Thane held up his spyglass and scanned the area, pausing when he saw movement.

"What can you see?" Cat asked anxiously. "Should we be worried? Do they look dangerous?"

Thane silenced her with a gesture, and kept focusing on the riders. Squinting, he started to make out details. Both men, both armed—and not lightly. One dark haired and one practically blond. The dark-haired one was bigger, so big that he required a massive stallion to ride properly. It was a far distance, but Thane could sense the determination in both of the riders. These men had a purpose, and no one would deter them from it.

"Yes, they're dangerous," he said, offering the spyglass to Cat. "It's Struan and Calan."

Chapter 24

THANE CARED DEEPLY ABOUT HIS friends, but their imminent arrival brought the brief idyll he had with Catriona crashing to a halt, like a ship grounded on a hidden shoal. Except it wasn't really hidden, because both of them knew the forbidden intimacy couldn't continue. It never should have started.

On seeing the men riding in the distance, Cat's whole demeanor changed in the course of a moment. It wasn't anything overt—just tiny things like her chin lifting, her shoulders rising, and a coolness covering her expression.

"I'd best go make myself presentable," she said without inflection. "If they're here, Aunt Tacita will likely be along soon in a carriage." The faintest wash of pink in her face let him know that she was not actually calm about this. But was it embarrassment? Shame? Anger? That he couldn't say.

"Wait," he told her. "Before you go. How do you want to handle…what happened?"

She looked at him in what seemed to be completely honest surprise. "Nothing happened. Nothing that concerns any of them. Or in fact anyone at all. So we'll say nothing."

She left down the spiral stairs. Thane very briefly considered the long drop down over the parapet, decided it wasn't for him no matter how maddening Cat was, and went down the more conventional way to prepare the house for his visitors.

Calan and Struan rode in through the gates, and Thane hurried to greet them. He was slightly surprised to see Struan had come, though an instant later, he regretted his reaction. Struan had always been there for him during the war. His character hadn't changed after his injury, just his appearance. And perhaps his general mood. But he'd always help when there was a need.

"Struan," he said, briefly embracing his friend. "I'm glad you could make it."

"My life's not too busy at the moment," Struan replied, deadpan. "How are things here?"

"Quiet, at least in terms of Miss Ross's safety. No word of any strangers about, and not even a hint that her attacker knows where she is."

"Good." Calan was looking around the courtyard, but he was clearly thinking hard. "She's all right here, then? Not clamoring to get out?"

"She'd love to go back to her home, but she's intelligent. She knows it's not wise until we can identify who's after her." Thane paused. "I almost wish we could leak out the news, and maybe draw the man here, where we control who can get in and out."

Struan shook his head. "Too risky. We know the man is willing to kill others along with Miss Ross. The last thing we need is for someone to taint the food supplies and poison half the castle."

"You're cheery."

"I think the worst so I'm not surprised by what happens. That's all."

"Is it just you two?"

Calan shook his head. "Tacita is following in a carriage, escorted, of course. She offered to ride but Duncan wouldn't have it."

As expected, the carriage arrived an hour later, and Thane was surprised to see not just Tacita and Duncan, but Kai as well.

"Kai, what are you doing here? I thought you were staying in Edinburgh."

"I'd planned to. But I got an idea about something and pursued it. And I think I've got the answer to why Miss Ross is being targeted. It's not about her politics."

"Wait. I just sent you a letter based on a hunch I got after speaking with Cat, I mean Miss Ross, about potential reasons men have to kill. She mentioned that her mother settled a trust in her name… I thought someone might be after it…"

"Great minds think alike! We had the same notion." Kai looked pleased for a moment, but then his expression turned. "However, the situation is worse than you imagined." His eyes went cold, and Thane saw the tiniest glimpse of another side of Kai. The young man was normally easygoing to the point that most people assumed he was harmless. He wasn't. When Kai felt a deadly response was necessary, he never hesitated.

"We'd better gather everyone and have it all out, then, yes?" Thane wanted to know exactly what Kai knew so they could plan their next steps. Protecting Cat was essential, and it seemed they finally had the key to discovering who was after her.

* * * *

Cat had never felt more unsettled. She embraced Tacita when she came into the great hall. "Oh, I missed you so much!" She wanted to sob all over her aunt.

"That bad, was it?" Tacita asked wryly. "The place looks quite lovely to me."

"Oh, Kinlochlie is a fine house, and everyone is very

kind. You'll meet Thane's sister Effie. She's wonderful. Come, I'll show you to your room. This place is nothing but rooms; he could host a battalion without doubling up."

"Let us hope it does not come to that," her aunt murmured.

The ladies were to come to the large parlor at noon. "Sort of a council meeting," Tacita said. "The men have all been working on your…problem, and I believe there's been some sort of breakthrough."

"They didn't tell you on the way?"

"Only bits and pieces. They wished to all be together, with you present, before sharing."

"I see." Cat didn't see, but within the hour she'd at least know as much as they did.

"I'm sorry I missed your birthday, lass," Tacita said. "I hoped to be here in time."

Cat nearly choked. In time to witness Cat's utter breakdown and then her ruination, courtesy of Thane? "Effie made a cake," she managed to say, her voice not shaking at all.

The enormity of what she'd done last night was starting to sink in. She still didn't regret it, but to assume that she was…unchanged…by the events would be a lie. She prayed Thane wouldn't blab to his friends about his conquest. Men did that, didn't they?

No. He wouldn't. He asked how she wanted to handle it and she told him in no uncertain terms that there was nothing to handle.

In this disturbed and distracted state of mind, she joined the group at noon. The men all greeted her politely, and Thane behaved exactly as he always did, which was some relief. She glanced at him once, trying very hard not to remember the way he'd felt in bed. She looked at the floor quickly. *Never think of that again*, she told herself.

Easier said than done.

Luckily, the men had begun to talk, each one giving his report on the progress he'd made in the matter of her attacker. Through his steady work with the newspapers and the magistrates' offices, Duncan had more or less eliminated the possibility that any other woman in the city was being similarly targeted.

"Oh, thank goodness," Tacita said. "How horrible to think of others suffering from such hate."

Cat, sitting next to her aunt on the settee, reached over to squeeze her hand. "Indeed."

Calan had been watching the men who had signed their names to the threatening letters sent to Cat, as well as Patrick Melrose.

"I uncovered nothing to suggest he is involved," Calan said. "Nor the other men, unfortunately."

Struan nodded. "I was helping Calan. I believe we can safely eliminate all those names."

"So where does that leave us?" Cat asked. "It's all well and good to know that most of the citizens of Edinburgh didn't want me dead. But it only takes one madman."

"Perhaps I can offer a different angle."

It was Kai who spoke, and Cat noticed him look to Thane. The men seemed to share some hidden communication.

"What is it?" Cat asked, suddenly quite sure that it was bad news.

Kai stood up, addressing everyone. "Following a guess I had, which it turned out was also on Thane's mind, I conducted some research along quite a different tack."

"You'd been damnably hard to track down in the city," Duncan said. "Always out when I called."

"Sorry. I had to go to a lot of places and find the right people to talk to." Kai took a breath. "Here's the gist. I believe that Miss Ross is in danger not because of her politics, but because of her name."

"What?" Cat asked.

"She's vulnerable precisely because she is the last Ross of her generation. After Brodie's death, there are no more known male heirs who can claim direct descent. Somewhat unusually, according to the family's traditions, the next in line is *not* the oldest male heir of the following generation—which doesn't seem to exist in any case. Aunt Tacita was very helpful in providing me with some information." Somehow, it felt perfectly normal for him to address the woman as Aunt.

"I couldn't fathom why you wanted it," Tacita admitted.

"You were kind to allow me to pursue my hunch," Kai told her. "To get to the point. The heir isn't the next available male in the family. Rather, it's the closest blood relation to the previous heir, whether male *or* female. As Brodie's twin, Catriona is indisputably the closest. And that means on her twenty-fifth birthday, which just happened, she is due to inherit nearly all of the family holdings, whether real estate or chattel."

"No, that can't be." Cat shook her head. "I could have saved you all that work. You see, my mother informed me that I had a small trust set up in my name, which I have control over for my lifetime. She was a very forward-thinking woman. She told me she arranged it that way so I wouldn't ever be at the mercy of another. She certainly would have had no need to do that if I were an heiress."

Thane seemed about to say something, then didn't.

"What?" she nearly snapped.

"Just that…your mother made those arrangements when Brodie was alive," Thane said, too gently. "When he *was* the heir."

The simple statement hit Cat like a cartload of bricks. The grief she continually tried to push away rushed over her again. *Brodie. Alive.*

"Yes. I suppose that's true," she said softly. Her mother made those plans because she thought Brodie would be alive and able to take on the responsibilities of inheritance. And of course she also would have assumed that Cat and Brodie's bond would mean that Brodie would be watching out for her as a brother, thus making it unnecessary for her to worry about anything. "She was already ill when we got the news of Brodie's death, so she ignored…matters she otherwise would have addressed. If we hadn't had Aunt Tacita living with us, I'm not sure either of us would have managed to brush our hair, let alone deal with matters of the law."

Duncan said, "Perhaps we should let Miss Ross rest for a while, before we continue."

"No, no, I'm quite rested." She waved a hand to dismiss the idea that she needed a moment, like some fragile creature.

"Are you," Thane muttered, and Cat had to bite her tongue to keep from snapping at him. This was him being circumspect?

"The good news is that there's a clear solution to the problem," Kai went on.

Cat looked at him. He did appear optimistic. "And what is that?"

Kai nodded. "I've spoken to a few different solicitors in Edinburgh, just to ensure that we're understanding the law correctly. And it's not that complicated. All you have to do is get married."

Cat stared at the young man, so earnest, so bright.

"You want me to *what*?" she asked.

Kai said, "Marry. Listen, it's quite simple. The moment you're married, your husband takes control of everything you own and everything you could own in the future, so he would get everything and you'd be perfectly safe. There's no more incentive for any attempt on your life." He smiled at her, evidently completely unaware of the nonsense he'd just spouted.

"Wouldn't the husband just become the target?"

"Mmm, unlikely. With your inheritance being controlled by him, if he died, the law would follow his will. So that would mean you'd get whatever was settled on you, and whoever his heirs are—whether they be your children or his siblings or perhaps cousins—the point is that the inheritance rules all change the moment you become *femme covert*. And whoever is after your fortune will have to sort through your husband's legacy, and it would be practically impossible that he's anywhere on the list of heirs. So he'll give up at that point. I'd hope."

Cat felt as if the floor was giving way beneath her feet, inviting her into an abyss. She looked at all the men, and realized that they had most certainly discussed this before she and Tacita got to the room. "Are you all mad? I'm not getting married just to not die!"

"What's so bad about marriage?" Duncan asked tentatively.

She whirled on him, about to enlighten him on the cavalcade of evils the institution of marriage brought upon hapless women. But before she got more than two words out, Thane stepped between her and Duncan.

"They're just explaining the situation," he told her. "You don't need to do anything yet."

"Anything? I've only been given two options: wedding cake or death."

"You'd really choose death?" he asked curiously. "Over cake?"

"I'd rather go to hell than go to the altar!" Cat declared. Then she stormed out, not quite making it to the door before tears started streaming down her cheeks.

Chapter 25

THERE WAS A MOMENT OF uncomfortable silence after Cat left. Then Kai said, "So I suppose we should hold off on sending out invitations for the wedding breakfast?"

"Aye," Struan said, looking as though he was trying very hard not to laugh. Normally, Thane liked to see his friends enjoying themselves, particularly Struan, who'd had a rough year to say the least. Now, however, he wasn't feeling so magnanimous.

"It's not funny," he snapped. "And the problem remains to be solved."

"Honestly, we didn't think she'd have such a strong ob-jection," Calan explained.

"Or any objection," Struan added. "Aren't most young ladies looking for marriage?"

"Not her," Tacita said sadly. "I do wish you'd mentioned this to me before announcing it. I could have told you what would happen."

"But not marry at all?" Kai asked. "Even to save her life?"

Thane shrugged. "She's said as much before." Except that was before she'd been compromised by Thane. He was un-comfortably aware that he now had the perfect weapon to wield over her should he want to force a marriage. A ruined, potentially pregnant Cat would find life even more difficult, and he doubted her attacker would take kindly to the idea of a baby, which would put him further away from inheriting.

"Aunt Tacita, why does she hate marriage so?" Kai asked.

"Though she is adamant that her objection is philosophical, I'm sure it stems from watching her own parents' unhappiness from a very close vantage point. Mr Ross was not a good husband or a good father by the end of his life, and it's my understanding that Mrs Ross did not conceal anything from the children. She was an outspoken woman, you see."

"That's completely believable," Thane muttered.

"Catriona told all this to Brodie after she ended her first engagement. He understood—though I suppose he would not have mentioned it to you gentlemen, it being a rather personal topic."

"He did ask all of us if we intended to marry in the future," Calan recalled suddenly. "Now that I think about it, that must have been shortly after the showdown with Melrose."

"Aye, and Brodie said himself that he wasn't as sure about the whole idea of marriage as he used to be," Kai added. "Not that he ever got the chance to come up to scratch for any lady."

Thane grimaced. That was his fault too. But aloud, he said only, "Sounds as if his sister made him reconsider."

"You ought to ask her yourself why she thinks as she does," Tacita suggested. "I was not present for most of her life, I'm sorry to say. She would undoubtedly offer you more details for you to counter."

"What, I'm a barrister now?" Thane asked.

"I merely point out that you and Catriona have often had lively discussions." The older lady smiled charmingly and excused herself. Thane recognized a rout when he saw it.

"Stop smirking, all of you," he muttered to the other men, who did not stop.

But Thane never got the chance to ask her, because Cat was impossible to find the whole afternoon, and when she appeared at dinner, she was withdrawn and aloof toward him, still clearly furious at the idea of marrying as a method of self-preservation. She was polite, and to everyone who wasn't Thane, she was even sweet. But frustration radiated from her like summer heat. Cat looked cornered, about to be caught and caged, and desperate for an out.

He'd have to watch her even more closely now.

Thane managed to get a word with Cat as she got up from the table. "We need to talk about your options."

"Oh, do I have any?" she asked sarcastically.

"Sleep on it, and we'll talk tomorrow." He tried to keep his tone even.

"Don't tell me what to do." She strode off, head held high. Thane watched her go, annoyed and…annoyingly aroused.

After dinner, the men met without the ladies to discuss the issue. Thane had fortified himself with a very stiff drink.

"So who's going to be the victim?" he asked. "Can't go to Melrose and ask him to offer again. The man's already got a wife."

"You'll offer," Duncan said flatly.

"Me?"

Calan said, "We thought you and she had some kind of rapport."

Thane glared at him. "Why would you think that?"

"You can't keep your eyes off her," Duncan grunted.

"That's not true."

"It is," Calan said. "Granted, she's a beautiful woman, so it's no surprise she's turned your head. But the question is more why you don't want to turn it just a bit more and get the girl to happily agree to a marriage proposal."

"She would more happily traipse to her death," Thane pointed out.

Duncan didn't look impressed. "Ach, she'll come around. Especially if you ask nicely."

"Why should I be the one who offers for her?" Thane asked, mostly because the old Thane, the before-Cat-upended-his-life Thane, would ask that.

"Oh, would you prefer one of us to do the honors?" Calan asked, rather too eagerly. "I'm only a second son without much at all to my name, but I'm willing to take the plunge."

Thane stepped up to his friend before he could stop himself. "Don't even try it!"

Calan's knowing smile hit harder than any punch to the stomach. "Ah, there it is. The jealousy at the mere thought of another man offering for her."

"It's got nothing to do with that. You all heard her. She's opposed to the very idea of marriage."

Calan snorted. "You're just scared she'll turn you down."

"You don't know what the hell you're talking about!" Thane blustered. "If you want to propose to her to *save her life*," he added sarcastically, "then by all means go ahead and do it! I don't care. Just don't be surprised when she says no."

Thane left before Calan opened his stupid trap again. If he did, Thane was liable to answer with his fist. He stalked away, so disturbed by the idiotic exchange that he nearly collided with one of the maidservants as he went. He needed another drink.

About an hour later, Calan found him in the library, nursing a glass of scotch. After pouring his own, Calan walked to the window near Thane's chair. "Ready to talk now? Or are you still thinking about punching me in the face?"

"That obvious?"

"Oh, no, it's just I have a very developed sensitivity to it by now. A lot of men have wanted to punch me over the years."

"Don't you mean over their wives?"

Calan chuckled. "Progress. I'm glad to see you're no longer going to rant and rave."

"I neither rant nor rave," Thane objected. "It's not my way."

"I know," Calan countered. "Which is why it was so re-vealing when you did so this time. But the fact remains that Miss Ross still has a serious problem, and you are in a posi-tion to help her solve it. A marriage would be quick, easy, and painless. And then her problem is solved."

By introducing a whole new problem, Thane thought. Aloud he said, "Why should it be *me* who has to marry her?"

"Hmm, I wonder. Perhaps because out of all of us, you're the only man here who addresses Miss Ross as *Cat*."

He shrugged. "So we've gained some familiarity." If by *some familiarity*, one meant that he knew what she looked like naked and breathless after coming undone on his bed.

As if reading his mind, Calan raised an eyebrow. "Some?"

"Look, she's not interested in marrying me or anyone else, so what does it matter?" Thane wanted, needed to de-flect his friends' attention from this. Especially Calan, who was no stranger to illicit relationships.

"If it keeps her alive, it matters."

"You saw her reaction before. It won't change. And I for one have no intention of shackling myself to a woman who will resent me for it for the rest of our lives. It would be a nightmare."

Calan told him he needed to get all his brooding done with so he could talk reasonably again. "Or if it will be faster, I can kick your arse."

"Either way, I just want another drink."

"I'm leaving, then. Come out when you're ready."

Thane continued to sit, alone. Brooding.

He'd never be ready. Not for a life with Cat. She was the one woman he truly desired, and the one woman he didn't deserve. God, he wanted to make her feel so good and so satisfied that she'd never be sad again. And never be able to hate him.

Thane fell back to earth, hard. Cat was still going to hate him, probably more than ever now. He'd made a choice, and unsurprisingly, it was the wrong one.

* * * *

Cat went to her room at the same time Tacita did, for appearances. But she paced in her chamber, her mind constantly turning over the news the men had brought. She believed the new theory to be the correct one. Kai and Duncan especially seemed like they weren't the type of people who committed to something until they were certain. It was in one way a relief. It meant that her choice to pursue the calling of advocating for women was not a mistake. She'd do it anyway, of course, but it helped to know that all the angry letters and mockery was just that, and nothing more nefarious.

On the other hand, it suggested a deeply callous individual who was willing to do anything to claim something he considered already his. How was Cat to ever sleep easy until that man was captured?

She walked the halls, finding the place mostly quiet, though she could hear the voices of men in the great hall… No doubt Thane and his comrades were having a grand time. Then she passed the room that Thane used as his office, and noticed a light burning there. She peeked in, and saw Thane sitting behind the desk, his long legs stretched out with his feet propped on the top edge. He was holding a glass of amber liquid, swirling it as he gazed at the minor maelstrom he was creating within.

He looked troubled, unhappy. Why wasn't he with his friends downstairs?

Cat pushed the door open more, and he looked up. His eyes widened, and he took his feet off the desk. "Cat, what are you doing here?"

"You said I ought to be reasonable and talk about my options. Well, I'm here, ready to talk."

"I said tomorrow."

"I couldn't wait till tomorrow, and anyway, why pretend that the answers would be any different? Why aren't you enjoying the evening with the men? You don't get many chances to all be together."

"No one wants my company tonight," he said, taking another sip of his drink. "I'm a miserable bastard who, I'm told, needs a swift kick in the arse."

"I'm surprised none of the others performed the favor for you. They all seem so obliging."

He chuckled. "They would. But I prefer to sulk alone." He gestured for her to sit opposite. "Not that you ever care what a man prefers."

"I could leave," she offered.

"No. Please stay." He looked up at her with an almost guilty expression. "Don't mind me. I'm a—"

"Miserable bastard, yes. We covered that."

"Drink?" he asked.

"No, thank you." She took the seat. *My goodness*, she thought. Here they were, being so civilized less than a full day after they'd behaved in perhaps the least civilized way possible.

"Why do you hate marriage?" Thane asked. "Tacita hinted that it's not just a principled stand against tradition. It's about your parents, specifically."

Cat frowned. "She should not have said anything."

"She's worried about you, kitty cat. We all are. We want to help you. Kai's suggestion makes sense. If you're married, you're no longer a target, even if we don't ever identify who's after you."

"And all it costs is my freedom!"

"Don't be dramatic. You could choose someone who will allow you to live as you like."

"It's the *allowing* part I object to. You don't understand, Thane. If I need my husband to allow me my freedom, it's not really freedom. It's an indulgence. It could be revoked at any time."

"Men aren't monsters, Cat."

"My father was. And he didn't start out that way," she said hotly. "From the stories I heard from my mother, from Tacita, from others…he was charming and kind and romantic. At first. But then my mother had us, and he grew cold and hard and distant over the years. He scarcely saw us, and he fought with my mother every time he came home…which proved to be less and less often as Brodie and I grew older. The man seemed to despise my mother, and he didn't like us much either. Brodie knew how to manage him better, because he was a boy, I suppose. But it got worse as time went by. You must know that Brodie bought his commission— well, made our father buy it for him—at the youngest possible age. It was because he wanted to get away from home. When my father died, I can't pretend it wasn't a relief."

"He died while Brodie was in the army," Thane recalled.

"Yes, less than two years after he joined up. Papa liked that Brodie was in the army. Good solid work for a man…the killing of other men." She winced, remembering who she was talking to. "I'm sorry."

"Don't be. It's an accurate description. I killed a lot of

men." Thane took a sip. "In fairness, they were also trying to kill me."

"Is that why you're drinking?" she asked.

"Not directly. Not tonight. But sometimes, yes." He put the glass down. "Brodie told us when your letter arrived, announcing your father was dead. I didn't realize it at the time, but he was a bit odd about the news. Not as sad as one might expect. Now that I think about it, his father was the one subject he never wanted to talk about. But he did always want to know about our fathers. And mothers. Maybe he was trying to understand how parents ought to be."

"My father's death was sudden," Cat said. "His heart, we were told. Just gave out one night while he was playing cards with his cronies. Nothing untoward or unusual. But life did get a little more…sedate in the house. Mama wore black, but she never looked better. Well, until she started getting ill. That was much later, though."

"So you lost your father, then your brother, then your mother in the space of a few years."

"I wouldn't group my father's death with theirs. Brodie and Mama were…I wasn't…" She stopped, the grief welling up in her chest again.

"Drink?"

"Perhaps a little."

He got up and went to a side table. Curious, Cat followed.

"Anything catch your eye?"

Well, he did, but Cat wasn't going to say that. "Please choose something you think will suit me."

He nodded, then selected a bottle and poured out something gold into a glass and handed it to her. "Try that."

Cat sniffed it experimentally, and inhaled something like whisky, but also heather and spices and honey and somehow a whole blue sky. "What is this?"

"A local drink. Sort of a whisky and mead blend, but not

exactly."

She took a cautious sip, then nodded approval. "It's very good."

"Of course it is. It's from the Highlands."

Cat smiled at him. "You are somewhat biased."

"If you stay here, you can drink it whenever you like."

"That's an interesting…proposal."

He leaned forward. "I can include it in the formal offer. Brodie did ask me to take care of you. I think that does include an offer of marriage, especially if you're in danger by remaining unmarried."

"Brodie would never have asked you to shackle yourself to me. Would you have wanted him to marry Effie?"

"He'd have liked Effie," Thane said, smiling. "Of course, she's married already, but to answer your question, if things were otherwise, yes. I would have been relieved to know she had a man as good as Brodie."

Cat sighed. "Perhaps not what I meant to argue. What I'm saying is…I don't know what I'm saying."

Thane reached out to her, removed the drink from her hand, then pulled her into his arms. "You're tired."

"I'm not."

"You should be. I kept you up all night, and it's been a demanding day, and you're not even able to argue right now…and when has *that* ever happened?"

She laughed softly. How nice it was to have Thane hold her. His hands were stroking her hair, and she felt the heat off his chest.

The arousal that had been smoldering in her belly all day, every time she thought of Thane, suddenly kindled into a higher flame. She tipped her head up, finding him looking back at her.

"Thane, kiss me."

He went still, but it was the sort of stillness a lion possessed before pouncing. "You said you only wanted to talk."

"I was wrong. Please, Thane. We're alone, and I don't know when we'll be alone again."

"I'm slightly drunk," he said in a tone of confessing something.

"Are you saying you don't want me?"

"I'm saying I should know better, but I'm going to use the alcohol as an excuse to misbehave."

Something dark and sweet uncoiled lower in her body. "I can't wait."

He pushed her against the wall, his mouth hot on her neck. He bit her hard enough that she winced, and then felt the heat flood her core. "Thane, you make me lose my mind."

"Good." He kissed her again, hungrily.

He was fully ready to take her, she saw with lust-tinged vision. Cat kept her eyes on his face as she reached down to circle his cock. His head tipped back as he let out a low moan of pleasure.

"Cat," he groaned once. "Why are you torturing me like this?"

"You sound like you like it," she countered.

"I do, I do." He reached for her, catching her shoulder. "But it's still torture."

She smiled. "Get used to it."

"You can't keep doing this to me. We should stop. I should stop anyway. I shouldn't be doing this with you at all, I just can't help myself…"

"It helps me," she said in a rush. "What we're doing helps me. And I know it's selfish but—"

"All right. That's all I need to hear," Thane told her, his voice low and gruff against her ear. "I will do anything for you, Cat. And if it helps you, you never need to apologize for it."

She started to pull up her skirts, giving him access. But he shook his head. "Go to the desk," he ordered, his voice hot. "I have plans for you."

Cat managed to get there, despite her knees going weak at the sight of him so hard for her.

"Put your hands on the top. Lean over, all the way. There's a good girl." He practically purred now, and his hand absently pulled at his cock.

He strode to stand behind her. Cat whimpered in anticipation.

He pulled her skirts up slowly, exposing her bare bottom and thighs above her stockings. "Oh, that's very lovely," he murmured.

Cat looked over her shoulder to find him smiling at her in the most wicked way.

"What should I do?" she whispered.

"Look ahead, kitty cat." He stepped closer and she felt him rub his erection against her bottom. It was erotic in a way she couldn't describe. Then he slid one hand around and dipped it between her legs, where she was so warm and wet.

"Kitty cat," he said, sounding inordinately pleased with her. "You're ready for me."

"Yes. Please, Thane."

"I've imagined taking you this way. It will feel different. Spread your legs wide for me."

She nodded, and then moaned as he slid into her from behind. Was she always going to be so wild for him?

"How do you feel?" he asked, his mouth by her ear, the whisky scent in his breath actually quite pleasant. She realized he was worried he was hurting her.

"Full of you. I like it."

"Mmm." He began to thrust, very slowly, telling Cat how tight she was, how hard she made him. He said things that would have been appallingly crass if he didn't say them in such a gentle tone that she wanted to melt at the sound of his voice. He drew out her pleasure, teasing her with his hand, timed to his thrusts, until Cat writhed and gasped and couldn't endure a single second more. She came undone, her hands pressed into the top of the desk and Thane holding her tight.

He waited for her to come down, and then thrust again, harder. He was so savage that she was sure he would finish inside her with a howl, but he withdrew and spent himself across her lower back, groaning.

Cat reached back to grip his thighs, holding him near her. Even the midst of her frantic pleasure seeking, Cat sensed a truth she'd denied until now, after sharing the story of her parents with Thane. She was using the bliss he offered her as a way to blunt all the pain she'd been carrying. A lust for life to avoid the agony of death. Was it fair to make Thane a part of this twisted path she was walking through her grief? Did he even realize the darkness inside her that was the very thing making her so responsive to his attention, so greedy for the fleeting happiness he could summon in her?

She looked over her shoulder. "Thane?"

His eyes opened, showing brilliant green. "Have I shocked you?" he asked.

She gave him a smile, smothering her rather unpleasant revelation. "Yes. I hope you do it again."

"Give me a moment." He sighed, running his hands over her bottom. "Don't move, sweetheart. I have to clean you up. Cost of safety." He pulled away and moved to a pitcher in the corner of the room.

He called what they just did safe? Yes, she understood that he withdrew, which was one way to lessen the risk of getting her with child. But that was just one risk. Cat's heart thudded as she thought of how much she still wanted him. That was far more dangerous.

He returned with a wet cloth and washed her very carefully, then did the same for himself.

Pulling her skirts back down and straightening her gown, Cat thrummed with the aftermath of lovemaking. It was like a pleasant buzzing all up and down her body.

"We haven't solved anything, have we?" he asked then. It took Cat a moment to remember that she'd come to *talk*.

"No, I suppose not. But I don't consider the time a waste."

"Well, thank you for that." He'd managed to rebutton and retie himself into the image of a respectable, boring, duty-bound man.

Absolute lies, Cat thought with a surprising burst of fondness.

Then he stepped closer and touched her face, the gesture much more tender than she was prepared for. "Kitty cat, you do need to consider the option of marriage."

"I really don't."

"It's not a death sentence."

"Neither is respectable spinsterhood. What I *need* is to know the name of the person trying to usurp my inheritance. And I believe that you and your comrades could find that name." She smiled at him with what she hoped was confidence.

He just looked more duty-bound. "Kai started the search as soon as he realized the possibility. It's extraordinarily time-consuming to search every random branch of a family tree, trying to track down possible heirs. Solicitors do this all the time, you understand, as part of selling estates. From them, we know it could take months, possibly years. And remember, we don't know which bad apple on which branch thinks he's better suited to be heir than you. We have to search them all."

Cat paused. "Months? *Years?*"

"Potentially. And that whole time, if you remain un-attached and alone, you'll be a target. Are you ready for that?"

She wasn't. "I could leave the country?"

"And go where? You'd abandon Tacita?"

"Of course not!"

"So you'd uproot her instead."

"Don't be hateful."

"I'm being practical, which you claim to pride yourself on."

Cat glared at him. "I'll find some solution."

"One has been found."

"I don't care for that one." She strode to the door, then turned. "You haven't actually asked me to marry you. In a formal sense."

Thane slowly shook his head. There was a darkness in his face that she didn't like at all.

"So you have reservations too."

"It's complicated," he said. "You don't know everything you'd need to know about me."

Why did that sound like a threat? She could think of only one thing that would stop him from making an offer. "Are you married already?"

Now he blinked. "*What?*"

"You could have married some fresh-faced lass like An-dra before you went off to war, and now you have to hide it."

He shook his head. "No. Do me a favor, Cat, and get the hell out of here. I can't think when you're around."

"I'll leave you to think, then."

"Cat."

She looked back over her shoulder. "What?"

"Leave your door unlocked tonight."

There was no mistaking that expression.

"I shouldn't. Anyway, aren't you drunk?"

"Not anymore. You don't have to make a production of it. Just leave the door unlocked."

"Perhaps," she said, leaving the room. She already knew she would.

Chapter 26

SHE WENT TO BED, BUT didn't even try to fall asleep. After the clock chimed one, Thane slipped in, closing the door behind him.

"You came."

"You let me," he responded, leaning over her on the bed, kissing her like he'd been gone for years.

She reached for him, and within moments they were skin to skin, exploring each other with abandon.

There was something different in Thane's mood that night, something more serious. He would sometimes pause and just look at Cat, like he was memorizing her.

"What is it?" she asked once.

"Nothing," he said with a half smile. "You're just so beautiful."

"I'm not more beautiful than last time, and you didn't stop to regard me then."

"Oversight," he said, his smile growing. "But you don't want my regard. You want something else?" His kiss was savage then, his mouth hot on her breast and his tongue doing things that left her weak and clinging to him.

"I want whatever you can give me," she said, hearing her own voice come harsh and needy from her throat.

"I'll give you everything," he swore.

Cat arched her back as she gave herself up to his touch.

By now, he knew exactly how to stroke her. He knew what she liked, and when she would start to pitch over the top, he brought her back before she could tip, over and over. He seemed to love the way she cursed him in a breathless begging whisper.

When he entered her, she felt like he belonged there. "No more teasing," she gasped.

"I was never teasing," he protested, and kissed her before she could say more.

Oh, why did it feel so good? Cat wrapped herself around him, pressing closer. When she climaxed, he held her tightly.

She bit her lip to stop from crying out so loud it would expose their secret to everyone within a mile. Thane bore down hard and wrung out the last few bits of her sanity. She whimpered a protest when he withdrew and spent himself in the sheets. But he then gathered her close and touched a finger to her lips.

"You're bleeding," he said, his finger coming away spotted with red.

"Am I? I didn't realize."

He leaned in and with one dart of his tongue licked the blood away, then kissed her so tenderly she nearly melted.

She tucked her head under his chin, resting against him, loving the warmth and solidity he provided.

This would be a good life, she thought dreamily.

With a bolt to her heart, she understood what she wanted. Cat craved that closeness even more than the physical release he offered. Maybe, maybe this was meant to be. Maybe there was a reason she crashed headlong into him in that hallway oh so many lifetimes ago. Though it had taken a while to unpeel the shell from his core, she finally knew the real Thane, the man hidden behind the duty-bound image. And she felt herself reacting to him, letting herself find out how to meet him. Not physically, but in spirit, molding herself so that they could match their flaws and their strengths. Less like a key in a lock, and more like sand filling a gouged-out beach after a storm. It might not be what anyone intended, but it was what nature used to heal.

And if they could live like this, together, then would it be so bad to put a formal mark on the relationship and call it a marriage? Surely that was the ideal of marriage—not the owning of a wife by her husband, but a true partnership of equals. Thane had shown time and again that he was willing to listen to her, willing to value her ideas and thoughts, and that he cared about her enough to keep her safe despite having no claim on her at all.

Not to mention the way he could respond to her unspoken, and sometimes unknown, desires, and give her ways to feel pleasure without demanding anything but the chance to do it again.

Then he spoke. "Kitty cat, there's something I need to tell you."

"I was just going to tell you something as well, but you go first." She curled up languorously. A kitty cat indeed. When he dared call her that, maybe it was because he knew her better than she knew herself.

Thane held her tightly for a long moment, so long that it gave Cat a premonition, the first hint that his words would not be as welcome as she'd intended hers to be.

"Cat, I've wanted to tell you this for a while. But something always seemed to interrupt…no," he interrupted himself. "That's not true. Or if it is, it's only an excuse."

She lifted her head, searching his face. "Thane, what is it?"

"God, Cat, this isn't easy."

"Whatever it is, I'm willing to hear it, love."

The endearment seemed to hurt him. He sucked in a

breath, fixed his gaze just beyond her face, as if staring into a void, and said, "I killed Brodie."

For a moment, Cat couldn't even make sense of the words. "I'm sorry, you what?"

"Brodie's death was my fault."

"Thane, he was shot by an enemy soldier," she said patiently. "I can see now that you felt a responsibility for him —I didn't really understand until I spent some time with you all here what it truly means to have a friendship forged in battle. But that doesn't mean you could alter his fate. Not you or Duncan, or Calan or Kai, or even Struan. War is terrible, love. Don't take on more than your due."

"It is my due," Thane insisted stubbornly. "Brodie wasn't killed the way you think, in a field full of thousands of men, the air turned to smoke and the sound of guns everywhere. He was killed performing an assignment I gave to him, an assignment I should have performed myself."

Her heartbeat faltered with the shock of it. What was he saying? What did she even know of what happened? Was anything she knew the truth?

"I don't understand," she got out, her voice as unsteady as her soul.

"Our superior officers had received some information from a soldier in the British army who'd overheard a conversation in the village. Some Prussian or German was going to meet with the enemy to sell them more weapons, enough to rout us out of our position and drive us back. It was my duty to follow up on the situation. But before I left to be at the meeting, I happened to mention it to Brodie. He grew excited at the prospect, and he pointed out that he speaks some German—and Lord knows I don't speak a word of it. He pestered me to let him take the assignment."

Cat inhaled. "You didn't."

Thane closed his eyes. "I did. He was eager for it, and I

was tired. It wasn't expected to be very dangerous," he added, sounding defensive.

"Oh, no? It got Brodie *killed*!" Cat burst out. She wanted to rush at him, hit him, hurt him. "Why did you let him go? Why did no one stop you..." She gasped. "Oh, Lord. You never even asked permission. It wasn't a sanctioned change. Brodie just went in your place."

He hung his head. "Yes. That's why it took longer to report his death. He wasn't even supposed to be there. And he damn well shouldn't have died."

"But he did. And you lived."

"I'm sorry, Cat."

"Sorry? You *lied* to me."

"I didn't." But there was no strength in his voice. "I just...didn't tell you."

"Until now," she spat. "You lied to me with your whole being, until now. Because you thought by now I was so besotted with you that I'd forgive you *anything*."

"It's not like that, Cat. I wanted to tell you before. I tried. Something always stopped me."

"Such as the opportunity to tumble me into bed?" Cat jumped up, pacing. "Lord, I should have known something was wrong. You hated me, until you got the chance to bed me. Then you just strung me along, making me into your little pet, letting me fall..." *in love with you.* Cat recoiled as the words nearly passed her lips. She had fallen for Thane, as simply and completely as any woman on earth. She ought to have known better. She did know better. And yet she still succumbed to his seduction. Hell, she encouraged it. Because it felt so much better than what she'd felt before. And because she wanted to believe Thane loved her.

Now she knew the truth.

* * * *

This was a new form of pain. The blows to her spirit that hit after the death of her brother and then her mother knocked her to her knees, leaving her hunched over and sobbing with grief.

This was an altogether different, sharper wound. More like a knife blade in her back. Yes, that was it, wasn't it? The deaths of her family were horrible. But Brodie had been a soldier, and she'd seen her mother's death coming for days, even weeks, before the awful moment occurred. She could, in some way, prepare.

Nothing prepared her for Thane's betrayal.

In fact, he'd weakened her first, carefully exposing her heart before he crushed it with a few words. With his truth that he didn't see fit to tell her until she was at her most vulnerable.

Cat pulled her black clothing around her like armor, unwilling to risk sharing her feelings with anyone. Even Tacita, who she loved so dearly. The next day, her aunt asked her what was wrong, saying she could see that something terrible had happened. What news did Cat learn that hadn't been shared with the others?

Naturally, Tacita assumed Cat's devastation had to be linked to the issue of her attacker. She couldn't dare tell her aunt what actually happened between her and Thane. Tacita would surely insist on him doing the honorable thing. Bu how could he, when he had no honor?

Besides, Cat wouldn't give him the satisfaction of laying claim to not only her, but also to her newly revealed wealth. Hell, for all she knew, Thane seduced her because he suspected she was an heiress. Didn't Kai mention that Thane and he got the same idea? But Thane never told *Cat* of his hunch. Why would he? She was a mere woman.

Such thoughts circled her mind like crows after a battle, a cacophony that left her angry and restless.

Worse, Effie had left the day after Tacita arrived, needing to return to her own home. Cat didn't begrudge her that, but she wished the woman might stay. Effie did, however, tell Cat to visit whenever she liked. Since Effie knew nothing of the rift between her and Thane, Cat didn't dare mention that she might well need the refuge.

Over the next few days, she avoided Thane completely, disappearing with the skill of a stage magician whenever he came near. It was easier to avoid the others as well, for they didn't hound her as Thane did, always trying to speak to her, always with a look in his eyes that seemed so sincere.

She knew better now.

But it was his home, his domain, and she had no peace in the walls of Kinlochlie. Only when she managed to get outside of it did she seem to be able to breathe. And she had things to take care of, and some of them could only be done away from the castle.

So she dressed to ride and walked to the stables. Unfortunately, Thane knew her routine by now, and he waylaid her in the hallway outside her room.

"Cat, I have to talk with you."

She kept walking, her head held high. "I assure you we have nothing to discuss."

He kept pace with her easily. Cat could run and he'd be able to stride along without a problem. "Cat, I never meant to hurt you."

"Well, you did." She whirled on him and glared, her eyes burning. "I *trusted* you."

"I know. And I should have told you…before. I set a trap for myself and then was dumb enough to wander into it. Secrets are like that, they strangle you. But I swear everything I've done was to protect you."

"From everyone but yourself," she retorted.

"Yes, fine, I'm a bastard. I know that. I don't deserve

you. I also know that. But Cat, please, please let me explain."

"There's nothing to explain."

"I didn't say it to be cruel, Cat. I had to tell you. I care for you—"

"If you cared for me as you claim to, you'd leave me alone!"

"I have!"

"You have not! You're…everywhere. This whole place just stinks of you. That's why I have to leave."

"Where are you going?"

She glared at him. "I intend to go riding. On my *own*."

"Of course." He didn't tell her not to, which she expected he would, and she was perversely annoyed that he didn't.

"That's all? No pronouncements of how reckless I am to be riding alone? How unreasonable I'm being to wish to make my own decisions?"

"I only want to protect you."

"Aye, to wash away your own guilt."

His jaw tightened.

They'd reached the stable by now. She stalked in and told the boy standing there she wished to ride. She hated that the boy glanced at Thane to receive a short nod of approval before dashing away to saddle her horse.

Now alone again, he said in a low voice, "Nothing will wash my guilt away. But I couldn't keep lying to you, Cat. You deserved to know everything."

"But not till after you took everything."

"I thought your liberated world view meant that you put no stock in things like virginity. How could you care about me taking what you never valued?"

"Virginity is a medieval concept designed to hobble women. But that doesn't mean I—"

She broke off. She couldn't put it in words. *It doesn't*

mean I didn't want to value the memory of my first time? It doesn't mean I granted it lightly?

"What, Cat?" Thane stepped closer. "What did it mean to you?"

"Nothing," she said reflexively. "It meant nothing. As I'm sure it meant nothing to you."

"Not true." He moved in front of her, preventing her from passing by. "Cat, don't pretend it meant nothing. I know you better than that."

"You don't know me at all." She tried to push him aside, which went as well as expected.

He didn't budge. He caught her hands and held them to his chest. "I know you in ways no one else does, Cat." His voice wrapped around her, searing her heart. "Tell me how I can make things right."

She took a deep breath, then said, "There's a grave in France you can occupy."

Chapter 27

CAT'S WORDS HIT LIKE BULLETS. Numb, Thane moved aside. Cat shoved past him, not willing to spend another second on him.

If only she knew he thought about that grave in France every day.

From the shadowy interior of the stable, he watched Cat ride off. Then he looked at one of the guards, who'd wandered close and was now leaning against the wall of the stable as if resting.

"Follow her," he ordered.

"Aye, sir." The man hurried to get the horse the boy had already saddled, anticipating the order.

Thane sighed. He'd never see Cat smile at him again, but he could still keep her alive.

With nothing else to do, Thane wandered around the grounds.

Thane found Struan at one side of the main house, not too far from the kitchens. Oddly enough, the man wasn't alone. Two toddlers swarmed around him, and he was holding a sleeping baby. The scene brought Thane to a stop, since he'd never once seen Struan with children.

"You're a nursemaid now?"

Struan grinned at him, his normally stern face alight.

"Aye. For a little while. The woman who usually minds the wee ones got ill," Struan explained. "I offered my services. Jack, don't go so close to the mule. Remember about the kicking?"

The boy stopped, regarded the mule with serious eyes, and then crawled sideways, well out of range.

The other boy decided that it would be a good idea to climb Struan, a barely achievable goal, since the man was sitting down. Struan allowed it, but steered the boy to his left slope. "Mind your sister, now. She's sleeping and she's much quieter when she's not awake, aye?"

"She's horrible when she's awake," the boy agreed, tumbling off Mount Struan onto the ground.

Struan gently set the boy up on his feet again, and told him to play tag with his brother. He watched the children run off, a rapt expression on his face.

Then Thane remembered that he had in fact seen Struan with children before. It was during the war. Their company had been given the task of going through a village to ensure that enemy forces weren't using it as a hiding place to launch raids from. The inhabitants had understandably assumed the worst, cursing and screaming at the soldiers as they looked into every building.

Thane, Brodie, and Struan had come upon a shabby house hiding soldiers within—except that the soldiers were four small children armed with a paring knife, a broom, a cooking ladle, and a rock. Brodie took the lead, telling them fluently in his typically easygoing way that the men were no threat. However, these children were still wary and edgy, having been tricked too many times in their short lives.

Thane was about to sweep them aside, but Struan instead shouldered his gun, and knelt down to the children's level. He explained in passable French that they weren't here to hurt anyone but it was important to look in the house. The eldest child, a girl, looked angry and accused them of coming to steal food, except it would do no good because they had no food on account of their mother not having money to buy any.

Struan instantly offered some rations from his pack, and within moments, the children were devouring chunks of dried sausages and inviting all three men inside (Brodie having also given up the bread he'd tucked away). Over the next hour, the men learned the names of every child, met the sunken-eyed, too-slender mother (who'd been hiding behind the door with a butcher knife while the children stood guard outside). Brodie even repaired a faulty stovepipe that had made the house too smoky to cook in. During that time, the children freely shared information about *other* soldiers who were using a nearby abbey as a base, largely because the monks had a wine cellar.

"They've already taken all the food and beer *here*," the eldest girl explained, her tone fierce with the anger that comes from hunger.

Struan promised to return the next day with more bread, and Thane saw when he slipped a few coins to the astonished mother. On their way back to camp, Thane chided his friend gently. "Those children could have been lying about everything."

"They didn't seem like liars to me," Brodie interjected.

Struan added, "Most children tell the truth, and when there's a group of them, no lie lasts very long. They were hungry, and they did pay a lot of attention to troops moving through. The mother told me her man was killed last year, so she's on her own with the young ones. She's French, but she wants this war over more than anything. Think it matters who wins when there's no food to eat? All these villagers would take peace in a heartbeat if it was offered. Plus, now we know where the army's hiding." He grinned. "Never underestimate a child."

Andra's arrival brought Thane back to the present moment. She neatly avoided being drawn into the game of tag, with a promise to the older boy, "I'm busy now, Ian, but I'll read you both a story later."

"The one with the giant who stomps all over England?"

"Again? Yes, if you like. Now play. I've got to speak to the boring old men."

"Old?" Struan asked in mock offense. He shifted the baby in his arms. The infant looked ridiculously tiny lying next to Struan's massive torso, but it was evidently quite content, opening its eyes slowly and gurgling as it smiled up at Struan. "Ah, this bairn's awake. I thought she might sleep all afternoon, till I have to pass her back."

Andra's eyebrows rose. "You *asked* to mind the children?"

"Aye. I like children. I'd always hoped to have a family." Struan kept his gaze on the baby in his arms.

He used the past tense, and Thane's gut twisted for his friend. The war had taken too much from him.

"Struan, I wanted to talk to you about how to address Cat…triona's problem."

The big man looked up. "Aye. She should marry someone. Anyone. Not me," he added. "Obviously."

"I shouldn't say it's obvious at all," Andra told him, rather saucily.

He looked away. "What's on your mind, Thane?"

"So, our new theory is that someone views her continued existence as an obstacle to their own inheritance. Let us say Catriona won't marry anyone to thwart her attacker. That only leaves one option."

Struan grunted. "We identify the man and tell him to stop what he's doing."

"Tell him to stop? That's supposed to have an effect?"

Andra asked skeptically.

"Struan is a very persuasive man when he wants to be," Thane said, not going into details. Then he turned back to Struan. "Do you think we can speed up the process of finding him?"

"Not without endangering Miss Ross," Struan said. "Who does appear to like being in danger, seeing as she won't do the one thing that everyone else agrees is a simple solution. To answer your question, I don't see how we can speed up the process, short of hiring an army of solicitors. Which would attract attention, which would make our man go to ground. It's a delicate balance."

Andra rolled her eyes. "You men! So roundabout when a simple approach will do."

"What's simpler than hunting the man down?"

"You don't *need* to do that. Just take away his reasons for wanting to harm Catriona."

"She won't marry anyone," Thane explained, again.

"She doesn't have to. Just announce the wedding date as if it were going to happen. The miscreant will give up the moment that day comes."

"I'm not sure he would stop at that. He might see through such a ruse, especially since there would be no proof of a marriage." Thane would bet the attacker was paying close attention for news of Cat.

Andra, however, was fond of her idea. "You could post banns in the papers. Wouldn't that work?"

"Who's she marrying? Supposedly?"

"You, of course."

"Cat hates me."

"Did you have a fight?" she asked.

"Not exactly. I told her something she didn't want to hear."

"You should apologize."

"I tried." He took a breath. "It was…not something she'll forgive. Ever."

"She'll come around," Andra said.

"I assure you, she won't."

"Well, luckily you know how to spell her name. That's all you need. You can have banns posted here to make it look proper, and then have this nice gentleman with the baby send a message to the city. I'll wager he knows how to get the announcement in all the papers."

Andra seemed quite impressed with Struan. Thane still thought the plan was daft. A fake marriage announcement? Would they need to host a fake wedding breakfast too?

But it *was* a plan that didn't require Cat's cooperation, and that was a strong point in its favor.

* * * *

Most of the way through her ride, Cat looked over her shoulder, and saw the rider perhaps a quarter mile behind her. God damn Thane, sending a guard to follow her, even when she made it clear that she meant *alone.*

Well, she'd anticipated this. She rode a little further, up to the circle of stones on the top of the hill. For a few moments, she was hidden from the guard's sightline, and that was when she dropped the small bundle she'd put in her saddle bag, making sure it was secure, hidden by the green leaves of some wild roses. Then she rode onward, not even glancing back.

The next day, Cat avoided Thane, as usual. She ate her crowdie alone, took a walk around the grounds alone, and tried to write a new speech alone.

None of those things proved to be pleasant to do when she was such a quaking mess of rage. Thane's betrayal flashed into her mind every few minutes, usually right after a too-vivid memory of him in bed. How could she have been so…persuadable? So willing to believe in a fantasy?

She was sitting on the lawn, alone, when Andra walked by and asked, "Have you seen the boys? Jack and Ian?"

"Not lately," Cat said.

"They must be at hide and seek again. I shouldn't have told them they were to have a bath today!" The redheaded beauty laughed at herself. "Ah, well, that's my mistake. Congratulations, by the way."

Cat was confused. "On what?"

"The banns were posted this morning."

"The *what* were posted?" Cat sprang to her feet.

"You and Thane. Getting married in a month." Andra finally seemed to realize that this was news to Cat. "Goodness, didn't he tell you the plan? The minister set aside the date. And I heard that Struan and Kai sent word to several newspapers in Edinburgh, since that's your home, and folks must have a chance to see the announcement. Tacita said it would be quite a surprise."

"Yes, primarily to me. Thane never asked! And if he had, I'd say no!"

"But you'd be such a fine match. And everyone likes you here. You don't like Kinlochlie?"

"It's not Kinlochlie. It's Thane."

"He's a good man."

"I'm sure *you* think so," Cat said, too tartly. "Anyway, it doesn't matter. I'll rip the banns down."

"Um, but they've been posted just so the person after you will—"

"I don't care what any paper may say! I'll die before I marry him."

She stormed off, leaving an open-mouthed Andra behind.

Cat could take it no longer. Alone in her guest chamber, she had never felt more acutely isolated. She had put her trust in Thane, but he had betrayed her in a more fundamental way than she ever could've imagined. Even with the other men at the house, the men who had demonstrated a willingness to help her out of a sense of shared friendship, she couldn't put aside the fact that they were Thane's comrades first. She knew that when it came down to it, they would side with him. The solution of a quick marriage surely seemed entirely reasonable to men who were used to solving problems in the most expeditious way. The fact that it would destroy her own life was irrelevant.

And now they'd decided to skip ahead and just carry that plan out without even letting her know.

So there was only one thing left to do.

Cat packed a small quantity of items that she had brought along with her, the items she absolutely needed and wouldn't trust to let out of her custody…including a few bank notes she'd hidden in the folds of a gown. It was just enough, she hoped, to suffice for a few days' travel.

Very early the next morning, she went down to the main hall, where she customarily took breakfast. She ate heartily, though without exchanging more than the bare minimum of polite pleasantries to others who passed through the room, mostly servants. When she had eaten her fill, she addressed Janet, who had come in to see if she needed anything else.

"Yes," said Cat, lifting a paper she'd written the night before. "Please give this to Mr MacPhearson. There is no need to wake him. It is not a matter of urgency. It merely tells him that I have decided to visit his sister Effie for the next few days. He will understand that I need a change of scenery."

The maid took the folded note with a small curtsey. Cat could read the worry in her eyes, for even though the servants had never been explicitly told what was happening, it was clear that they knew something well beyond the typical social interaction was afoot.

"I have already packed a small bag sufficient for a short visit, and I intend to ride there as soon as I am finished with my breakfast. I have no wish to trouble the household more than I already have done." She gave the housemaid a grateful smile. "Truly, I have felt very well cared for while I've been here."

The maid curtseyed once again, this time with a slight coloring to her cheeks. It never hurt to offer a compliment, particularly when it was true.

Once again on her own, Cat rose from the table and returned to her bedchamber just long enough to put on the riding habit she'd borrowed from Effie and grab the bag that she had packed the night before.

She went down to the stables and requested one of the boys to saddle up the horse she typically used on rides. She also let him know that she was riding to Effie's home and intended to keep the horse there for the duration of her visit. "Though of course if the horse is needed, someone can come and collect her."

"Don't see that happening," the stable boy said. "The master has more than he needs."

Cat didn't trust herself to reply to that, so she merely thanked the stable boy after he helped her saddle up and slung her bag across the horse's back. Cat rode out of the gates, mentioning to the guard posted there that she was heading to Effie's. The man gave her a polite nod, and told her to be careful.

Once free of the gate, Cat encouraged the horse to a trot, and then a gallop, moving in the direction of Effie's home. Cat was pleased that she had spent the last several days acquainting herself with the area, because by now she knew the best points along the way where she might be momentarily unobserved by the various watchers that Thane had placed all around his estate and the approaching roads and tracks.

Cat rode nearly the entire distance to Effie's home, only veering off before the house itself came into view because she didn't want anyone to notice her arrival. At the point where the rolling hills created a small valley, she abruptly turned her horse to the left and rode down the slope into a small copse of trees. Once under the cover of the green canopy, Cat slowed her horse's progress and picked her way through the woods, following deer trails as best she could. She waited about an hour, half expecting some thunderous pursuit from Thane. But no one interrupted her solitude at all. It was perhaps the first time since the beginning of this entire saga that Cat felt she had been left truly alone.

Once she felt certain that no one was coming for her, Cat resumed her ride, this time sticking to clumps of bracken and small woodlands, moving in a very large half circle around Kinlochlie to reach the stones that she had noticed on her first ride.

As expected, the circle of stones was completely deserted. Cat left the horse tethered to a branch in the nearest arm of the woodlands close by. On foot, she moved swiftly toward the stones and retrieved the bag she had dropped there the day before. Part of her had hoped she would never need to do this, and that planning her escape had merely been a mental exercise. But at this moment, another part of her was glad she had done so. She walked the bag back to the horse and added it to her load. Mounting was somewhat of a struggle, until she found a fallen tree that she could clamber up and use as a stepping stool to swing herself onto the horse. Then she rode through the woodlands once again, aiming for the village to the north.

Go back, Cat, ye wee numpty!

She inhaled, not ready for her brother's voice to ring out so loudly in her heart. Brodie continued to tell her in no uncertain terms that she was behaving like a fool. But in a characteristic fit of contrariness, she pointed out that her behavior over the last several days had been a fine example of foolishness, and this could hardly be worse. Brodie's voice inside her was silent, and Cat had to conclude it accepted her point.

Thus, as she wrestled with dueling impulses within her own mind, Cat began her solitary journey. She had seen what came of trusting a man to help her. Now she was on her own.

Chapter 28

IN GENERAL, THANE PREFERRED TAKING action to sitting around. But ever since his last moment with Cat, when she told him what she thought of him and what he deserved, he was useless. He barely slept, he didn't eat. He couldn't let anyone say more than two words before he snapped at them.

Thane was utterly and completely miserable, in a way that he hadn't known it was possible to be. He'd experienced melancholy, and even abject despair during the war, as nearly every soldier had. But this was somehow worse. Perhaps it was because he was at home, during peacetime, and hadn't adequately prepared himself for the blow. Or perhaps it was because it involved a woman. It was a first for him to have his heart broken. Or perhaps, and this was the most likely, his misery was the direct result of him making a monumental mistake. And then repeating that mistake multiple times.

His confession to Cat had come far too late, and he was aware that merely saying the words out loud didn't absolve him of everything he had done. But he had allowed himself to hope that her reaction would be tempered by the knowledge that he loved her. That wasn't what had happened. He wasn't even sure she believed him when he told her how much he had come to care about her in such a short time. But then, why would she? Cat was right to denounce him, and she was right to punish him for the way he'd taken advantage of her trust. No wonder she'd fled to Effie's home. Thane nearly chased after her, but he was too afraid of what she'd say when he saw her.

But that didn't mean the punishment hurt any less. Thane would do nearly anything for her forgiveness; unfortunately, he'd have to perform the miracle of bringing Brodie back to life to achieve it, and that was a power he didn't have. No one had it. All of which left Thane even more miserable than before.

The other men at first attempted to cheer him up, but it was a losing proposition. So they left him alone to brood, applying the usually trusty theorem that time would heal whatever his wounds happened to be.

The morning of the third day after Cat had fled to his sister's house, one of the lads who worked in the stable came to see Thane, a pinched expression on his face.

"What is it?" asked Thane.

"A horse has come back to the stable," the boy told him, keeping his eyes downcast and nervously shuffling his feet.

"Was a horse missing?" There were still occasionally reavers working in the Highlands, usually small bands of men unable to find any honest work. But it was rare, and Thane hadn't heard any reports of thefts from neighbors since he returned.

"It's the horse Miss Ross used to go to your sister's." Now the boy looked up, and Thane could see the concern in his eyes.

"Effie keeps a good stable. I'm sure the boys there wouldn't let the horse run loose, but it's possible that the creature wanted to come home and found its own way during the night." Even as Thane said the words, he didn't believe them. The image of Cat lying on the ground after having been thrown from the horse came to his mind. She was a competent rider, but an accident could happen to anyone. And if Cat had been riding with Effie, his sister would've sent word if there had been any incident. So she must've ridden alone, which meant that if she was injured or worse—he didn't allow himself to consider what *or worse* would be—the situation required immediate action.

"Saddle my horse," said Thane to the boy. "I'm riding to my sister's."

The boy practically saluted, and dashed away.

Thane lost little time in throwing on boots suitable for riding, and then made his way toward the stables. He hesitated only slightly when he heard the voices of Duncan and Kai in one of the rooms, where they were probably relaxing or enjoying a card game. First, he would find out what had happened to Cat. If a search party was required, then he would involve his friends.

The situation with Cat was his own secret shame, and he hated the idea of turning it into a public spectacle. Not that his friends couldn't be trusted, but Thane needed to see Cat's face above all. He couldn't make a coherent decision without knowing what she wanted, without knowing if she was well.

Once astride his horse, Thane rode fast all the way to Effie's home. He didn't see any sign of Cat along the way, nor did he notice any unusual activity among Effie's servants. Perhaps there was another explanation for why the horse had returned. Perhaps he was allowing his imagination to run away.

As he slowed his horse, a footman came outside and nodded to him.

"Good morning, sir." The man was polite, but puzzled. "The mistress is still in bed, as far as I know. Is she expecting you?"

"No, I didn't send word. In fact, I am hoping to speak to Miss Ross."

"Sir?"

"Miss Ross. The young lady who is staying here. Has my sister been hosting so many guests that it gets confusing? Miss Ross has black hair and dresses in all black. You can't fail to notice her."

"Won't you come inside to the parlor, sir?" He gestured for one of the stable boys who had already approached to mind Thane's horse. "I'll let the mistress know that you're here."

Thane followed the footman into the house and walked into the pretty parlor room that Effie generally used. The footman went along upstairs, presumably to alert both Effie and Cat that he was here.

There was something odd about the footman's reaction to what Thane thought was a basic request. Was it possible that Cat had somehow conveyed to the household staff here that she was never to be at home to Thane? On the one hand, it seemed an almost absurd extension of command: for a guest to insist on such a thing as telling the *brother* of the home's mistress who would or would not receive him. But on the other hand, Cat had every reason to avoid Thane. She'd already demonstrated that by going to Effie's in the first place. And he could easily imagine servants being swayed by the idea of a young lady in distress and wishing to remain unseen by a man who had troubled her. Even though Thane was the person they knew, and not Cat, who until two weeks ago didn't even exist for them. Edinburgh may as well be in America for all the influence the city's society had here in the Highlands.

Well, the women would be down soon, and then he would discover what was going on.

After a few moments, his sister walked into the room, looking like she really had just woken.

"Thane, have you grown lonely for my company already?

I had assumed you had much else to occupy your mind."

"Effie, I've got to speak with Miss Ross."

His sister looked at him with a strange expression. "Why are you telling me such a thing? I assume you're not asking for permission or advice."

He shook his head. "I'm not in a position to ask for either. Just tell her to get down here."

"What? I haven't the slightest idea where she is. Don't tell me you mislaid her."

"She left a note saying she was staying here with you!"

Effie's eyes widened. "Here? No, Thane. I haven't seen her since I returned home."

"And I haven't seen her since she left home. That's almost three days ago." Thane cursed. Where was Cat? The distance between the siblings' homes was relatively short, but there was still plenty of space to get into trouble.

"We'll get to the bottom of this." Effie rang a bell on the table next to her and a maid hurried in.

"Ma'am?"

"Ask everyone if a young lady has called at the house anytime in the past three days. Her name is Miss Ross."

The maid curtseyed and left.

Effie gave Thane a worried smile. "I'm sure there's an explanation."

"The horse Cat was riding returned to Kinlochlie," he told her. "We should find out from the stable if any of your horses are gone."

"We've only got two," Effie said.

A quick query to the servants confirmed both horses were calmly cropping grass, exactly where they should be. "So horse thieving does not appear to be rampant," she noted.

"If she rode somewhere else and the horse she used has returned," Thane said, "we're looking at up to a day and a half's ride. That could get her to Inverness."

"Alone? Catriona's a fine rider," Effie said. "But she surely couldn't ride any great distance, particularly without some escort or protection. There would be far too many questions. And she'd have had to sleep one night on the way. Where would she have done that? She knows no one up in the Highlands, and…does she have money?"

Thane shrugged. "We have to assume she does. Christ, what was she thinking?"

Effie crossed her arms. "Well? What *was* she thinking? What might have set her off three days ago?"

Thane looked at his sister, realized she would never believe anything but the truth, and sighed. "We fought."

"Oh, dear. Over what?"

"I told her something that upset her."

Effie's eyebrow lifted. "Upset?"

"It's difficult to explain quickly. I did offer to marry her as well. Which also upset her. Not as much as the other thing."

"Thane, you're being uncharacteristically coy. Tell me what you did to evoke such a drastic response."

"Effie, if I died, and then someone came to you and announced that he had killed me, what would you do?"

His sister blinked in confusion. "What sort of question is that?"

"A hypothetical one! Just tell me."

"I'd probably want to throw something at him. Or have him arrested. Or kill him myself, I suppose."

"Now imagine the man who told you this was…close to you."

"How close?"

"What if it was Robbie who told you?"

"He would never!"

"Effie. Answer me."

"I'd be sick. I'd never want to speak to him again. I'd tell him to get out of the house, or I'd leave myself…" She trailed off, her features stilling. "Oh, Thane. Her *brother.* But…you didn't. You couldn't."

Thane told her everything. The bare bones of it, the worst truths he could speak. Effie listened, arms still crossed, her mouth open and her eyes distant.

At the end, she said, "So you became lovers, and then you offered to marry her for reasons having nothing to do with love, she refused you, you remained lovers, and then you told her that you're the reason her brother is dead."

"Essentially, yes."

"Oh, Thane." She stepped forward and wrapped her arms around him. "You must be in agony. All these months of mourning him, and then her coming into your life, and then this."

He hadn't expected sympathy from Effie. He didn't know what to expect, but it wasn't this gentle response. It destroyed him in a way that yelling or censure couldn't have. He closed his eyes, and felt his throat close as he choked back tears.

"I failed her so completely, and now she's *gone,*" he said, his voice rough. "I never deserved her, but I didn't care because I needed her. I just…did what I did, and when I tried to tell her the truth, she…"

"She wouldn't listen?"

"Oh, she listened. And then she left me. Which I understand. But she left Kinlochlie, Effie. She left the one safe place she had. And it's my fault because I made it unsafe for her."

"Thane, you made a mistake. But if Catriona loves you as much as you love her, she'll realize that it was just that, a mistake. Eventually."

"We don't have eventually. I need to find her *now,* before whoever is after her does."

"Then why are you standing here? Go and get your men and go after her."

So Thane returned to Kinlochlie and rounded up the others, Tacita included. He explained what happened and all the facts he knew, leaving out only the more personal and private details of his and Cat's relationship.

When he was finished, Calan asked, "How did she evade the notice of the men you've got posted around the estate?"

"She's smart. She's been here long enough to know where they would be, roughly, and she probably picked her route specifically to avoid them. Plus, I stressed that they ought to watch for strangers arriving. Even if one saw Cat riding by, well, she's done that before. Why would he think she was fleeing?"

"We'll find her," Struan said, standing up. "It's a matter of eliminating possibilities."

They started by riding to the village, the nearest point where Cat could reasonably start a journey.

They asked every traveler they encountered, and stopped in each shop.

The explanation finally came at the public house and a farmer from the village came up to them. "They've been saying you're looking for a black-haired lass. A lady from the lowlands."

"Aye, did you happen to see her?" Thane felt some hope in his chest.

"Indeed, sir. I was driving my cart up the road and she approached, asking where I was bound. Well, I had a load of carrots to take to town and I told her so. She offered to pay me to let her ride along. She was a very well-spoken young lady, and it seemed rude to refuse, so I let her on the cart and drove her to town."

"What did she say during the journey?"

"Not much. Just that she'd got word from her family, and

that she didn't want to inconvenience her hosts by asking for a horse or carriage."

Thane snorted at that. "No, she wouldn't."

"She thanked me when she left the cart, and then walked down the road toward the posting inn. I didn't see her after that, I had my own work to do."

Thane closed his eyes. Damn it. *This is your fault.* He cursed the voice in his head for being correct.

"She wasn't a criminal or something, was she?" the farmer asked worriedly. "She was dressed like a lady, and she was very polite. I thought she *was* a lady. I'm sure she didn't steal anything from me."

"She's not a criminal," Thane said wearily. "There's just been a misunderstanding, and I need to find her." He gave the farmer a few coins for his trouble, and then turned to Calan. "She's gone. She would have taken the first coach leaving town. Which means she could be anywhere."

"Let's find out if that's true. If she got a seat on a coach, someone will have spoken to her, or at least noticed her waiting. She's not the sort of lady who can be ignored."

No, she would not be ignored, Thane thought. More likely she'd use the time waiting to convince her fellow travelers of why women should hold seats in Parliament or something like that.

At the posting inn, a bright-eyed girl about fourteen years old remembered Catriona very well, from her costume ("The most wonderful black buttoned boots!") to her travel plans ("She aimed to get to Edinburgh and even asked about hiring a private coach, though as it turned out she only had to wait two hours for the scheduled one and there were three seats empty on it."). The girl recalled that Cat stepped on the coach just after the noon meal and also left behind a pamphlet advocating for women's rights, which the girl kept, tucked into the family Bible. "Oh, she was so kind, sir. She even gave half a roll to Tam, I mean the dog there, before she left."

On hearing his name, the old, half-blind setter raised his head. The girl said, "You remember the lady, don't you, Tam? The one who petted you and said you were handsome and gave you bread?"

The dog thumped his tail against the floor and gave them all a happy doggish grin.

Was there anyone Cat couldn't charm? Thane wondered in frustration. If any of these people had exercised the slightest bit of caution...for what? Thane had to remind himself that Cat's actions, while rash and dangerous and personally terrifying to him, weren't actually suspicious or illegal in any way. Cat had the right to travel wherever and however she wished, provided she had the funds to pay for it and was willing to deal with the social consequences of being a woman alone—consequences that Cat clearly had no fears about.

The men gathered in the tavern room of the inn, each with a drink. Thane felt he'd need several. They discussed the possibilities. Thane was worried the coach to Edinburgh could be a decoy.

Duncan said, "She's not from the Highlands, so she won't have much reason to stay. More to go, since she knows we all have connections here. We'd be able to locate her fairly quickly."

"She was upset," Kai said slowly, "so she'll want to go to familiar territory." He turned to Tacita. "Is there anywhere besides Edinburgh that she might go? A relative or friend somewhere else in Scotland?"

"Anyone I could possibly think of is in Edinburgh or very close to there. But Catriona wouldn't like to...expose her wounds," she said carefully, glancing at Thane, "to anyone. She's very proud and doesn't like to appear weak. I suspect she'll be heading for home. Our house."

"It's shut up, though, isn't it?"

"Cat would be able to get in, and she would be able to live there for quite a while even without any servants at all. What matters is that it's *her* home."

Struan nodded in understanding. "I'd probably do the same."

"That's not safe," Thane said.

"It is to her." That was Calan who spoke, and Thane always relied on Calan's insight. Even when he didn't know a person well—or at all—he seemed to understand their thoughts.

"Why?" Thane asked him.

"Because you're not there," Calan said.

Thane glared at him. "You're not helping, man. If Catriona did go back to Edinburgh, we need to get there as well. Goddamn it. She's three and a half days ahead of us now!"

"Maybe we can make up the time."

"How? A deal with the faeries?" Thane asked sarcastically.

"I don't think we need anything that drastic. You said the lady didn't enjoy the sea journey up from Edinburgh."

"She was sick the whole time."

"So she'll avoid taking a ship back. She caught a coach heading south. She won't go to Inverness or anywhere along the shore to get a ship. She's traveling by land, and that means slow going and overnight stops."

Thane felt a flicker of hope. "We can go north and catch a ship sailing to Edinburgh, which shouldn't take us more than a day on the water."

Struan nodded. "Day and a half, if the weather turns."

"Do you want to really be involved with this? It's not your fight," Thane told him. Struan, more than any of them, would be fully justified in staying away from the city, where too many people tended to look at him…or avoid looking at him.

Struan shrugged. "I have to go back to Edinburgh anyway. Why not rescue someone while I'm there?"

Thane almost laughed. "You would, wouldn't you?"

"We won't beat her," said Duncan. "But we can shorten the time that she's unprotected. Come on. Let's return to Kinlochlie and pack."

As the others headed off, Thane remained rooted to the spot for a moment, just thinking how lucky he was to have friends who kept their heads. And who were willing to fight battles that weren't theirs, over and over.

* * * *

On the ship, the sailors handled everything, so all Thane could do was pace the deck and worry about Cat.

Calan came up to him as the sun was setting over the headland to the west. "You shouldn't be up here all night. If for no other reason than that if you fall overboard, you'll be cranky about that as well."

"I'm not cranky."

"You're the definition of *cranky*. This lass has you so enchanted you can't think of anything else."

"She's impossible to ignore."

"You keep pretending that she irritates you. Just stop, man. It's obvious that you're mad about her."

"Look, the fact is that we…well…"

Calan rolled his eyes. "How old *are* you? So you bedded her, but you can't actually say you bedded her?"

"I can't say that because I wasn't supposed to do it! I didn't intend for it to happen."

"Oh, it was an accident? Just rolled into bed and—surprise!—it was her bed?"

"No."

"Aye, didn't think so."

"This situation isn't simple."

"Why not? The objective doesn't change. You still need to get her back."

"But even if I find her, she won't listen to me, because she hates me. The reason she left is because she's angry. At me."

"Well, that's your problem. But we'll help you get to her."

"You can't tell the others about…the sleeping with Cat part."

Calan laughed. "If they don't already know, they're idiots."

"What do you mean?"

"From the night you met, you looked like you planned to toss her into a bed the first chance you got."

"I did not."

"You did. Not blaming you. She'd catch any man's eye."

"Like yours?"

"Of course," Calan admitted. "But I doubt she would have been interested in anything I could offer. She needs someone more serious than me. Like you. Didn't expect things to go quite as far as they did, but…"

"Well, if you thought all that, why did you let me near her?"

Calan shrugged. "Because it was funny to watch you squirm."

"Kai and Duncan think this too?"

"Duncan's not blind, but he probably decided it wasn't his problem. Kai honestly might not have realized what's going on. That boy is going to need some serious education, and soon."

"I can't believe you didn't try to say anything, like, Mac-

Phearson, don't lust after Brodie's sister while you're supposed to be protecting her."

"Sounds like you already told yourself the same thing. But what would have been the point of warning you off? You wouldn't have listened." Calan put a hand on his shoulder. "Anyway, we have to get to her before someone else does."

Calan left, but Thane lingered on deck, watching the night take over. For a moment, he didn't realize someone had joined him. Kai's slender form and silent demeanor was easy to miss.

"I hope we find her," Kai said quietly.

"Me too." What else could he say? It was the only thought in his head: finding Cat, keeping her alive.

"What are you going to say when you see her?" Kai asked then.

Thane shook his head. He had about a thousand things to say, and also none. Besides, Cat wouldn't want to hear any of them. "Depends on where and when we find her, I suppose."

"Are you going to tell her you love her?"

"What?" Thane swiveled to regard his friend. Kai obviously did notice what was going on. Or had Calan blabbed to him so fast?

"Well, you do," Kai went on. "Don't you?"

"I don't know."

"I think you do."

"What the hell do you know about it? You know about as much about love as a monk in a cloister."

Kai nodded, not the least offended by this characterization. "Aye, I've never been in love. Maybe I never will be. But it seems like the sort of thing that you shouldn't hide."

"Maybe in a perfect world," Thane said with a snort. "And that's not this one."

"No. That's what Miss Ross was saying too—I mean

back in Edinburgh, when we first met her. About how she wanted to make an imperfect society better."

"For women."

"Making it better for women probably makes it better for everyone," said Kai. "The world is half women. They really ought to get more say about what it looks like."

"Fine, then you can join her stupid ladies' league when you get there."

"Think they'd let me?"

"I think they'd eat you up like a piece of meat."

Kai looked intrigued by that. Then he said, "Come below deck and get some rest. We should be there midday tomorrow. You'll want to be ready for anything."

Chapter 29

CAT WOKE UP, ALONE.

She was in her own bedroom in the house in Edinburgh, having arrived late the previous evening.

There was no breakfast tray with tea, no fire crackling, because all the servants were gone. Aunt Tacita would have instructed them that they wouldn't need to return until she sent word, and they were all very likely taking advantage of their unexpected holiday. Most of them would visit family normally out of reach, considering that most servants could expect only one day a month, besides half days on Sundays.

All of which meant that Cat would have to fend for herself until they either came back on some predetermined date, or she could send word to their housekeeper.

It was not the type of house meant to be lived in on one's own.

"Oh, don't be maudlin." Cat flung aside the covers and got out of bed.

The house was so still. Cat had lived in the place her whole life, but never before had she been completely alone inside. There had been her mother, her father (for a shorter time). Always Brodie, whether in flesh or in spirit. Then her aunt Tacita, stepping up to provide the care Cat needed when no one could have anticipated it would be necessary. And of course, the household servants.

The slightest sounds echoed strangely, bouncing off the walls and often tricking her into thinking that someone else *must* be there. Cat walked through rooms with little intention, but nearly every time she got ensnared in a memory, and more often than not, she found herself wiping away tears.

This place was meant for a whole family, generations living together with children and dogs running about, and friends visiting, and the servants making it all work. She sank onto a chair in the drawing room, which was dim and shadowy because no one was there to pull aside the curtains.

Finally, Cat had to admit to herself that she was lonely. For a brief time, she had been utterly swept up by Thane's attention, and she'd mistaken her infatuation for love. She couldn't have really fallen in love with him, could she? Not after what he revealed to her.

But if it wasn't love, why did the very thought of him make her soul ache? Why did the idea of a long life lived without one more moment with him in it give her chills?

Oh, because she did love him. And over the past few days, when she was essentially solitary while among other travelers, Cat came to the understanding that she'd been horribly cruel to him in a moment when he needed kindness. Telling her the truth had been an act of bravery.

And she punished him for it.

Granted, he hadn't chosen the best time to tell her. But there probably wasn't an optimal moment to confess such a thing. And it wasn't malice that got Brodie killed. It was…a misjudgment. She knew better than anyone how persistent Brodie could be when he wanted something. And if he decided that he ought to go on the mission assigned to Thane, he'd pester until he got it. Would Cat be angry if Brodie had successfully carried out the mission and returned to the camp unharmed? Of course not. She'd never know. So it wasn't the action that she objected to. It was the result.

And that part was out of Thane's hands, wasn't it? War was uncertain and dangerous. If Thane had gone, he'd have died instead. How was that any better?

"Brodie, I don't know what to do," she murmured.

Coming back to the city had been a mistake. Cat thought she'd feel secure in her own home. But a house was just a shell. She'd left Tacita up in the Highlands. She'd left Brodie's old comrades. She'd left Effie, who'd shown her nothing but hospitality when she didn't have to offer anything. And she'd left Thane, who had promised to protect her, and had done so over and over.

Oh, Lord. She had behaved like a spoiled child, running off without the slightest idea of what she'd need to do to live on her own.

How mortifying it would be to crawl back there, to stand in front of Thane, and Tacita, and the others, and say *Please forgive me, I was too busy being self-righteous to be sensible.*

Would Thane even take her back? Did he know she was *gone*, or did her note and her carefully placed comments to the servants convince him that she was still at Effie's home?

Cat curled up on the chair, her heart aching as she realized that what she truly, truly wanted was for Thane to hold her again, to kiss her and tell her that yes, they could be together.

She had to go back. As embarrassing as it would be, she had to go. A pilgrimage to burn away her pride.

It'll go faster if you take a ship, Brodie's voice said in her mind.

"Oh, shut up," she grumbled, a faint smile nonetheless lifting her a tiny bit above the darkness. "I'm taking a coach…but not till tomorrow."

Brodie's answering laugh seemed to echo around her, and Cat felt a tiny bit less alone. She'd always have Brodie… their souls were intertwined.

She sighed into the pillow she and Brodie had made so long ago. Why did life have to be so difficult?

Why couldn't she keep what she loved?

Then a sound, a real sound, jolted her into alertness. What was that?

The sound came again, and finally Cat recognized it as an energetic rapping on the front door. She rose, thinking that someone must be quite keen on talking to her, since the door knocker had been removed when the house was shut up. Ordinary people passing by would immediately know that the family was away. And yet, someone seemed to know she was here.

Thane.

Cat's heart leapt, and then her stomach dropped, a disconcerting pair of reactions that left her feeling a bit sick. He followed her! Even if he didn't know for sure that Cat was here, he'd damn well look. That was the kind of man he was, relentless until he was satisfied.

A memory of his relentless efforts to satisfy her came to mind, and she flushed.

Another knock, even louder. Cat hurried to the foyer, thinking that she'd just peek out the window to verify it was Thane. Thane wouldn't actually break into the house to satisfy his curiosity, would he?

Oh, he would.

Cat steeled herself.

It wasn't Thane.

On lifting the curtain just enough to peep out to the steps, she saw the bottom third of a woman's gown. Robin's-egg blue, which was certainly not Thane's color.

Suddenly weak with relief, Cat reached for the key in the

lock and turned it. She could speak to a stranger without losing her composure. This woman must have the wrong address, or she was collecting for charity or some other purpose. Cat opened the door. "Excuse me, but—"

"Catriona Ross!" Miss Fairchild said with evident relief. "My goodness, am I glad to see you. We were so worried after that terrifying scene in the park! I wrote several times, but never got an answer."

"I was away," Cat replied dumbly. The scene in the park? It took her a moment to recall it—it seemed to have occurred *eons* ago. "I thought it best to get out of town for a while."

"You poor dear, you must have been beside yourself."

After a moment, Cat realized that she was being rude by making the other woman stand on the doorstep. If the footmen had been here, this all would have gone so smoothly. "Would you like to come in? Pardon me, I'm not quite up to entertaining. All the servants are still gone…"

Miss Fairchild stepped inside, saying, "I'll just stay for a short while, to ensure you're taken care of. Goodness, it's like a tomb in here! Are you really all alone? Have you informed the servants they ought to return? How are you *eating*, dear?"

"Oh." Cat frowned. When had she eaten last? She remembered buying a meat pie from a vendor on the street when she arrived in the city, but had she eaten since? "I believe there's something in the pantry. If you'll wait in the parlor…"

"Nonsense, dear. Let me help." Miss Fairchild put an arm about Cat's waist and steered her toward the kitchen. The woman seemed perfectly at home, firing up the little coal stove and filling the kettle with water from a bucket (Cat *had* remembered to get fresh water from the well, at least).

Between them, they managed to find cups, plates, and some shortbread from a tin to assemble on a tray. The result looked almost like a proper tea. The whole time, Miss Fairchild kept up a chatter about events in Edinburgh, what the ladies' league had been up to, and how much Catriona had been missed by her compatriots. "Mrs Roberts talks about you incessantly, you know. I expect she wants to pass the torch of leadership to you when she's ready to retire."

"I don't deserve it," Cat mumbled. Lord, she'd been within inches of throwing away all her principles to give herself in marriage to a man just because he turned her head. She had no business telling other women how to live independently.

"I told her you'd say something like that. You're so humble, Miss Ross." Miss Fairchild smiled at her, her teeth flashing for just a moment as she turned toward the light. "Well, I think everything is ready. Lead the way to the parlor, won't you?"

Miss Fairchild took charge of the big tray, holding it firmly with lace-gloved hands. Cat led her to the parlor, and took a seat while Miss Fairchild poured.

"Sugar?" she asked, even as she dropped two lumps into the otherwise perfect brew.

Cat didn't take sugar, but it seemed churlish to refuse the offered cup, and anyway she'd have to go back to the kitchen to get another. She'd just drink one overly sweetened cup and then fill the next herself.

Miss Fairchild sat back, sipping from her own cup and then giving a sigh of satisfaction. "Ah, there's nothing like a proper cup to set one to rights. Don't you find tea so restoring?"

Cat managed one sip and nodded, trying not to grimace. Lord, the sugar was cloying. She wished there was cream. But alas, that was one of the many luxuries she got only when the servants were at work, making the whole house run so smoothly it didn't look like work at all.

"What have you been doing these past few weeks, Miss Fairchild?" she asked politely as she took another tiny sip. If she got the liquid level down halfway she could pour more tea in, diluting the intense sweetness.

"I've been in an agony of waiting," the lady confessed. "And I must say, I've been wondering where you've been, Miss Ross. To disappear from a scene of such drama, and then no one in the whole city could say where you'd gone! It's all very mysterious. Can you not give a hint?"

"I was in the Highlands," Cat said, knowing that it was statement of such vagueness that she might as well have said nothing at all. "I felt I needed to get away for a while."

"You could have *told* someone!" Miss Fairchild chided, wagging her white-laced finger playfully.

"I told my aunt Tacita."

"Who also absconded a few days later, so what good was that?" Miss Fairchild chuckled, then nibbled a biscuit.

"Wait, you knew she left?"

"Well, I called at the house, didn't I?" Miss Fairchild replied. She tapped the remaining half of the biscuit so that the crumbs fell to the carpet.

Cat found herself annoyed by the gesture, even though it was probably done without the slightest thought. "Would you like a plate?" she asked, leaning forward to pick one up from the tray.

The sudden motion made her head spin. Cat lost her hold on the plate and it fell on the floor. The thickness of the carpet was the only thing that kept it from shattering.

"Goodness," Miss Fairchild said, her eyes widening, though a smile played on her lips. "How are you feeling, dear?"

"A little dizzy," Cat confessed. "I may need to lie down."

"You want a nap," her guest said, nodding. "That's quite understandable."

"Yes, I've been under rather a strain the past few days. The travel down from the Highlands and being alone in the house…" Cat had to stop a yawn with her hand. "Excuse me!"

"Take more tea," Miss Fairchild said, lifting Cat's cup to her mouth.

She drank another sip, grimacing at the sugary sweetness. Then she leaned back in her seat. "It was very kind of you to call," she said. "I truly didn't mean to worry everyone."

"They'll manage, and after all, people have such short memories, don't they? I do like this house," Miss Fairchild said, looking around with a gleam in her eyes.

"Oh…thank you?" Cat was getting rather muddled, and she wasn't entirely sure where this conversation was going.

Miss Fairchild looked directly at Cat and smiled. "It needs a dog."

"We had a dog. He died not very long ago."

"I know. It was unavoidable, but it was necessary. I didn't do it to be cruel, of course."

Cat heard the words, but they didn't make any sense. At least, not in her head. Meanwhile, her stomach dropped. "What…what do you mean? What was unavoidable?"

Miss Fairchild said, slowly and patiently, as if to a child, "Killing the dog. We put poisoned meat out in the yard, and he went for it immediately. We were going to get in the house that night, just as soon as the dog went to sleep. We needed him to not bark an alarm, you see. But then some damn housemaid was awake when everyone ought to have been asleep, and we had to retreat anyway. Very frustrating."

"You…killed Check?"

"Yes, Miss Ross. Goodness, do try to keep up. The tea is supposed to make you sleepy, not stupid."

"The tea?" Cat inhaled. "The sugar! You poisoned my tea with something in the sugar lump."

"Full marks! Yes, it was easy. And fast. And you needn't worry. Once you drop off, I'll get you all comfy on the chaise over there. It will look like you swooned, and then your heart just failed. Happens all the time! Healthy women seem to be full of life one day, and the next day they're in the kirkyard in their finest gown."

"Are you talking about marriage or burial?"

Miss Fairchild actually leaned back and laughed. "Clever to the end, Miss Ross. Your funeral will be well attended, I've no doubt."

"Why do you want to kill me, Miss Fairchild?"

" *Mrs* Fairchild, in fact. Speaking of marriage, I feel I ought to share the good news about mine. My husband is a cousin of yours, actually. Not that anyone in this house ever recognized him or offered the slightest hint of familial warmth. But he *is* the closest male descendent in your father's line. When Brodie Ross died, my husband should have been the next heir."

"But I'm Brodie's twin. I'm the next in line."

"And a blow that news was, I assure you." Miss—no, *Mrs* Fairchild glared at her. "What need have you for the inheritance? You've got a pretty face and fine manners. If you did what you ought to have done, you'd have found a gentleman to marry and he'd take care of you. The estate belongs to my Thomas. He needs it to take care of me."

"If you believe that, why did you even join the League?"

"Not for the yammering about ladies' rights!" The woman rolled her eyes. "Such caterwauling! The system we have works very well so long as everyone knows their place in it. I joined to get closer to you, Miss Ross. To learn your movements and make it easier to get rid of you when the time was right." She smiled happily. "And after a few missed opportunities, the right time has finally arrived!"

Cat tried to stand. She needed to get out of the house,

now. But her legs felt wobbly as she rose, and she collapsed back down onto the seat.

The other woman shook her head indulgently. "Just go to sleep, dear. You always have to make such a fuss. For once in your life, do as you're told."

"I will not."

Miss Fairchild picked up the embroidered pillow, the one Catriona and Brodie had worked on so painstakingly as twelve-year-olds, determined to give their mother the most beautiful gift in all of creation. Her tormentor gave it a cursory glance, which turned into an expression of actual curiosity. "My word, this is hideous. What possessed anyone to create such a thing, let alone keep it?"

Cat could have told her about the sort of love that resulted in an object like that, mocked and mourned, teased and treasured. But she could barely speak now. Just keeping her eyelids open was a chore. All she got out was "My...family."

Miss Fairchild just laughed. "The plan worked well up till you. You proved rather difficult. But now I've got you, and it's time for you to rejoin your family, dear." She held up the pillow and stepped toward Cat. Cat lifted up her hand to ward off the descending pillow, but her muscles had turned to water, and there was no force in her arm.

She inhaled, aiming to get as much air as she could, to fight the inevitable attack. But it was not a fair fight, and despite her struggle, within moments she was swallowed up in enveloping, eternal velvet night.

Chapter 30

WHEN THEY REACHED EDINBURGH, THANE announced he'd go directly to Catriona's home.

"You can catch up later," he told his friends.

"Like hell," Calan retorted. "We're all going."

The others agreed, and Kai was hailing a carriage before Thane could respond.

He looked to Tacita, who had just stepped onto the dock. "Go," she said simply. "I'm quite capable of hailing my own ride." Indeed, one of the men unloading the ship overheard and immediately offered to track a carriage down for the lady once her luggage was secured.

"There, see?" She put a hand on Thane's arm. "Just go find our Cat and stay with her. I'm sure all will be well. I'll be along shortly."

He nodded, grateful for the woman's endless understanding.

Kai shouted that the driver was waiting and they all piled in.

The ride didn't take long, but it felt like ages to Thane. He was jumpy and tense, dogged by the feeling that he was wasting time, that when he got there it would be too late.

He had no reason to feel that way. Probably, when they arrived, Cat would lean out a window, perfectly beautiful and perfectly angry, and tell him to go to hell.

God, let that be what happens, he thought.

As soon as the carriage jolted to a stop, Thane got out and hurried up the steps to the house. Everything was closed up, the ground floor windows shuttered and the knocker removed from the door. He knocked anyway, pounding on the heavy wood.

There was no answer.

"I'll head around back," said Kai, already moving.

"There's a side garden with doors into one of the rooms," Calan recalled. "I'll try to get in that way."

"Are we going to be taken for thieves?" Struan asked.

"If we must." Thane *had* to get inside. He pounded on the door again. "Catriona Ross! Open up!"

Duncan looked back at the street. "We're going to be noticed, and the neighbors won't like it."

Struan leaned past Thane and put his hand on the doorknob. It turned easily, the door inching inward.

"Oh." Thane felt like an idiot.

Struan clapped a hand to his back. "Never hurts to check." He pushed the door open all the way and stepped inside.

Thane and Duncan followed, closing the door afterward. The men stood in the foyer, listening hard. It was entirely quiet, but the kind of quiet that felt wrong.

Struan raised his hand and gestured silently to indicate that he was going to move toward the dining room. Thane nodded, gesturing back that he intended to go the other way, toward the back study. Duncan pointed to the stairs going up.

Why the hell did this feel like they were in enemy territory? They'd reverted to the wordless communication they'd learned during the war, but this was a house in Edinburgh, for Christ's sake.

It wasn't as if Cat were going to drop boiling oil on him.

Well, maybe him. But not the others.

But even as Thane moved through the foyer, he felt watched. He moved down the hall to the little study, intending to open the glass doors for Calan to be able to enter without smashing the panes.

He was just in time, for he saw Calan on the other side holding a rock, ready to throw it at the glass. Thane hurried to the door and unlocked it with the key that lay on the desk nearby.

Calan gave him a grin as he slipped in. "You're taking all the fun out of this."

"I'm sure Cat prefers her doors unbroken."

Calan sighed, but kept the rock in his grip. "Is she here?"

"If she is, she's being very quiet," Thane told him. "But she has to be here. Where else—"

At that moment, a gunshot rang through the house. Both men went still for a moment, then Thane muttered, "Upstairs. Duncan's up there."

They charged to the door and headed back for the foyer and the main staircase. Struan was already near the top and gestured that Thane could advance. Nonetheless, Thane pressed himself against the wall and kept his eyes up as he moved up the steps, Calan close behind.

At the top of the stairs, they saw Duncan, clutching his shoulder with one hand. He glanced at them, and said, "I'm fine. He's over there."

Thane looked, and saw a man leaning out from a doorway, holding a gun in one hand. "Everyone stop! If anyone moves, I'll shoot the bastard again."

So this was Cat's attacker, the man who had shot at her multiple times, poisoned her dog, and wanted to take all her inheritance. He looked familiar somehow.

"You don't want Duncan dead," Thane yelled. "He's no one to you. Let him leave the house."

"Not likely! He's seen me, so he'll have to be killed. You all as well now. Should have let the lass alone!"

"Where is she?" Thane called.

The man gave an ugly laugh. "Gone."

Duncan frowned, making a show of sounding dense. "Gone from the house or gone—"

"Shut up! You should be bleeding to death!" the man yelled, his voice sounding almost panicked, despite him being the one with the gun.

He didn't expect so many of us, Thane realized. *He's not sure he can take us all.*

"Listen," Calan called out, his tone deliberately calm and smooth. "You can't spend the inheritance if you're dead. Let's come to some arrangement. We're all reasonable men."

"Reasonable? You kidnapped the girl I was trying to kill! What's your game? I won't stand—" The man's rant ended with a surprised grunt, and then the sound of a body sliding to the floor.

Thane leaned forward and saw the man crumpled near the doorway, clutching his chest. Kai stood behind the man, a large kitchen knife in his hand.

"Where the hell did you come from?" Thane asked.

"Servants' stairs up from the kitchen," Kai responded, breathing hard. "It's at the end of the hall, and you all kept his attention away from my angle. I decided it was worth the risk. He's still alive," he added with a tinge of relief.

"I'll get him downstairs," said Struan, swinging his arms. "We can tie him up in the kitchen until the law hauls him off —"

Another shot cracked the air, and all the men ducked.

Thane was shoved aside by the injured man, who used the distraction to grab his gun from the floor, jump up, and flee.

"*He* didn't just shoot now," Kai said in confusion.

"There's two of them with guns! Stay down," Duncan ordered.

Thane slid over to use a toppled table as better cover. Another shot whistled past him.

"They're pinning us down here," Thane said.

Duncan touched Kai's arm. "Where's the servants' stairs?"

Kai pointed. "Last door on the left."

"I'm going to circle around," Duncan said, and was off before they could protest.

To cover Duncan, Struan grabbed a vase off the table and hurled it toward the shooter. They all heard it shatter, the sound followed by an oddly high-pitched yelp of surprise.

"Was that him?" Struan muttered.

"Let's find out." Calan lunged forward, intending to go after the fleeing figure.

"Wait." Struan put his arm out. "We go together."

They stormed into the room, and found a figure in the corner, aiming a gun at them.

"Careful," he warned them. "I've reloaded."

"I'm sure you have," Kai said, putting his hands out in a calming motion. "But just consider that a murder charge will mean you'll be declared a criminal and you'll never see the money you fought for."

"I'm not giving up now," the man snarled. "And anyway, why should I listen to you? You're on her side."

"We're on Brodie's side," Struan said.

"Ah, Brodie Ross." The man's smile turned cruel. "Sad loss. So young. So determined to serve, even when he wasn't asked."

"What do you know about Brodie Ross?" Kai asked, frowning.

"Enough. After all, I'm his heir."

"You're not."

The man glowered at them all. "I should be!"

"I understand how you feel," said Thane.

"I don't think you do." The man laughed and hurled the oil lamp toward the corner, where the carpet touched the wall under a window. The carpet and the draperies, soaked in oil, caught instantly.

Struan yelled something Thane couldn't catch, and then two more shots were fired. Thane dropped to the floor defensively, but looked up when Kai called out that the man had run out.

"He used the fire as a distraction!" Thane was annoyed at himself for not seeing it. "We need to find Cat. Now."

"Fire's spreading," Kai said, as if noting the approach of a carriage. "We need to locate Miss Ross and get her outside. We have perhaps five minutes."

The flames jumped to the next drape.

"Or less," Kai corrected.

"Come on, room to room," Thane said.

The others moved, but Struan stood there, unmoving, horror written on his face.

Hell. Thane realized that the fire was not just a present danger to Struan, the way it was to him and the others. Struan was being sent back in time to the war, when another fire blazed up around him and nearly killed him.

"Go!" he shouted to Struan. "Get the hell out of here! Get outside and organize a fire brigade!"

Nothing from Struan, just that wide-eyed, terrorized stillness.

"I've got him." That was Kai who spoke. Somehow the smaller man maneuvered Struan around and got him walking toward the entrance. He looked over his shoulder to Thane. "I'll handle the situation outside. Just go find her!"

Thane nodded, then looked back to where the conflagration was already taking over the room.

"Calan, clear all these rooms. I'm going to her bedroom." He pointed to the door, thinking she was most likely there. People retreated to where they felt safe, and for most women, that would be the one room they could call their own. Cat had told him that.

But she wasn't there. He flung open the door and looked in on an empty room with an unmade, and uninhabited, bed.

"Damn." Where the hell was she?

A shot streamed past him, and Thane spun around. The other gunman! Except…it wasn't a man.

"Miss Fairchild?" he said, recognizing the blonde woman.

"Mrs," she corrected with a sneer. "You never thought to look for a woman, did you?"

Thane silently admitted they had not. "So you're a full partner in your husband's scheme?" he guessed.

"Of course. A wife should be a helpmeet to her husband."

"And of course, it's rather a lot of money."

"Don't be vulgar. It's about what's right. My husband, Thomas, should have been announced the heir!"

"Except for the inconvenient fact that he wasn't actually the heir," Thane pointed out.

Mrs Fairchild grimaced, and adjusted her shooting arm to settle her sight on Thane's head. "It doesn't matter now."

"Of course it does."

One advantage of living through a war was that he no longer froze at the prospect of being shot. The woman thought she had him pinned. But Thane had been scanning the room the whole time, and he knew exactly what he needed to do to even the situation.

"Looks like your Thomas is bleeding out," Thane said conversationally, lifting his chin to indicate the doorway behind her.

"I'm not going to be fooled by that," she said. But she

cast the briefest glance over her shoulder—instinct was hard to overcome.

At the same moment, Thane dropped to the floor, and grabbed the edge of the large rug, yanking it toward him. Mrs Fairchild was standing on the other end, and she lost her balance when the rug moved underneath her. She stumbled and fell to her knees. She didn't drop the gun, but by then Thane was already moving. He charged over to her, and stepped down on her forearm. She couldn't use the gun any more than she could stand up.

"Let me go," she demanded as if he were some brute who attacked her.

"Tell me where Cat is." He leaned down and plucked the gun from her.

"You're too late. Even with your friends along to help you. They're going to die too."

She smirked at him, or rather she smirked until he laid a boot across her neck.

"Tell me where Cat is."

"Dead, or on her way to dead. You can't save her."

"Care to wager?" he asked.

She choked as she tried to get in another breath, but her eyes blazed with triumph. "I used poison."

Thane's heart shuddered. Cat dying of poison? While her home burned around her? Well, if he couldn't save her, then he could damn well serve her. He wasn't going to let her die alone.

"Where is she?" Thane demanded, pressing harder.

Miss Fairchild snarled, until she began to choke.

"Tell me, or you run out of breath," he said, keeping his tone even. He couldn't let her see how much he loathed using this method to get information from a woman, even in such dire circumstances. "Funny, you dying in the same house as the woman you killed. Makes you look pathetic, as a murderer anyway."

Her eyes were bulging when she finally wheezed out, "Parlor."

Thane released the pressure on her throat and jumped toward the door. Behind him, he heard the woman roll over and let out a hacking cough in between gasps for air. Flames licked the walls, giving a hellish look to the place.

The parlor doors were shut, which was why Thane and the men had run past initially. Now he pushed them open, only to feel an immense gust of heat rush out. The parlor was on fire too.

Smoke plumed out of the doorway, and Thane ducked as he entered, holding his sleeve up to his mouth to give him something to block the smoke.

"Cat! Are you in here?"

He looked around the room, everything made hazy and orange-tinged from the spreading fire. Christ, this was worse than the battlefield shells. At least that had happened outside. The fire had spread thanks to a nest of curtains that had been half flung into the fireplace to function as a sort of fuse. Now flames caught all along it, and they'd reached the furniture and the other window curtains as well.

"Cat!" He couldn't see any sign of her. Had the woman lied after all? "Cat, answer me!"

Then he noticed a slight rise under a blanket thrown onto the couch. The curve of a woman's hip.

He rushed to the couch, at last seeing Cat's unconscious form and her pale face at one end, head cradled by that hideous pillow.

"Cat! Wake up!" He reached for her shoulder and shook her. God, she wasn't dead already, was she? Poison, smoke, fire. Any one of those could finish her.

She coughed once, weakly.

"Cat!" He reached down to scoop her into his arms.

"You're alive. Thank Christ. I've got you, love. I'm getting you out of here."

"Go away," Cat whispered. "I don't…want you…."

Ignoring the sting of her slurred words, Thane lifted her up. She didn't have to love him to be worth saving. He'd run into fire for her even though she despised him.

The foyer was thick with smoke. He could see no one, though he heard the shouts of his comrades. Thane turned to the right and took the final distance at a dead run. He didn't dare breathe, and the added weight in his arms made it feel as if he were running underwater, his legs heavy and his feet dragging.

Then someone pushed him from behind. A low grunt of encouragement as an arm went around his shoulders, steering him.

It was Calan, providing the extra force Thane needed to get free of the smoke-choked building and out into the night air.

He stumbled across the street and laid Cat down on the ground. Her head lolled to the side, and she didn't open her eyes.

"Cat? Cat!" Thane tipped her head and saw her mouth open. She coughed out a grey mist—smoke from the fire. He told himself that was all it was. Not her soul.

"I need a doctor!" he yelled to the gathering crowd, remembering Miss Fairchild's smug reveal of using poison. Thane couldn't save Cat from poison. He never felt so helpless.

"Cat, it will be all right. I'll make it right. I promise."

"Get away," she whispered, her eyes opening. But she didn't focus on him. She seemed to be staring beyond.

"Cat, a doctor will be here soon. Please just stay with me," he pleaded.

A neighbor thrust a cup of water toward him, and he took

it, lifting Cat enough to help her drink. She sipped and spat it back up. "Bitter."

"Try again, love. If you drank something bad, the water may help dilute it."

Beyond him, he was dimly aware of Duncan yelling something, and bucket after bucket of water being hurled at the house, and the fire hissing like a dragon each time. He heard Kai and Calan struggling with a woman, her cries sounding inhuman. Then Struan appeared from somewhere and simply caught the woman in an embrace that might as well be iron.

"You killed him! You killed him!" she continued to shriek, flailing against Struan's bulk without effect.

Thane ignored the rest, and turned back to Cat. She managed a few sips of water, but he hated the ashen tone of her skin.

He didn't know how much time had passed when an older man edged up to him, holding the leather bag that seemed to be the badge of the medical profession.

"This young lady was injured in the fire? Breathed in smoke?"

"Probably, yes. But she was also poisoned."

"Poisoned!"

"We think. The woman screaming over there…she said she poisoned Miss Ross."

"With what?"

"I've no idea." Thane called for Calan, who came over instantly. "Find out the name of the poison Fairchild used."

"Aye." Calan went away, his face like stone. He'd get the answer.

Thane looked at the doctor. "What can I do?"

"One of the neighbors offered the use of her house." The doctor pointed to the home two down from Cat's, a safe distance from the fire.

"Can you pick her up? Good. Take her inside there and I'll do what I can," the doctor said with a bleak expression.

Thane had seen that expression many times during the war, on the faces of doctors and nurses who worked at bedsides where they knew Death waited on the other side.

Chapter 31

CAT WOKE UP SLOWLY, UNWILLINGLY. Her whole being ached.

She looked to the side, and there it was. The ugliest pillow in the known world, the lace ruffle on one side badly singed, but otherwise in one piece.

"How…"

"When MacPhearson carried you out of the house, he grabbed the pillow as well." It was Tacita's voice, soft and gentle in the dim lighting. "He says he doesn't remember doing it."

Cat grabbed the pillow and cried, fat tears dripping onto the already blemished fabric. The smell of smoke welled up when she hugged the pillow tight. She didn't care.

After a few moments, she got hold of herself and tried to sit up, only to collapse back as a coughing fit overtook her.

"Don't strain yourself," Aunt Tacita told her. "You've had an ordeal, what with the smoke and the poison."

Cat had forgotten about the poison. She remembered reading somewhere that poisons could take a while, leaving the victim a walking ghost, awaiting the inevitable conclusion. "Am I expected to die?"

Tacita suddenly smiled. "Apparently not! The doctor's come around twice to check on you, and he seemed surprised that you were still alive the second time. He said that people who ingest that particular poison usually die within a day. You are a marvel."

"I only took a very small amount of the tea she put it in," Cat said, feeling as if that fateful moment was both long gone and quite recent. Everything after the tea was as broken up and jumbled as the ruins of a stained glass window. "What *happened*?"

Over the next half hour, Tacita told her everything from the moment Thane and the other men discovered she was gone and gave chase. They had sailed (naturally), which allowed them to gain three days over her land-based route. They rushed directly from the wharves to the house.

Evidently Miss Fairchild and her accomplice did their best to eliminate the men, but were badly outmatched, considering Thane and his friends had military training and experience that meant they could counter nearly everything the couple threw at them. Until they set the fire.

"I can hardly believe the house is still standing," Cat said.

"Oh, it'll take more than that to harm this pile of bricks. The fire was seen immediately, and the neighbors came with water to quench the blaze. There's a lot of damage to furniture and curtains and other items, but what matters is that no one died."

"What of Miss Fairchild...or Mrs Fairchild?" Cat asked, frowning. "And her...husband? Is he really my cousin? It's all so confusing."

"I wonder that you remembered any of that, dear. Yes, as it turns out Thomas Fairchild was a second cousin once removed on your father's side. I suppose he technically had a claim to the inheritance, using the most stringent interpretation of only male heirs being allowed to inherit. But according to the solicitors, who have shown commendable promptitude in responding to this incident, the fact is that Scottish law favors explicitly written contracts over tenuous claims based on tradition. The man would have had a very difficult time defending his claim in court."

"Unless I was dead, and unable to press my own claim."

"I certainly wouldn't have stood by while some miscreant tried to steal your family's legacy!" Tacita sniffed at the cheek of it. "And I must say, your gentleman and his comrades were impressive in defending you."

Cat looked down at the pillow still clutched in her arms. "I don't know why. I treated him very badly before I left the Highlands. And I don't know why the others should have joined in. They have no stake in the matter."

"They all called Brodie friend," her aunt said. "For them it was enough."

Cat closed her eyes, still feeling the heat of the fire that had surged so close to her…before Thane carried her to safety. "I will have to thank them, but I don't think I can face them yet." Thane, she meant. It was Thane she was too ashamed to face.

"Well, you still need to rest, dear." Tacita poured a glass of water and offered it to Cat.

"I mean, I don't know how I could ever face them. They must think I'm vapid and silly for leaving Thane and running headlong into danger. Did he say anything?" Cat asked suddenly, peering hopefully at her aunt.

"Which he do you refer to?"

"Tacita, don't tease me. I mean…Tha…Mr MacPhearson."

"Mr MacPhearson said that he was glad he got here in time so your death wouldn't be on his conscience."

"Oh." A little part of Cat's heart died, and it had nothing to do with any lingering poison. He merely sought to clear her from his conscience, a final act to resolve his obligation to Brodie. There was nothing more. Well, after she'd told him she hated him, why would she think he had any tender feelings left for her? "I think I'll sleep again. I'm…I'm not feeling well yet."

Tacita tucked her in like a child and turned the lamp very low, telling Cat to rest up.

But Cat wasn't sleepy at all. She clutched the smoke-scented pillow close and tried not to burst into tears once more. Thane had followed her just to fulfill his oath to Brodie, and not for any other reason. And what other reason had she given him? Why had she made such a mess of everything? Why did she find it so difficult to accept that Thane had made a mistake when she herself made so many as well?

* * * *

Cat's recovery was swift, in the physical sense. Her lungs cleared, and she could sit up in bed and walk about the house for short periods. She slept a great deal—or more accurately loafed in bed, unable to rouse herself to any action. She knew she ought to write to Thane. But every time she approached the desk to pick up a pen, she found herself turning back to her bed, crawling under the safety of the covers.

However, she was not bereft of visitors. Mrs Roberts came the next day, and expressed her genuine horror at what occurred. "To think that woman used our noble goals as a cover for such a nefarious scheme! We shall have to vet our members much more closely in the future. And I suppose I shall never again be able to convince you to speak in public, my dear."

"Of course I shall speak," Cat said. "Indeed, now all I have to fear is the usual mob of angry men and whatever rotten vegetables they may hurl. And I am not afraid of that."

"That's the spirit! You are such an example to the young women of our nation."

But Cat did not feel like an example. Not a good one anyway. She'd first assumed she needed no man in her life, then allowed her heart to be stolen by one, then threw herself at him, only to have her heart broken the moment she truly thought she could be his wife. And she *still* yearned for him.

Later that same day, she received a visit from Kai.

"I'm an ambassador," he explained after handing over a bouquet of cheerful yellow roses. "We didn't want to crowd you, but we're all very concerned. How's your recovery?"

To Cat's ears, Kai seemed to be tactfully avoiding the names of any specific men who were concerned, which allowed him to evade the mention of any who weren't…namely Thane. But she said, "The doctor says I am doing well and should be back to my usual self any day now."

"How wonderful!" He beamed at her. "I'll tell the others. We've all been worried that there would be permanent damage, either from the fire or the poison."

"Not from those," she said softly.

If Kai caught her meaning, he said nothing. Instead, he spoke of minor news in the city and the country, obviously hoping to engage her interest in the larger world. He was so sweet and earnest that Cat conjured up the courage to ask a question that had been dogging her ever since Miss—Mrs— Fairchild had revealed the truth.

"Kai, I've no right to ask it, but I need a favor, and I think you're the only one who can manage it."

"Me? Are you sure you don't want to ask MacPhearson, or…"

"He can't help with this," Cat said abruptly. "Even if he wanted to. But I know you have a gift for finding things."

"I'll be happy to try, Miss Ross."

"It's about Brodie."

Pain flashed across Kai's face, but he said, "Anything."

Cat told him what she wanted to know, and while puzzled

by her request, Kai promised to do his best to fulfill it.

She received more visitors the next day: a few neighbors, more ladies from the League, then Duncan and Calan together. They conveyed Struan's regrets that he couldn't join them, with Calan adding, "It's the smell of smoke, I think. He doesn't do well with it, not since the war."

Cat said she quite understood, and she intended to write Struan a letter to express her gratitude. The men didn't stay longer than was socially acceptable, but Cat rather wished they did. When they left, the house felt much emptier.

Thane was not among the callers, and Cat doubted he would ever set foot in her home again.

Chapter 32

THANE REQUIRED A PURPOSE. HE currently had none, and the resulting feelings of being extraneous, useless, and lost were more than he could bear. He wandered the city, walking up and down streets until he wore holes in his boots. He'd climbed to the top of Arthur's Seat multiple times, out of a misguided hope that by seeing the city laid out below him, he'd somehow find a pattern he'd missed before. But each time, his gaze kept returning to the spot far below where he knew Cat's home to be.

Naturally, he couldn't actually see the house, let alone the damage from the smoke that left ugly streaks of charcoal across the cream-colored stone. Despite the fire, the house remained habitable. He'd half hoped that wouldn't be true— then he could have offered to let both women stay with him, by way of apology for nearly letting two killers take Cat's life.

But Cat didn't need his hospitality. She didn't need his protection. And she didn't want anything else from him, not after learning he was responsible for what happened to Brodie.

So apart from his solitary excursions around the city, he remained in his rooms, useless and restless.

Five days after the fire, Struan found him. The big man

walked into Thane's sitting room, looked around at the empty glasses of whisky, and said, "Have you even eaten a meal these past few days?"

"Probably."

Struan snorted. "I'd offer to drag you down to the nearest pub, but as it happens I don't care to dine out much myself anymore." He revealed a package that he'd brought in, which contained freshly baked bread, two meat pies, and a few wedges of cheese. Thane was suddenly famished.

Over the meal, Struan told him that the other men visited Cat and she appeared to be perfectly healthy, if still rather subdued.

Thane wanted to ask if she asked after him, but he was too much of a coward to do so.

"Everything seems to be resolved," his friend concluded after sharing that Mrs Fairchild, the only surviving accomplice, was expected to spend the rest of her days in either a prison or an asylum…which were much of a muchness in any case.

"Aye," Thane responded. "Damsel saved, evildoers captured, all that sort of thing."

"You don't sound happy about it."

"Of course I'm happy about it. I mean, that's what the whole point of this was, yes? Protecting Brodie's sister."

"Catriona Ross," said Struan.

"Yes. He hasn't got another sister hidden away, has he?" Thane was feeling decidedly testy this morning.

"I just thought you might want to use her name, as if she were a full person and not merely half of her brother." Struan's voice was low and even, but the censure was clear. And Thane knew he was being an ass.

"Look, I know she's her own woman. Christ, she never lets anyone forget it. I only meant that our job is done. She's safe now, and has no more need of us."

"She never had need of me," Struan pointed out. "Nor for most of us. You, however, are a slightly different matter."

"She's made it quite clear that I am neither needed nor wanted. And to be honest, she's correct."

"You made a mistake."

Thane gave an ugly laugh. "Aye, I never should've gone near her."

"No, I mean during the war. It was a mistake, Thane. You made an error in judgment when you allowed Brodie to take the assignment, but it was an understandable error. Brodie did have a qualification you didn't. And Brodie did ask for it. You didn't foist it on him. You didn't skip out on it to avoid the risk. It wasn't even supposed to be a high-risk assignment. You couldn't have known what would happen."

"But it did happen…Brodie's death. And then I said nothing."

"What good would saying anything have done at that point? Wouldn't have brought him back. Wouldn't have changed the war."

"I should have told you and the others, at least."

"We've all got memories we don't want to share," Struan said. "And we've all done things we're not proud of. War isn't polite or fair or kind. But those who survive it do get another chance to live. So you'd better bloody take yours. If you mope around here any longer, I'll fight you myself."

"Please don't." Struan was not the sort of man anyone wanted to fight one-to-one.

"Then are you going to explain yourself to the lass, or not?"

"If I go to her, will you promise not to crush me?"

"I'll think about it," Struan grunted. "But in any case, I'm leaving the city soon. Though I won't go before I hear that you've at least tried to speak with her."

"I'm surprised you stayed this long."

"Matter of business. There's a debt that needs paying." Struan did not look happy about it.

"You've a debt to pay?" Thane asked in surprise. He always thought Struan to be very comfortably off, and he certainly didn't spend money frivolously—or at all.

"No. This debt is owed to me. And it's past due. The war kept me busy, but it's time to attend to all the loose ends in my life."

"Oh, so you can retreat to your home in the Highlands and live like a hermit forever."

"That's the plan." Struan didn't appear to be open to discussing it, and Thane knew by now that it was wise to pick his battles.

Chapter 33

THE NEXT DAY, THANE BATHED, shaved, and dressed for the first time since the fire. He was going to Cat's house, and he wanted to look like a respectable man while he was there. With his luck, he'd be turned away at the door, but at least he would have tried. And that should keep Struan from exacting the physical punishment he threatened. Not that Thane really believed his friend would ever do such a thing.

When he knocked on the door, the footman not only didn't kick him to the curb, he gave a cordial bow as he ushered Thane in. "Good day, sir. Mrs Murray has been hoping you'd call. Won't you come to the study? The usual room is unavailable," he added with a meaningful look.

So Tacita wished to see him? Was she intending to tell him to never approach Cat again? He'd understand if that was the woman's stance. If he hadn't first lied to Cat and then told the truth in exactly the wrong way, she never would have fled the Highlands and been at risk in her own home.

They passed the main parlor, which still stank of smoke. The study was more or less unscathed, perhaps because it was in the back corner. He walked to the doors to the garden, which were open to allow the breeze in. He remembered when he'd come upon Cat practicing her speech in the garden. How defiant and how utterly enchanting she'd been.

God, to be able to go back to that moment.

"Mr MacPhearson," Tacita's familiar voice came to him. "I am glad you called on us."

He turned to see the older woman smiling at him, her arm out to indicate that he should take a seat. "Tea?" she inquired.

"No, thank you, ma'am." he said, feeling like a schoolboy for some reason.

"Catriona is asleep, I am afraid. She's recovering but seems to require much rest."

He nodded, though he suspected that it was just a polite lie to account for Cat's refusal to see him at all. "She must do whatever she thinks is best for her."

"Oh, she does," Tacita said with a light laugh that still somehow held a little sadness. "Usually, that is."

"I am returning to Kinlochlie," he said, too abruptly. He saw her blink at the news, which he had intended to lead up to. Clearly, he had yet to master a simple social conversation. "What I meant was, I wished to verify that you and Miss Ross had all that you required before I left town. After the… recent event, I imagine that you have not yet found…" He trailed off.

"Equilibrium?" Tacita supplied.

"Something like that," he said, nodding gratefully for her ability to decipher his bumbling words.

"It's true that life is not quite back to routine. But we're trying. It will be a relief to be on an even keel again."

"May I assist you at all?"

Tacita shook her head. "You have done more than we could have imagined, you and your companions."

Her tone was kind, excruciatingly so, so Thane had to conclude that the woman didn't imagine exactly what Thane had done to—with—Cat.

"Well, if you do require anything, anything at all, I hope

you will write to me at Kinlochlie. I will be at your service." He stood up, feeling that awkward sense of ending. Of having said his last line, but not yet off the stage.

"Must you leave so soon?" Tacita asked, still sitting. She probably never felt awkward. The woman seemed to have a very strong sense of—what was it—equilibrium.

"I have a number of tasks to complete before I travel," he said, even though that number was in fact laughably small.

"Perhaps you would care to look in on Catriona before you go."

"You said she was asleep?" he said, surprise making it a question.

"Yes, but I thought it would do you good to just see her face. To reassure yourself that she will be well."

Thane did want that, very much. He was desperate to see her. "I don't wish to…presume." As if he hadn't already *presumed* far more than that.

"Oh, Mr MacPhearson, after all we have been through, after all you have done for Cat, it's not a matter of presumption. She would be sad if you did not."

He doubted that, but it was obvious that Tacita thought him far better than he was. "In that case, I'll look in on her. Shall we?" He offered his hand to help her up.

Tacita waved him off. "Too many people would bother her. You may go on your own. You know the way, of course."

Why did this feel like a trap? Thane couldn't imagine the lady setting him up to be cornered by Cat so that she could once again tell him how little she thought of him. Perhaps she'd written a new speech just for the occasion.

No, Tacita would never be an accomplice to something mean. So Thane went up the stairs, still wary as if heading into an ambush. No servants were about. Not unusual…but still disquieting.

Cat's door was not fully closed, probably so that Tacita or the maids could enter without disturbing her rest. He pushed the door open and slid in, letting his eyes adjust to the dimness.

Everything was in shadow, the furniture merely a suggestion, all edges smoothed by the darkness. He saw the bed, but couldn't discern anything more. He moved closer. He just wanted to see her face. Then he would leave.

He was practically touching the bedpost when a voice came from the deepest shade. "Who is it?" A figure shifted and sat up in the bed. "Thane?"

"I'm sorry. I didn't mean to bother you. Tacita told me you were sleeping. I just wanted to see you before I left the city."

She blinked, as if coming slowly out of slumber. "You're leaving?"

"Yes. I'm returning to the Highlands. I came to say goodbye."

"How could you say goodbye if I was asleep?"

He shook his head. "I don't know what I was thinking." Other than that it might be easier to say goodbye to her while she was sleeping…and that he needed one last look at her. "If I knew you were awake, I wouldn't have intruded. I'll go." He half turned, cursing his luck. Why could he never know what to say to Cat?

Why can't we ever keep what we love?

"Wait," Cat said, stopping him in his tracks. "I don't believe you, that you simply wanted to say goodbye. You always have a purpose, Thane MacPhearson. Did you come to find out if I'm carrying your child, so that you can offer for me to save the bairn from life as a bastard?" She spoke softly, with no rancor or rage. With nothing, really. Not at all like the Cat he knew, who spoke with passion whether she was discussing politics, or dreams, or breakfast.

"You needn't worry," she continued, looking at the curtained window instead of at him. "As of this morning, I know I'm not."

He winced. Bitterness he could take. Not the deadness in her tone. He swallowed hard, then said, "That's not why I came here. I didn't even think…that is, I assumed you'd tell me if…Christ, why do I assume anything when you're involved?" He sighed. "Anyway, if you do need something from me, you only have to ask. You should know that."

"I think I've asked for quite enough. Haven't I nearly gotten you killed?"

"You didn't. The people who came at me were really just trying to kill you. And you know I don't stand for that sort of thing." *Keep it light*, he told himself. If he got too serious, or too sincere, he'd drown.

"No, you don't."

God, he hated to hear her so…lifeless.

"I really must go," he said again. But he didn't move.

"It's good you're here."

"It is?" Hope was a nigh-unkillable thing, and it leapt again in his heart.

"Yes. There was something I'd meant to send you. Go to my desk," she ordered. "There's an envelope there, with Kai's handwriting on it. Look inside. You'll need to light a candle."

Thane frowned, but did as she asked. He pulled a few sheets of paper out the envelope, and recognized the wording of a formal military report. He'd written dozens in his own career, and read hundreds more.

Now he read this one, and was suddenly thrown back into the war, to the night he always tried to forget. It was a report written by one of his superior officers regarding the fiasco of the mission that Brodie had begged to take from Thane. Much of the information felt familiar—far too much—but he saw that a passage had been underlined in bright red ink.

He read the last, crucial phrase aloud, "'...acting on information discovered by Lieutenant *Fairchild*.'"

Cat's mouth actually pulled into a twisted half smile. "A common name, but it sounds different now, doesn't it? Something Mrs Fairchild said to me that night stuck in my mind. She said the plan had worked well *up till me*. I kept thinking about it, and when Kai stopped by a few days ago, I asked him to find any information about Brodie's death, no matter how trivial."

"Kai is damn good at finding anything his company needs," Thane murmured.

"I can't prove it, of course. And with Lieutenant Fairchild dead, we'll probably never know. But I suspect that he engineered Brodie's death by inventing the false witness and the timing of the supposed meeting, knowing that Brodie had better German than you and that he'd want to go in place of you on the mission. I suspect he made sure Brodie heard about it. Whatever happened, Brodie's death wasn't your fault. Even if you had gone that time, Fairchild would have tried something else. Just as Miss Fairchild tried with me. They were the only people to blame for all that happened. Not you, Thane."

He read the words over and over, while Cat's words trickled into his brain. If this was true... "Why didn't Kai let me know this?"

"He only just got it. It arrived in the post this morning. I asked to see the information first, and then I planned to send it on to you if it revealed anything useful. And I think it did."

Thane sat down in the chair by the desk, feeling woozy. After bearing the guilt so long, it was almost shocking to have it lifted away. "I don't know what to do."

"You don't have to do anything now," she said. "Any obligation you felt you owed to Brodie...it's over. You're free, Thane."

He didn't quite like the way she said it. "No one's ever completely free. Brodie was my friend, and I'll always remember that."

"Yes, but you needn't rip yourself to pieces now. I appreciate what you did do," she said with a sad little laugh. "You were even willing to risk your freedom to keep me alive—just imagine, Thane, if I'd accepted your offer. We'd be wed by now, and you'd never have needed to pull me from a burning house."

"It would have been an easier path," he said, thinking of the pain that might have been avoided. But then, Cat never would have learned who was stalking her, or been able to move on after they'd been neutralized and taken away.

"At the beginning, it would have been," she said in a musing voice that sounded very far away. "But I'm sure you're grateful you dodged that bullet." Then she blinked, and looked at him, coming back to the present. "Why *are* you here?"

Thane shook his head. "Not to find out if I've got an obligation to you, or ask you to marry me, even if there's no child to force the issue. You've made it clear, over and over, that you don't want to marry anyone, let alone me."

"About that…" she said, fidgeting as she spoke, twisting the sheet in her hands. "It's true that I believe women should not *have* to marry simply to get on in the world. We should be able to make our own money, own our own property, speak our thoughts, and not fear that merely by existing we are at the mercy of some man's whim. But I never thought myself better than you. Or that I didn't want to have you in my life." The topic that she devoted so much time to gave some heat to her voice. She sounded more…*herself.*

"But you still refused when I did ask, back at home." His home, the home he hoped to make hers as well.

"You did it out of a sense of obligation to Brodie. I didn't want to trap you into a marriage that you didn't want either."

"You daft lass," Thane burst out. "I wouldn't have asked if I didn't *want* you for my wife! Christ, any of the men would have been happy to step up if I would have let them. Calan offered more than once. Duncan is a better catch than I'll ever be. Or you could have married Kai."

Cat wrinkled her nose. "Goodness. Kai? That would be like gaining another brother, not a husband. And I'd wallop Calan within a day, the rake." She paused, then said, "I'm sure that Duncan is…very nice."

Thane laughed, but inwardly he was relieved that she hadn't been disappointed to miss other potential offers.

"You didn't mention Struan," she pointed out.

"Oh, he'll *never* marry," Thane said. "He's said as much."

"Funny that when a man says it, everyone accepts his decision without protest. And yet when I told people that marriage wasn't for me, they all assumed I was a silly girl who just needed convincing."

Thane couldn't deny the truth of it, so he said, "It's not fair, Cat. I know. But you have to believe that I love you."

She looked up suddenly, and he was struck by the pain in her eyes. "You must stop loving me."

It would be easier to stop breathing. "Can't do that, kitty cat. I see you in my sleep, and you're the first thing I think of when I wake. The thought of you in danger makes my heart seize up. You don't have to love me—you don't ever have to see me again after today. But I couldn't leave without telling you that I do love you, and always will. If you can't see that, it's because you don't want to."

Cat closed her eyes. "Oh, God, Thane. I love you so much it hurts."

He had to take a moment to understand what she said.

"You do? Even knowing what I did?"

She sighed. "I know it wasn't as simple as I pretended it was. I was a beast to you. To everyone really, but especially to you. I tried not to see what you did for me. How good you were, how you never hesitated to help, even when I was acting like an ungrateful wretch. I didn't dare love you. I'd lost both the people I loved most, and the thought of loving again scared me too much. Since Brodie died, I built a wall around myself. And kept building it higher when I lost my mother."

Thane couldn't stand the hollow tone she used, but he didn't know if she'd allow him to touch her.

"Cat," he said, stepping closer, his hand extended. She ignored it, too intent on her own words. He sat on the edge of the bed, drawn to her, as always.

"I only know how to put more stones in the wall around me," she said, her arms around her drawn-up knees. "It's the only thing I've done for months. I thought it would keep me safe, but it's really just a way to die without dying."

"God, Cat." Thane pulled her close, feeling her heartbeat flutter like a bird in a cage. "No one's meant to be alone. Not like that." He'd seen soldiers react that way, when the violence got too much to bear, when they lost the last thing keeping them sane. He'd seen men break down, and stop speaking, eating, sleeping, too haunted to go on. Or they'd just walk toward the enemy, leaving their weapons behind, inviting death to find them. The official line was the men got confused by smoke and gunfire. Thane knew the truth. They felt too much alone and too much alive at the same time.

He just hadn't realized that anyone could stumble into that horror, no matter where they were. That's what she'd been fighting when she first met him, and why she'd thrown herself into his arms, no matter what the consequences. It was her attempt to not be alone.

And even knowing that, he couldn't stop loving her. "Cat, I'm so sorry," he said, cradling her head against his chest, cherishing this last touch. "Just tell me what I can do, Cat. Anything you need."

She choked up, and murmured something against his chest. He pulled away enough to hear her clearly.

"Could you forgive me?" she asked.

It took too long for the words to register. Thane just stared at her like an idiot, and before he could speak, Cat just crumpled into him.

"I knew it. I knew it was too late to try again."

"Cat…"

"Thane, if I thought you'd forgive me, I'd beg you for another chance. But I burned all my chances up."

Chapter 34

THANE PULLED AWAY FROM HER, putting his hands on her shoulders. His gaze was so intense that Cat felt scorched by it. Why wouldn't he say *some*thing, if only to fill the awful silence?

Then he moved one hand to touch her face, lightly, as if she would break. Maybe she *would* break.

"Cat, you own all the chances you could ever want," he said roughly. "You own me. Or at least you've got my whole heart in your hands. When you left the Highlands to come here, I was nearly mad with worry. Just the thought of you getting hurt, love…and then reaching the house and finding you half-dead…"

Cat took his hand and squeezed tight. "You saved me. I was a fool to leave in the first place, and even though I was a fool, you still came for me. You wouldn't let me suffer for my mistake."

"I wanted you safe, love. Nothing else matters."

"I don't want you to protect me because you think it's your duty, Thane."

"It's not duty. It's because I love you."

Cat inhaled. He said these words before, but they were still so unexpected, so tantalizing. It had to be a trick. "After everything?"

"Yes. Always and forever."

"I love you," she said, dropping each word like a gem. "I tried not to. At first because I didn't want to trust anyone. When you love someone, you can lose them. Or they betray you."

"Like I did." His voice was bitter, but the bitterness was all directed inward.

"No. You kept the truth from me to protect me."

"And myself."

"But your silence didn't protect you," she said, looking up at him in time to see the pain in his face. "It only hurt you more, because you couldn't talk to anyone about it. And you couldn't know what *really* happened because Fairchild engineered things that way."

"I should have told you. I never meant to hurt you, Cat."

"I was angry when I heard your confession, but it wasn't fair of me to accuse you of having no feelings for me. If you didn't care for me, you would have never told me at all, because you wouldn't have thought it worth confessing. You told me because you loved me, and you needed me to see all of you...what you despised about yourself as well as what you were proud of."

As she spoke, she reached to touch his face, hoping to shatter that frozen expression. "Thane?"

"Cat, what can I do to make things right between us?"

She leaned forward, and let her mouth brush against his. "I want nothing between us," she told him, her voice now raw with suppressed desire.

He held still for a beat, then suddenly took her shoulders in his hands and drew her closer.

It was slow, but not soft. Cat needed him too badly, and he seemed to feed off her desire, teasing her to a state of need that had her slicked with a sheen of sweat and whimpering into her pillow. And it felt divine.

When he took her, it was with her on her back and Thane on his knees. "So I can look at you, lovely," he said in a rough voice. "Really look at you."

She wrapped her legs around his waist, desperate for him to enjoy her as much as she enjoyed him. He thrust deep and strong, bringing her to her peak before she was ready. Cat was still thrumming with the aftermath of her orgasm when Thane urgently ordered her to let him go. He spilled on the sheet, and she wrapped her hand about him, drawing out the last of his pleasure.

Afterward, he spent a long time stretched next to her, kissing every part of her body just to make sure he hadn't missed any. Her feet, her legs, her stomach, her breasts.

"You're perfect, love," he said softly. "Every inch of you is glorious."

"Are you trying to flatter me, Thane MacPhearson?"

"I'm trying to compliment you, you daft girl. Can't a man just tell his woman she's beautiful without there being some underhanded motive for it?"

"I thought you might be trying to butter me up for a marriage proposal."

"Mmm, if I butter you up, it will be for quite a different purpose," he said with a low chuckle that promised some salacious future act. When Cat demanded an explanation, he told her, and she nearly fainted.

"People can do that?" she asked.

"Can and do. If you're curious, we can explore the possibility another time. When you're fully recovered."

"I'm fine," she protested.

"You're gorgeous and wonderful, but you're still in bed by doctor's orders."

"You seem to like me in bed."

"That I do. Tell me, Cat, are you still opposed to marriage?"

"Why do you ask?" Cat murmured, dazed by the way he was laying kisses down the inside of her arm. "Do you intend to force me to the altar after all?"

"Not force," he protested mildly, sucking on her ring finger. "I just thought that you might appreciate some of the benefits."

"I think you heard how much I appreciated the benefits a little while ago, and I didn't even have to marry you for that."

She gave a little shriek when Thane suddenly tickled her side. She wriggled to get away, but without any warning, she found herself pinned beneath him, staring up at a face she now knew as well as her own.

"Don't think you can intimidate me into agreeing to your demands, Thane MacPhearson."

"I haven't made any demands."

"You will. You're going to ask me to marry you."

"Asking isn't demanding."

She rolled her eyes. "Well?"

"Well, what?" he teased her.

"Ask! If your intentions are honorable, that is."

"My intentions…!" he sputtered, and Cat bit back a grin. "You're the temptress who's naked in my arms."

"You didn't take much tempting," she pointed out.

"I'll take as much as you give, Catriona Ross." He smiled slowly. "Oh, by the way, will you marry me?"

Cat pursed her lips, making a show of thinking it over. Then she said, "No."

"No?" Thane looked wounded.

"However," she said, "I am considering taking a lover. A long-term position, and the duties are, I trust, not too onerous."

"What qualities does this lover need to possess?"

"Hmm, well, he'll have to be a magnificent physical

specimen, of course." Cat ran a hand over Thane's chest and down his stomach, enjoying the way his muscles contracted as she grazed each one. "Able to satisfy me in myriad ways."

He groaned. "Ugh. Did you just use the word *myriad* in bed? Bluestocking." Then he groaned again, for an entirely different reason.

"My lover will respect my views," Cat said softly, watching Thane's eyes grow dark with lust. "He'll recognize that I'm intelligent and independent and worth all consideration."

"He'd better," Thane growled, "or I'll kill him."

"It's you, you dolt," she told him.

"I know. But the principle stands. I will defend you against the whole world, my lovely Cat. Until you take it over, of course," he added.

She demurred, "I have no ambition to run the world. I just want to live in the best version of it."

"And that version includes me?" he asked, showing a trace of uncertainty.

"If you're content to love me and know that I love you, without some silly ceremony that makes me your property."

"That's enough," he said. "It's more than enough. I intend to spend the rest of my days making you happy, Cat. In every way you could dream or desire."

"Now that sounds quite promising," she purred, a specific desire already stirring in her body. "And I swear that you'll not regret being with me."

"I've regretted many things in my life, but being with you is not one of them." He kissed her slowly, drawing out a moan of anticipation. Then he pulled away, frowning slightly. He said, "People will talk. Both here and in the Highlands."

"Let them." Then Cat smiled. "In fact, we ought to give them something to talk about."

"I've got a few ideas."

Cat was more than willing to listen, and Thane was a very persuasive man.

As if he heard her thoughts, he said, "I'll be asking again. I mean, I'll be asking you to marry me."

"You may ask as much as you like," she told him. "But for now, I have other plans for you."

ABOUT THE AUTHOR

Elizabeth Cole is a romance writer with a penchant for history. Her stories draw upon her deep affection for the British Isles, action movies, medieval fantasies, and even science fiction. She now lives in a small house in a big city with a cat, a snake, and a rather charming gentleman. When not writing, she is usually curled in a corner reading...or watching costume dramas or things that explode. And yes, she believes in love at first sight.